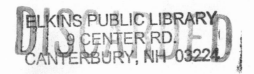

White Christmas Pie

WANDA &
BRUNSTETTER

**Doubleday Large Print
Home Library Edition**

BARBOUR
PUBLISHING

© 2008 by Wanda E. Brunstetter

ISBN 978-1-60751-269-1

All scripture quotations are taken from the King James Version of the Bible.

All German-Dutch words are taken from the *Revised Pennsylvania German Dictionary* found in Lancaster County, Pennsylvania.

This book is a work of fiction. Names, characters, places, and incidents are either products of the author's imagination or used fictitiously. Any similarity to actual people, organizations, and/or events is purely coincidental.

For more information about Wanda E. Brunstetter, please access the author's Web site at the following Internet address:
www.wandabrunstetter.com

Cover Design: Müllerhaus Communications Group

Published by Barbour Publishing, Inc., P.O. Box 719, Uhrichsville, OH 44683,

Our mission is to publish and distribute inspirational products offering exceptional value and biblical encouragement to the masses.

ecpa Member of the
Evangelical Christian
Publishers Association

Printed in the United States of America

**This Large Print Book carries the
Seal of Approval of N.A.V.H.**

DEDICATION/ACKNOWLEDGMENTS

With special thanks to Anna Yoder for
sharing her delicious
White Christmas Pie recipe with me

**"And ye shall know the truth,
and the truth shall make you free."**
JOHN 8:32

CHAPTER 1

Three-Year-Old Girl Abandoned in Small Town Park.

A lump formed in Will Henderson's throat as he stared at the headline in the morning newspaper. *Not another abandoned child!*

The little girl had been left alone on a picnic table in a small Michigan town. She had no identification and couldn't tell the officials anything more than her first name and the fact that her mommy and daddy were gone. While the police searched for the girl's parents, she would be put in a foster home.

Will's fingers gripped the newspaper.

How could anyone abandon his own child? Didn't the little girl's parents love her? Didn't they care how their abandonment would affect the child? Didn't they care about anyone but themselves?

Will dropped the paper on the kitchen table and let his head fall forward into his hands as a rush of memories pulled him back in time. Back to when he was six years old. Back to a day he wished he could forget. . .

Will released a noisy yawn and rolled over. Seeing Pop's side of the bed was empty, he pushed the heavy quilt aside, scrambled out of bed, and raced over to the window. When he lifted the dark green shade and peeked through the frosty glass, his breath caught in his throat. The ground and trees in the Stoltzfuses' backyard were covered in white!

"Pop was right; we've got ourselves some snow!" Will darted across the room, slipped out of his nightshirt, and hurried to get dressed. He figured Pop must be outside helping Mark Stoltzfus do his chores.

When Will stepped out of the bedroom, his nose twitched, and his stomach rumbled. The tangy smell coming from the kitchen let him know that the Amish woman named Regina was probably making breakfast.

"It didn't snow on Christmas like Pop said it would, but it's sure snowin' now!" Will shouted as he raced into the kitchen.

Regina Stoltzfus turned from the stove and smiled at Will, her dark eyes gleaming in the light of the gas lantern hanging above the table. "Jah, it sure is. It would have been nice if we'd had a white Christmas, but the Lord decided to give us some fluffy white stuff today, instead."

Will wiggled his bare feet on the cold linoleum floor, hardly able to contain himself. "I can't wait to play in the snow with Pop. Maybe we can build a snowman." He rushed to the back door, stood on his toes, and peered out the small window. "Is Pop helpin' Mark milk the cows?"

Regina came to stand beside Will. "Your dad's not helping Mark do his chores this morning," she said, placing one hand on his shoulder.

Will looked up at her and squinted. "He's not?"

She shook her head.

"How come?"

"Didn't you find the note he wrote you?"

"Nope, sure didn't. Why'd Pop write me a note?"

Regina motioned to the table. "Let's have a seat, shall we?" When she pulled out a chair, he plunked right down.

"After you went to bed last night, your dad had a talk with me and Mark," she said, taking the seat beside him.

"What'd ya talk about? Did Pop tell ya thanks for lettin' us stay here and for fixin' us Christmas dinner yesterday?"

"He did say thanks for those things, but he said something else, too."

"What'd he say?"

Regina's eyes seemed to have lost their sparkle. Her face looked kind of sad. "Your dad said he would leave a note for me to read you, Will. Are you sure there wasn't a note on your pillow or someplace else in your room?"

"I didn't see no note. Why would Pop leave a note for me?"

Regina touched his arm. "Your dad left early this morning, Will."

"Left? Where'd he go?"

"To make his delivery, and then he—"

Will's eyebrows shot up. "Pop left without me?"

She nodded. "He asked if we'd look after you while he's trying to find a different job."

Will shook his head vigorously. "Pop wouldn't leave without me. I know he wouldn't."

"He did, Will. That's why he planned to leave you a note—so you would understand why."

Will jumped out of his chair, raced up the stairs, and dashed into the bedroom he and Pop had shared since they'd come to stay with Mark and Regina Stoltzfus a few days ago. There was no note on the pillow. No note on the dresser or nightstand, either. Will

**ran over to the closet and threw open
the door. Pop's suitcase was gone!**

Will's knee bumped against the table,
bringing his thoughts back to the present.

He lifted his head and glanced down at
Sandy, his honey-colored cocker spaniel,
who stared up at him with soulful brown
eyes. "Did you bump my leg, girl?"

Sandy whimpered in response.

Ever since Will had been a boy, he'd
wanted a dog of his own, but Pop had said
a dog wasn't a good idea for people who
lived in a semitruck as they traveled down
the road. Papa Mark had seen the need
for a dog, though. A few weeks after Will
had come to live with Mark and Regina,
he'd been given a cocker spaniel puppy.
He had named the dog Penny because
she was the color of a copper penny.
Penny had been a good dog, but she'd
died two years ago. Will had gotten another cocker spaniel he'd named Sandy.
He'd bred the dog with his friend Harley's
male cocker, Rusty. Sandy was due to
have her pups in a few weeks.

Sandy nudged Will's leg again, and he
reached down to pat her silky head. "Do

you need to go out, girl, or are you just getting anxious for your *hundlin* to be born?"

Sandy licked his hand then flopped onto the floor with a grunt. Maybe she only wanted to keep him company. Maybe she felt his pain.

The lump in Will's throat tightened as he fought to keep his emotions under control. A grown man shouldn't cry over something that happened almost sixteen years ago. He'd shed plenty of tears after Pop had gone, and it had taken him a long time to come to grips with the idea that Pop wasn't coming back to get him. Tears wouldn't change the fact that Will had been abandoned just like the little girl in the newspaper. He wished there was a way he could forget the past—take an eraser and wipe it out of his mind. But the memories lingered no matter how hard he tried to blot them out.

Will's gaze came to rest on the propane-operated stove where Mama Regina did her cooking. At least he had some pleasant memories to think about. Fifteen years ago, he had moved with Papa Mark and Mama Regina from their home in Lancaster

County, Pennsylvania, to LaGrange County, Indiana, where they now ran a dairy farm and health food store. On the day of that move, Will had made a decision: He was no longer English. He was happy being Amish, happy being Mama Regina and Papa Mark's only son.

Now, as a fully grown Amish man, he was in love with Karen Yoder and looked forward to spending the rest of his life with her. They would be getting married in a few months—two weeks before Christmas. Will didn't need the reminder that he had an English father he hadn't seen in almost sixteen years. As far as he was concerned, Papa Mark and Mama Regina were his parents, and they would be the ones who would witness his and Karen's wedding ceremony. Pop was gone from his life, just like Will's real mother, who had died almost a year before Pop had left. Will's Amish parents cared about him and had since the first day he'd come to live with them. They'd even invited Will and Karen to live in their house after they were married.

As Will's thoughts continued to bounce around, he became tenser. Despite his resolve to forget the past, he could still see Pop's bright smile and hear the optimism in his voice as he tried to convince Will that things would work out for them after Mom had been hit by a car. Pop had made good on his promise, all right. He'd found Will a home with Regina and Mark Stoltz-fus. In all the years Pop had been gone, Will hadn't seen or heard a word from him. It was as though Pop had vanished from the face of the earth.

A sense of bitterness enveloped Will's soul as he reflected on the years he'd wasted, waiting, hoping for his father's re-turn. *Is Pop still alive? If so, where is he now, and why hasn't he ever contacted me? If Pop stood before me right now, what would I say? Would I thank him for leaving me with a childless Amish couple who have treated me as if I were their own flesh and blood? Or would I yell at Pop and tell him I'm no longer his son and want nothing to do with him?*

Will turned back to the newspaper article about the little girl who'd been aban-doned. "It's not right," he mumbled when he got to the end of the story. "It's just not right."

"What's not right?"

Will looked up at Mama Regina, who stood by the table with a strange expression. He pointed to the newspaper and shook his head. "This isn't right. It's not right at all!"

She took a seat beside him and picked up the paper. As she read the article, her lips compressed into a thin line, causing tiny wrinkles to form around her mouth. "It's always a sad thing when a child is abandoned," she murmured.

Will nodded. "I was doing fine until I read that story. I was content, ready to marry Karen, and thought I had put my past to rest. The newspaper article made me think—made me remember things from my past that I'd rather forget." He groaned. "I don't want to remember the past. It's the future that counts—the future with Karen as my wife."

Mama Regina leaned closer to Will and rested her hand on his arm. "The plans you've made for the future are important, but as I've told you many times before, you don't want to forget your past."

"What would you have me remember— the fact that my real *mamm* died when I was only five, leaving Pop alone to raise me? Or am I supposed to remember how it felt when I woke up nearly sixteen years ago on the day after Christmas and discovered that Pop had left me at your house and never said good-bye?" As the words rolled off Will's tongue, he couldn't keep the bitterness out of his tone or the tears from pooling in his eyes.

"I don't know the reason your *daed* didn't leave you a note when he left that day, and I don't know why he never came back to get you." Tears shimmered in Mama Regina's eyes as she pushed a wisp of dark hair under the side of her white cone-shaped head covering. "There is one thing I do know, however."

"What's that?"

"Every day of the sixteen years you've lived with us, I have thanked God that your daed read one of the letters I had written to your mamm when she was still alive. I'm also thankful that your daed brought you to us during his time of need and that Mark and I were given the chance to raise you as if you were our own son." She smiled as she patted Will's arm in her motherly way. "We've had some wonderful times since you came to live with us. I hope you have many pleasant memories of your growing-up years."

"*Jah*, of course I do."

Mama Regina glanced down at Sandy and smiled. "Think of all the fun times you had, first with Penny and now with Sandy."

Will nodded.

"And think about the time your daed built you a tree house and how the two of you used to sit up there and visit while you munched on peanut butter and jelly sandwiches and sipped fresh milk from our dairy cows."

Will clasped her hand. "You and Papa Mark have been good parents to me, and I want you to know that I appreciate all you've done."

"We know you do, and we've been glad to do it."

"Even so, it was Pop's responsibility to raise me. The least he could have done was to send you some money to help with my expenses."

Mama Regina shook her head. "We've never cared about that. All we've ever wanted is for you to be happy."

"I know." Will slid his chair away from the table and stood. "I think I'll get my horse and buggy ready and take a ride over to see Karen. Unless you're going to need my help in the store, that is."

Mama Regina shook her head. "An order of vitamins was delivered yesterday afternoon, so it needs to be put on the shelves. But Mary Jane Lambright's working today, and she can help with that."

"Guess I'd better check with Papa Mark and see if he needs me for anything before I take off."

"I think he plans to build some bins for storing bulk food items in my store, but he'll be fine on his own with that." Mama Regina smiled. "You go ahead and see Karen. Maybe spending a little time with your bride-to-be will brighten your spirits."

"Jah, that's what I'm hoping."

"Don't forget your *zipple* cap," she called as he grabbed his jacket and headed for the door.

"I won't." Will smiled as he pulled the cap from the wall peg. He was glad he and

Mama Regina had talked—it had made him feel a little better about things. He figured he would feel even better after he spent some time with Karen.

CHAPTER 2

Do you need any help with that?"

Karen Yoder looked up and smiled when her sixteen-year-old sister, Cindy, stepped up to the kitchen table where Karen was cutting material for her wedding dress. "I'm just about done, but if you'd like to help put things away when I'm finished, we can get lunch going."

"Jah, sure, I can do that." Cindy tucked an unruly strand of blond hair under her head covering and smiled. "It won't be long until you and Will are married. Are you getting excited about the wedding?"

Karen nodded and sighed as she slid

her fingers over the soft green material. "December's only two months away, and I really should have my wedding dress made by now. I just wish Will's father could be here for our wedding."

Cindy quirked an eyebrow. "How come Mark won't be at the wedding?"

"I'm not talking about Mark Stoltzfus. I was referring to Will's real daed—the man who left him with Mark and Regina when he was six years old."

"I can't imagine how Will must have felt when his daed left him like that." Cindy grunted. "I don't see how any parent could do such a thing."

"It's not our place to judge. We don't know all the circumstances involving Will's daed leaving him with Regina and Mark."

"Even so, it doesn't make sense that the man never came back for Will." Cindy pursed her lips. "Maybe he didn't come back because he's dead. What does Will think? Does he believe his real daed is dead?"

Karen shrugged. "Will rarely talks about it, so I don't know what he believes."

"Why don't you ask?"

"Because every time I bring up the sub-ject, Will closes up like a star tulip."

"Are you sure Will's the right man for you?" Cindy wrinkled her nose. "I mean, if he won't talk about his past—"

"I know he loves me, and I love him. That's enough for me."

The distinctive *clip-clop* of a horse's hooves could be heard outside. Cindy dashed over to the window and peered out. "Speaking of Will, I see his horse and buggy out there right now."

Karen joined her sister at the window. Sure enough, Will was getting out of his buggy and heading toward the house. A sense of excitement welled in her soul as she hurried to the back door and stepped onto the porch to wait for him. She was always glad to see Will. He was the right man for her, no matter what Cindy thought.

"*Wie geht's*, Will?" Karen asked when he joined her on the porch.

"I'm doing okay. How about you?"

"I'm fine. It's good to see you." She opened the back door. "Can you come in-side and visit awhile, or did you need something from my folks' store?"

He shook his head. "I knew today was your day off, so I came to see you—if you're not busy, that is."

"I've been cutting out my wedding dress, but I'm almost done. Then I'll need to get lunch going, but that won't keep me from visiting with you. Come inside, and we can visit while I finish up."

"Okay."

"Hello, Will," Cindy said when Karen and Will entered the kitchen.

Will ran his fingers through his thick, wavy red hair. "Hi, Cindy."

Karen motioned to the material on the table. "Do you still like the color we chose for my wedding dress?"

He nodded and shuffled his feet a few times, the way he always did whenever he had something on his mind. "It's a real nice shade of green."

Karen looked over at Cindy. "Would you mind going to check on the laundry? With the cold wind we've been having today, the clothes ought to be dry by now."

Cindy's eyebrows furrowed. "I thought you wanted my help clearing the table so we could start lunch."

"We can do that after you get the clothes

off the line. Besides, Mom's not back from Grandma Yoder's yet."

Cindy shrugged, grabbed her jacket from the wall peg, and went out the door.

"If your mamm's over at your *grossmudder's* house, and you and Cindy are here, who's minding the store?"

"My sister-in-law Mavis is helping Dad today. She started working a few days a week after her youngest son started school. I thought you knew that."

"Guess I forgot." Will shuffled his feet a few more times. "Does your brother Evan still like his job at the trailer factory?"

"He seems to. All four of my brothers have jobs they enjoy a lot more than working in the family dry goods store, and they're much happier these days." Karen motioned to the pot sitting on the stove. "Would you like a cup of coffee, Will?"

"Jah, sure, but I can get it." He headed for the stove, calling over his shoulder, "Would you like one, too?"

"No, thanks. I've already had two cups this morning."

Will poured himself a cup then took a seat at the far end of the table where there was no material. Karen appreciated his thoughtfulness in keeping the coffee away from the dress material. She picked up her scissors and began cutting again.

"I was surprised to see Cindy. Is this her day off, too?"

"Not really, but since they aren't too busy in the store right now, Cindy came home a little early to see if I needed help getting lunch on."

Will stared into his cup, and a muscle on the side of his neck twitched a couple of times. Something wasn't right. He obviously had something on his mind.

"What's wrong, Will? You look *umgerennt*."

The smattering of freckles on Will's nose scrunched together as he frowned. "I am a little upset, but I'll get over it." He continued to stare at his coffee.

Karen wondered if Will's pensive mood signaled that he might be nervous about their upcoming wedding.

"Are you having second thoughts about marrying me?" she dared to ask.

Will's pale eyebrows lifted high on his forehead. "Now where'd you get a notion like that?"

"You're not acting like yourself, so I thought maybe—"

"I'm not having second thoughts about getting married. I just have a lot on my mind."

"Such as?"

He blew on his coffee. "Just things, that's all."

Karen nibbled on her bottom lip as she contemplated what to say next. If Will didn't want to talk about whatever was bothering him, she didn't want to push. Maybe they needed a change of subject.

Snip. Snip. She cut the last piece of her dress and set the scissors aside. "Evan mentioned the other day that they've begun hiring at the trailer factory again."

"So I heard. Abe Miller started working there a few weeks ago. He says he likes the work, and they pay pretty well."

"Have you ever thought about working in one of the trailer factories?"

Will shook his head. "Papa Mark needs my help with the dairy cows, and when I'm not helping there, I'm either busy with other chores or helping out in Mama Regina's health food store."

"Maybe after we're married, I can help

in your mamm's store. I think it would be interesting."

"I'm sure Mama Regina wouldn't turn down such an offer. She won't be able to work there forever." Will lifted his mug to his lips and took another drink. "She's probably hoping the two of us will take over someday."

The back door creaked open, and Cindy stepped into the room. "Some of the clothes on the line aren't quite dry, so should we start lunch now?"

Will pushed his chair aside and stood. "Guess I'd best be on my way home."

"We have plenty of leftover soup from last night, so you're welcome to stay and have lunch with us," Karen was quick to say.

"Okay, maybe I will." Will sat back down.

A knock sounded on the back door, and Cindy scurried out of the room. A few seconds later, she was back with Karen's old boyfriend, Leroy Eash. "Leroy just came from the store," she announced.

Leroy nodded enthusiastically. "Jah, and when your daed said you were over here, I decided to stop by and say hello." He

smiled at Karen. "I didn't interrupt anything, did I?"

"Will and I were visiting, and I just invited him to stay for lunch." Karen scooped
the material and scissors off the table and
placed them in the cabinet.

Leroy sniffed the air. "I don't smell anything. What are you having for lunch?"

"We haven't started it yet," Karen replied.

"But we will soon." Cindy gave Leroy a
wide smile. "Say, why don't you stay and
eat with us, too? We'll be having leftover
chicken-corn soup, and there's plenty to
go around."

"Chicken-corn soup sounds real good."
Leroy's gaze remained fixed on Karen.
"You made that soup a time or two when I
joined you and your folks for supper dur-
ing our courting days." He winked at her.
"I'd be a fool to turn down that offer."

With an undignified grunt, Will jumped
out of his seat, brushed past Leroy, and
made a beeline for the door.

Karen hurried after him. "Aren't you staying for lunch?"

He shook his head. "I don't think there'll
be room enough for two guests around

your table." Before Karen could think of a response, Will rushed out the door.

Karen's forehead puckered as she stood in the doorway, watching him head for his buggy. What had made him seem so moody today, and why had he changed his mind about staying for lunch? Was Will jealous of her old boyfriend?

Karen ran down the stairs and dashed into the yard. "Will, wait up! We need to talk!"

He whirled around, and when she caught up to him, a blank expression crossed his face. "What's there to talk about?"

"I'd like to know why you changed your mind about staying for lunch."

"Do you really have to ask?" Will grunted. "What gives Leroy the right to come over here and practically invite himself for lunch?"

"It wasn't that way. He just said—"

"Couldn't he see that you already had company? I mean, you'd just told him I was staying for lunch." Deep wrinkles marred Will's forehead. "Doesn't Leroy know that you're going to be my wife in a couple of months?"

"Of course he knows. I'm sure he only—"

"What's he trying to do—come between us?"

A gust of wind tossed a stray curl across Karen's forehead, and she pushed it under her *kapp*. "I'd appreciate it if you'd stop asking questions and listen to what I have to say."

He folded his arms. "Okay, I'm listening."

Karen held up one finger. "Number one: Leroy didn't invite himself to stay for lunch; Cindy invited him." A second finger came up. "Number two: Just because Leroy showed up and you were already here doesn't mean he should turn right around and head out the door." She extended a third finger. "And number three: Leroy knows I'm going to marry you, and I don't think he's trying to come between us."

Will shrugged. "Think whatever you like, but I've seen the way he looks at you. He wishes you were still his girl. Probably wishes it was him you were marrying, not me."

"You're wrong, Will. Leroy's just a friend."

Karen clasped his arm. "Please come back inside and join us for lunch."

"No thanks, I'd rather not." Will turned and started walking toward his buggy again.

Karen debated about going after Will but decided it wouldn't do any good for her to say more. Maybe once he had calmed down and thought things through, he would be willing to listen.

CHAPTER 3

Will sure took off in a hurry," Leroy said when Karen stepped back into the kitchen. "Talk about unpredictable. I thought he was planning to stay for lunch."

"He changed his mind." Karen headed for the refrigerator to get the soup.

"He seemed like he was in kind of a weird mood," Cindy said.

Leroy followed Karen across the room. "Will's always been kind of hard to figure out. How do you think things will go being married to someone so moody and unpredictable?"

She removed the soup and some cheese. "We're all moody at times."

"Will's probably nervous about your wedding. I'll bet his moodiness will improve once you're married." Cindy spoke to Karen but looked at Leroy as she leaned against the cupboard with a silly grin.

Karen didn't understand what had brought on this change in her sister. Just a short time ago, she'd asked if Karen thought Will was the right man for her. It made no sense.

"What if Will's moods don't improve?" Leroy asked.

Karen placed the soup and cheese on the counter and turned to face him. "Why are you making such an issue of Will's mood? Doesn't he have the right to be moody once in a while?"

Leroy grunted. "Ever since that fellow moved to Middlebury with his folks, he's been kind of strange."

"Will is not strange. He's hardworking, dependable, and—"

"My horse is hardworking and dependable, but that doesn't mean any mares would find him appealing."

Cindy snickered, but Karen, not the least

bit entertained, stared at Leroy and said, "If you'd have let me finish, I was going to say that Will is also a kind and generous man, and I enjoy being with him."

Leroy folded his arms. "I can't imagine what's so enjoyable about being with someone who's moody and unpredictable."

"He's not unpredictable!" Karen's hands shook as she poured the soup into a kettle. She didn't know why this conversation was upsetting her so much or why Leroy kept going on about Will. Usually she enjoyed talking to him. Maybe the things he'd said upset her so much because she had concerns about Will and didn't want to admit them. She didn't like the fact that Will had come here with something on his mind but hadn't told her what it was. It made her feel left out—like he was afraid to take her into his confidence.

"Are you okay?" Leroy asked. "You're shaking."

"My sister always trembles whenever she's been with Will." Cindy rolled her eyes as she placed both hands against her chest. "That's because she's *so* much in love."

Leroy shook his head. "She didn't start to tremble until after Will left. I think there's something more going on than her being jittery because she's in love." He nudged Karen's arm. "If something's bothering you, just say what it is; maybe I can help."

"I'm fine. There's no need for you to worry."

"Okay, whatever." Leroy's forehead crinkled as he moved toward the door.

"Where are you going? I thought you were gonna stay for lunch," Cindy called out to him.

"I've changed my mind. My mamm's probably getting anxious for me to get home with the stuff I bought at your folks' store, so I'd better head out before she sends my little *bruder* lookin' for me." Leroy turned and smiled at Karen. "If you ever need to talk about anything, just remember that I've got good ears for listening."

"*Danki*, I appreciate that, and I'll keep your offer in mind."

When Leroy went out the door, Cindy dropped into a chair at the table and sighed. "I think Leroy still likes you, Karen."

Karen grabbed a wooden spoon and

started stirring the soup. "He does not. We're just good friends."

"Did you notice how muscular Leroy's arms are?"

"He's muscular because he's a black-smith."

"I think his dark hair and green eyes make him look so *gut-guckich*, don't you?"

"He is good-looking, but he's not right for me."

"Are you sure about that?"

"Of course I'm sure. Things have been over between me and Leroy for a long time, and I was never really serious about him."

"You think Leroy believes that?"

"I'm sure he does. He knows we're just friends, and I don't think he expects any-thing more." Karen opened the cupboard door and removed a stack of bowls. "Do you want to set the table, or would you rather make some sandwiches?"

"I'll set the table." Cindy took the bowls. When she returned for the silverware, she paused in front of Karen. "Do you think I'm pretty?"

Karen tipped her head and studied her

sister. "Well, let's see now. Your blond hair is nice and shiny."

"Your blond hair is shiny, too."

"You also have nice-shaped eyes."

Cindy nodded. "Same as yours, only my eyes are brown and yours are blue."

Karen touched Cindy's cheeks. "And your cute little dimples look like they're winking whenever you smile."

"Danki." Cindy's cheeks turned pink. "Do you think there's a chance that Leroy thinks I'm pretty?"

Karen's mouth dropped open. "Do you have your eye on Leroy? Is that what you're saying?"

Cindy's cheeks darkened further as her gaze dropped to the floor. "Maybe."

"Need I remind you that you're only sixteen? Leroy's almost twenty-four, for goodness' sake!"

Cindy lifted her gaze. "Mom was only eighteen when she and Dad got married, and they're seven years apart."

"But you're not eighteen, Cindy. You're too young to be thinking about marriage or being courted by a man Leroy's age."

Tiny lines formed across Cindy's forehead. "You make him sound like he's an old *mann*."

"He's not an old man—he's just too old for you."

"Mind if I ask you a personal question?"

Karen shrugged.

"I think Leroy's more fun and easygoing than Will, and he's sure a lot cuter, so I'm wondering how come you broke up with Leroy and started going out with Will."

Karen turned the gas burner down on the stove. "Good looks, humor, and big muscles aren't everything, Cindy. Leroy can be overbearing and too much of a jokester at times. He can also be a bit pushy."

"But you liked him once. Isn't that right?"

"Jah, but now I'm in love with Will, and we have a lot more in common than Leroy and I ever did. That's why Will and I are getting married in two months. Now can we drop this silly discussion?"

When Cindy nodded, Karen breathed a sigh of relief.

As Will guided his horse and buggy down the road, all he could think about was seeing Leroy standing in the Yoders' kitchen, grinning at Karen and making comments about the soup she'd fixed during their courting days. Despite what Karen had said, Will was sure Leroy still had an interest in her.

Will flicked the reins, giving his horse the freedom to trot. *Leroy probably wishes Karen was going to marry him. He might think he'd make a better husband for her than me.*

He snapped his teeth together with a click. *Maybe Leroy would make a better husband for Karen. After all, he does have part ownership in a busy blacksmith business, and he doesn't have a past that haunts him and makes him feel moody at the most unexpected times. I wonder if Karen regrets breaking up with Leroy and agreeing to marry me.*

Beep! Beep! Beep!

Startled by the horn of a passing car, Will realized his horse had drifted over the center line. He pulled on the reins, guiding Ben back into his own lane of traffic. Some roads in this area had a lane for horse and buggies, but not this one. He had been careless to let his thoughts wander.

Beep! Beep! Another horn honked from behind. Why was everyone so impatient?

The car whipped around Will's buggy, going too fast and coming too close. Apparently Will's horse thought so, too, because he reared up and tore down the road.

"Whoa, Ben! Steady, boy!" Will pulled back on the reins, but Ben kept running. As the horse picked up speed, the buggy began to vibrate and rock from side to side. Will's hands shook as he struggled to gain control. "Slow down, Ben! You've got to stop running!"

CHAPTER 4

Will gripped the reins and continued his struggle to gain control. Finally his horse slowed to a steady trot, and the buggy quit rocking. Will breathed a sigh of relief.

Feeling the need to steady his nerves, he guided the horse to the side of the road and brought the buggy to a full stop. He drew in a couple of deep breaths and sat very still, hoping to calm his racing heart.

It took several minutes until he felt relaxed enough to head back down the road. He was about to get the horse moving again when another horse and buggy pulled up behind him. A few seconds later, someone tapped on the driver's side of his buggy.

Oh no, it's Leroy! Will opened his door. "What's up?"

"I was behind you a ways and saw your buggy weaving back and forth. When you pulled off the road, I figured I'd better stop and see if you were okay."

"My horse got spooked when a car sped past, blowing its horn, but I've got everything under control."

Leroy squinted. "Are you sure? Your face is awfully red, and you're breathing real heavy."

"I'm fine."

"How's your horse? You want me to check him over?"

Will's fingers dug into the palms of his hands. "Don't trouble yourself; Ben's fine, too."

"Okay. Guess I'd better get home with the supplies I bought from the Yoders' store."

"I'm surprised you're heading home already. I figured you'd still be with Karen and Cindy having lunch."

Leroy shook his head. "Decided I'd better get back to the blacksmith shop and help my daed and bruder get some work done. They'll be on their own again this afternoon while I make a trip to Shipshewana to pick up some supplies and get a gift for my mamm's birthday."

The mention of Lovina Eash's birthday caused Will to remember that his own birthday was coming up. He'd be turning twenty-two. When he'd stopped over at Karen's, he'd planned to ask if she would go to supper with him to help celebrate, but after Leroy had shown up, Will had forgotten to extend the invitation.

Leroy tapped on the side of Will's buggy. "Before I go, there's something else I'd like to say."

"What's that?"

"We both know I used to court Karen, and I was wondering if the reason you left Karen's without staying for lunch is because the idea of sharing the same table with me would make you feel uncomfortable." Leroy tipped his head. "Was that why you hightailed it out of there so fast?"

"It would take a lot more than sitting at the same table with you to make me feel uncomfortable."

Leroy shrugged. "Okay. Just wondered, is all."

"Jah, well, danki for stopping."

"Sure, no problem. Glad to see you're all right." Leroy sauntered back to his buggy.

I wasn't about to tell Leroy the reason I didn't stay for lunch. Will gathered up the reins and turned his horse in the direction of the Yoders'. *Since Leroy won't be sitting at Karen's table, I think I'll go back and talk to Karen about my birthday. If it's not too late, maybe I can get in on some of that tasty chicken-corn soup!*

Regina pursed her lips as she stood in front of the kitchen counter, cutting ham to make sandwiches for their noon meal. No matter how hard she tried, she couldn't get Will off her mind.

She bowed her head and prayed: *Dear Lord, please comfort Will. He's a good man with a kind heart, but it's obvious he's still quite troubled by his past.*

"You look like you're in deep thought," Mark said, stepping up to Regina.

She turned to face him. "I was praying for Will."

"Mind if I ask why you were praying for him?"

"I was thinking about how moody and despondent he acted this morning, and I was asking God to comfort him."

"Will's been a bit moody ever since he came to live with us." Mark pulled his fingers through the ends of his full, nearly gray beard. "Never know what's going to set him off."

Regina nodded. "Normally he does pretty well, though. It's just when something happens to remind Will of his past that he gets out of sorts."

"What brought it on this time?" Mark asked as he washed his hands.

"An article about a little girl who was abandoned by her parents and left on a park bench in a small Michigan town." Regina reached for the loaf of bread and pulled out four slices. "The article brought back unpleasant memories for Will about his daed leaving him with us."

Mark glanced around the room. "Speaking of Will, where is he?"

"He went over to see Karen."

"If anyone can put Will in a good mood

again, it's Karen." Mark pulled out a chair and sat down. "He always seems happy when he's with her. Maybe after they're married, Will's bouts of moodiness and depression will be over for good."

"I hope that's the case." Regina glanced at the battery-operated clock on the far wall. "Since it's lunchtime and Will's not back yet, he must have been asked to stay and eat with the Yoders."

"Probably so."

Regina worked in silence until the sandwiches were made; then she placed them on the table, along with two glasses of milk, and took a seat. After their silent prayer, she said, "Since Will's birthday is next week, I was thinking maybe we should have some of Will's friends over for supper."

"I thought we'd talked about taking Will and Karen out for supper."

"We did, but when I spoke with Karen after church last Sunday, she mentioned the idea of a surprise party. I'd be willing to host it here."

Mark reached for his glass of milk and took a drink. "A surprise party for Will is fine with me. If time spent with Karen doesn't brighten our son's spirits, then the party will do the trick."

When Karen heard a horse and buggy roll into the yard, she glanced out the kitchen window. "Mom's home," she announced. "I'm sure she'll be hungry, so let's get things set out on the table."

Cindy touched Karen's arm. "You won't mention anything to Mom about what I said about Leroy, will you?"

"I won't if you promise to stop thinking about him."

Cindy's lips turned down. "Since he's so good-looking and comes around here a lot, it's kind of hard for me not to think about him."

"I mean it, Cindy; Leroy's too old for you. You need to get any romantic notions you might have of him right out of your mind."

The back door opened, and their mother stepped into the kitchen. "Sorry I'm late." Mom patted her flushed cheeks. "Your grossmudder was especially chatty today, and it was hard to get away."

"It's not a problem," Karen was quick to say. "I got my wedding dress cut out, and then Cindy helped me get lunch going."

"Has your daed come in from the store yet?" Mom asked as she hung her heavy shawl and dark outer bonnet on a wall peg.

"Not yet. Should I run out and get him?" Cindy asked.

"Jah, please do." Mom flicked at the wisps of grayish blond hair on her forehead as she moved toward the bathroom door. "I'll be back as soon as I wash up and fix my hair."

"No problem. Take your time," Karen called after her.

Cindy grabbed her shawl and scurried out the door. A few seconds later, Karen heard another buggy rumble into the yard. She figured it might be a store customer. As she lifted the lid on the kettle of soup, a curl of steam wafted toward the ceiling. The delicious aroma made her stomach rumble in anticipation.

The *clump, clump, clump* of boots on the back porch, followed by a *rap-rap* on the door, let Karen know that whoever had driven the buggy in wasn't a customer.

She replaced the lid on the kettle and hurried across the room. When she opened the door, Will stood on the porch.

"This is a surprise! I thought you had gone home."

"I was halfway there when I decided to come back." The warmth of his dimpled smile helped calm her anxieties. Maybe he wasn't mad at her, after all.

"I'm glad you did." Karen opened the door wider. "Come on into the kitchen. I'm just about ready to serve up some soup."

"That soup does smell good. Is it too late to change my mind and stay for lunch?"

"Of course not. We'd be glad to have you join us."

Will glanced around the kitchen. "Where is everyone?"

"Cindy went to get Dad, and Mom's down the hall, washing up." Karen motioned to the table. "If you'd like to have a seat, I'm sure everyone will be here soon."

Will turned to face her. "I. . .uh. . .wanted to say I'm sorry for acting so moody when I was here earlier. I had a lot on my mind, and—"

Karen held up her hand. "It's all right. There's no need to explain."

"But I want to explain." He grimaced. "This morning's newspaper carried an article about a little girl who was abandoned—left on a park bench with no identification or clue as to who her parents might be."

"Oh, how terrible. I wonder what will become of the little girl if her folks don't come back."

"She'll probably be put in a foster home." Will leaned on the back of the nearest chair. "The article got me to thinking about how I was abandoned, and I guess it put me in a sour mood."

"At least your daed didn't drop you off in some park. He had the decency to find you a good home with Mark and Regina."

"I realize that, and I appreciate them taking me in, but that doesn't excuse my daed for leaving without telling me. . .or for not coming back."

Karen touched Will's arm. "I feel sad that I never got to meet your real daed. It would be nice if he could be here to see us get married."

Will shrugged. "Mama Regina and Papa

Mark are my parents. They'll be at the wedding, so that's all that counts."

"I know they've been like parents to you, but it might be nice if—"

"Can we please change the subject? There's something I'd like to ask you."

"What is it?"

"I was wondering if you'd go out with me for supper next week."

"What night next week?"

"Tuesday evening—on my birthday. I thought maybe the two of us could go to Das Dutchman in Middlebury for supper, and then afterwards we can go over to my place and have cake and ice cream with my folks."

Karen shifted uneasily as she tried to formulate the best response. She couldn't go out for supper with Will if she and Regina held a surprise party for him.

"Well, what do you say? Would you like to go out for supper on Tuesday?"

"I'm not sure I'll be free that night, Will."

"What do you mean you're not sure? You're either free or you've made other plans. Which is it?"

"Well, I—" Karen moistened her lips. "I'm going to be busy that night."

"Doing what?"

"I. . .uh. . .really can't say."

Will frowned. "What do you mean you can't say?"

"I can't say what I'll be busy doing."

"Fine, then! If you don't want to help celebrate my birthday, I'll celebrate alone."

"It's not that I don't want to help celebrate your birthday. I just—"

"Never mind; it's not important." He started for the door.

"Where are you going?"

"Home."

"But I thought you were staying for lunch."

He turned to face her. "I've changed my mind."

Karen frowned. "You're unpredictable, Will. One minute you say you're going to do something, and then you change your mind for no good reason."

"I do have a reason. You won't be honest with me, so it's time for me to go."

She fixed him with a wordless stare.

He shrugged, blinked a couple of times, and tromped out the door.

Karen leaned heavily against the kitchen

counter. *I couldn't tell Will the truth. It would have ruined the surprise. I'll need to speak to Regina as soon as possible. I can't have Will upset with me because he thinks I don't want to go out with him on his birthday.*

CHAPTER 5

Karen stepped outside and drew in a deep breath. The mist rolling over the farmlands surrounding Middlebury lifted the curtain on another day. She leaned her head back and looked at the sky. A small patch of sun peeked through the clouds, offering a promise to chase away the chill on this frosty Sunday morning. It was an off-Sunday in their district, so she and her family would be attending her aunt Jean's church.

As Karen headed to the chicken coop to feed the chickens, she thought about Will and how strange he'd acted the day before. She felt bad about the way things had gone when he'd invited her to join him for supper.

I wish I felt free to tell Will about the party, but if I do, it won't be a surprise. Maybe after we get home from church, I'll go over to the Stoltzfuses' and see if I can get Regina alone for a few minutes to discuss this problem.

Karen opened the chicken coop door and stepped inside. She bent to pick up one of the watering dishes and was startled by Herman, their biggest and meanest rooster. He flapped his wings, stretched his neck, and charged across the coop.

Karen jumped back and waved her hands, but the ornery rooster pointed his beak right at her ankle and—*peck, peck, peck!*

"Ouch! *Absatz*—stop that!" The water dish slipped from Karen's hands, splashing water all over her dress.

The rooster backed up a few steps, ruffled his feathers, and charged again. Quickly Karen bent down, lifted the lid off the chicken feed container, and threw some on the floor. Herman rushed for it, as did the other chickens. While they clucked around the coop, fighting for food, Karen hurried through the watering process. The job done, she headed back to the house.

Stepping onto the porch, she tripped on a loose board and fell on her knees. Gritting her teeth, she limped into the house, mumbling, "I think I should have stayed in bed this morning."

"Daughter, what's wrong?" Mom asked when she saw Karen.

"Our *nixnutzich haahne* is responsible for my wet dress and bleeding leg."

"Which naughty rooster?"

"Herman. As soon as I reached for the water dish, he charged across the chicken coop and pecked my ankle."

"Dad ought to take that rooster's head off." Cindy spoke up from where she was setting the breakfast table. "That ornery critter's always causing some kind of trouble."

Karen limped over to the sink to wash her hands. "Herman was fine once I put food out for the chickens."

Cindy let out an undignified grunt. "He pecked your ankle and made you limp; I don't call that fine."

Karen turned to face her sister. "I'm not

limping because Herman pecked my ankle."

"Why are you limping?"

"When I was coming to the house, I tripped on a loose board on the back porch and fell."

"I'll speak to your daed about getting that board fixed as soon as possible, and if Herman keeps up with his antics, he might end up in my stew pot." Mom went to the cupboard where she kept medicinal supplies. "You'd better have a seat and let me clean up those bloody spots on your ankle. Then I'll take a look at your knees."

"If you'll give me some antiseptic and a couple of bandages, I can tend to my own injuries," Karen said as she dried her hands on a towel.

Mom handed Karen a bottle of peroxide and some cotton balls. "If you'd like to take these over to the table, I'll bring the antibiotic ointment and bandages."

Karen started across the room but had only made it halfway to the table when the bottle slipped out of her hands and landed on the floor. The lid popped off, and all the peroxide spilled out. "Now I know I should have stayed in bed this morning," she said with a groan.

"Cindy, please clean the floor while I help Karen with her knees, and then she'll need to go upstairs and change out of her wet dress."

"I'm not a *boppli*, and I don't need help with my knees!"

Mom blinked a couple of times. "I'm sorry, Karen. I didn't mean to imply that you were a baby."

The heat of shame burned Karen's cheeks, and tears pricked the back of her eyes. "It's me who should apologize. I seem to be a ball of nerves this morning." She dropped the cotton balls on the table and sank into a chair.

Mom rushed to her side. "Karen, what's wrong? Is what happened in the chicken coop making you act so *naerfich*?"

Karen lifted her head. "I'm not really nervous, more anxious than anything. I'm concerned about Will."

"Has something happened to Will?"

Cindy spoke up. "Will was here yesterday, and he was in a sour mood."

Mom looked at Karen. "How come?"

Karen swallowed around the lump in her

throat. "He'd seen a newspaper article about a little girl who'd been abandoned, but he didn't tell me that until he came back the second time."

"He was here twice?"

"Jah, that's right," Cindy said. "He was acting kind of strange when he first showed up, too. But then Leroy came in, and Will got even weirder." She looked over at Karen. "Sister, are you sure you want to marry him?"

"Of course I do."

"What about the second time Will came over?" Mom asked.

"He came back to apologize, but then we had a misunderstanding."

Cindy wrinkled her nose. "I'll bet you argued because he was acting weird again."

Mom shot Cindy a disapproving look. "You'd best keep your opinions about Will to yourself and finish getting that floor cleaned up."

"I'm almost done."

"Good. Then you can start scrambling those eggs I never got started." Mom turned back to Karen. "What was the problem between you and Will?"

Karen told Mom about the surprise party and explained that Will had wanted to take her to supper. "Will was really upset when I said I had other plans on Tuesday evening." She massaged her forehead. "If I'd been thinking, I would have told Will that even though I wasn't free to go out with him on Tuesday night, I could go later in the week."

Mom patted Karen's shoulder. "I'm sure everything will be fine once Will finds out about the party."

"I doubt things will ever be fine as long as Will keeps acting so jealous," Cindy said. "He acts jealous every time he sees Leroy in the same room with Karen."

"A bit of jealousy isn't always a bad thing," Mom said. "When a man acts jealous, it means he cares for you."

"I'm sure I can make Will see that I have no interest in Leroy," Karen said. "Right now I'm more worried about what I should do about him thinking I don't want to have supper with him on his birthday."

"Since Will's mamm is helping you plan the surprise party, it might be a good idea to talk to her about this," Mom suggested. She handed Karen some antibiotic cream

and a box of bandages. "I'm sure everything will work out."

"I thought maybe the two of us could call
on a few of our friends after we leave
church in Cousin Emma's district today,"
Regina said to Mark as they finished eating breakfast.

"I'll go to church with you, but I don't
think I'll feel up to any visiting afterwards,"
he said.

"How come? Are you feeling *grank*?"

"I'm not sick, but my back's really sore,
and I think I'd better spend the afternoon
resting so I'll be able to get the milking
done this evening."

"I'm sorry about your back. Have you
rubbed arnica lotion on it?"

"Not yet, but I will after breakfast.
Thought I'd put an ice pack on my back,
too."

"That's a good idea."

Mark glanced toward the door leading
upstairs. "Did Will tell you he's got a *koppweh*?"

She nodded. "He said he was going
back to bed as soon as the milking was

done. Hopefully his headache will get better with some rest."

"Guess he won't be going to church with us this morning."

"That's what he said." Regina lowered her voice. "I think I'll stop by the Yoders' place this afternoon and talk to Karen. Will mentioned that he asked her to go out to supper on his birthday, and when she said she had other plans for that night, he left her house in a huff."

"He got huffy over a little thing like that?"

"He thinks she doesn't want to be with him."

"That's *lecherich*. If Karen's willing to marry Will, then he ought to realize she wants to be with him."

"It may seem ridiculous to you and me, but Will thinks his feelings are justified."

"Will's been irritable ever since he read that article about the little girl who was abandoned." Mark reached for his coffee cup and took a drink. "You'd think by now he could have let go of the past."

"Some things from Will's past are hard to get over. He was hurt bad when his daed left him, and I doubt he'll ever get over it completely." She leaned against the sink and sighed. "I wish Frank Henderson had left a note for me to read to Will like he said he was going to do. I'm sure it would have made a difference if Will had understood why Frank left."

"But we tried to explain things to him."

"That's true, but it wasn't the same as hearing it from Frank. I've never been sure that Will believed us. I think he believes we only told him that in order to make him feel better about his daed taking off like he did."

"He ought to know we wouldn't have lied."

"He was only a boy, Mark—a sad little boy who felt abandoned by his daed."

"But he's a grown man now and should see the truth for what it is."

"Be that as it may, Will has an ache in his heart that won't go away until he turns it over to God and forgives his father for leaving the way he did."

"Shouldn't he have done that when he got baptized and joined the church?"

Regina nodded. "During the baptism service, Will agreed to follow Christ and commit himself fully to the church, but that doesn't make him the perfect Christian. It doesn't even mean Will has completely surrendered himself to the Lord or sought forgiveness for the anger he's felt toward his daed."

"I see what you mean. Would you like me to speak to Will about this?" Mark asked.

She shook her head. "He might think you're trying to pressure him. Sometimes too much pressure can push a person in the wrong direction. For now, I think it would be better if we just keep Will in our prayers and don't say too much more."

"You're right." Mark rose from his chair. "Guess we should quit yakking so we can get on the road. I'll go out and get the horse and buggy ready while you finish up in here."

CHAPTER 6

Karen walked briskly across the yard, enjoying the cool late-afternoon breeze. If not for her concern over the way things were between her and Will, she might have felt at peace with the world.

She was almost to the barn when a horse and buggy rumbled up the driveway. Regina Stoltzfus stepped down.

"I'm glad to see you," Karen said. "I was just heading to the barn to get my bike so I could go over to your place and talk to you about Will's surprise party."

Regina smiled. "Now isn't that something? I came over here to talk to you about that very thing."

Karen stroked Regina's horse behind its ear. "A little problem has come up regarding the party."

"I think I know. Will told me that he asked you to go to supper with him on Tuesday and he was upset because you weren't free that evening. I'm sorry about that, but I may know how we can fix things."

"What did you have in mind?"

"I'd like you to tell Will that you're free to go to supper with him on Tuesday evening."

"What about the surprise party?"

Regina's lips curved into a sly smile. "You can tell Will you're free to go but that you'd like Mark and me to join you. Soon after we pick you up, I'll say I forgot something at home and need to get it. When we arrive at the house, I'll send Will inside to get whatever it is that I've forgotten. When he enters the house, he'll discover his friends, who'll be waiting to holler, 'Surprise!' "

"That's a good idea. I'll go over to see Will right now and tell him what you said."

Regina gave Karen's shoulder a gentle squeeze. "Will woke up with a koppweh this morning, and he went back to bed. But I'm sure he's feeling better by now." She motioned to the house. "And while you're gone, I'll go inside and invite your folks to the party."

"Where's Mama Regina?" Will asked when he found Papa Mark sitting on the back porch with a cup of coffee in his hand. "I didn't see her anywhere in the house."

"She went calling on a few of our friends."

Will frowned. "How come you didn't go with her?"

"My back's still hurting a little. I figured I'd better rest it so I'll be able to get the milking done this evening."

"I can probably manage on my own if you're hurting too bad."

"I'll be fine. My back's feeling better than it was this morning." Papa Mark looked over at Will. "How's that koppweh you had?"

"I took some white willow bark capsules, and after resting awhile, I feel much better."

"That's good to hear." Papa Mark motioned to the seat beside him. "Why don't you get yourself a cup of coffee and sit with me?"

"Jah, maybe I will." Will was almost to the door when he heard the sound of crunching gravel. He turned. Karen was riding in on her bike.

"Looks like you've got company," Papa Mark said, rising from his chair. "I think I'll take my coffee and go into the house so you and Karen can have some time alone."

Will didn't argue. Maybe he could find out why she'd been unwilling to tell him the reason she couldn't go out with him on his birthday. Maybe she'd come to apologize for hurting his feelings.

Karen parked her bike near the house, and Will stepped off the porch to greet her. "This is a surprise. Since it's an off-Sunday, I didn't expect to see you today," he said.

Karen smiled up at him. "I wanted to apologize for the way things ended between us yesterday and let you know that I'll be free to have supper with you, after all."

"That's good news." Will motioned to the porch. "Should we sit and talk about where we'd like to eat?"

"I thought you wanted to go to Das Dutchman."

"I do, but if you'd rather go someplace else, that's fine with me."

"It's your birthday, so you should be the one to choose." Karen sat in one of the wicker chairs.

"Okay, Das Dutchman it is. How about I come over to pick you up around six?"

"That's fine, but I'd like to make a suggestion."

"What's that?" he asked, sitting in the chair beside her.

"I think we should invite your folks to join us. After all, they're the ones who've raised you, and I think they might be hurt if they were left out of our plans."

Will nodded. "You're right; I should have thought to invite them. I don't know what I was thinking." He leaned close to her ear. "Guess I was thinking how nice it would be to spend time alone with my future wife."

She smiled. "We'll have plenty of time to be alone after we're married."

"Jah, that's true. You know, I'm thinking we should invite your folks to join us for supper, too. I wouldn't want my future in-laws to be mad at me for leaving them out of my birthday celebration."

Karen's cheeks turned pink as she shook her head. "That's a nice idea, but my folks have other plans for Tuesday evening."

"Oh. Guess they won't be upset because they weren't invited, then."

"No, I'm sure they won't."

As a soft wind whispered and the trees in the yard swayed lazily in the breeze, Will began to relax. The setting sun cast a golden hue against the porch, and he noticed that the little flecks in Karen's pale blue eyes were quite visible against the dark of her pupils. She looked so beautiful sitting there that he was tempted to kiss her, but he knew it would embarrass Karen if Papa Mark came back to the porch.

"I'm sorry about how I reacted when you said you had other plans for Tuesday." Will reached for Karen's hand and gave her fingers a gentle squeeze. "I've been feeling a little insecure lately and probably overreacted."

"I understand. You've been upset ever since you read that article about the little girl who was abandoned."

Will nodded. "That's true, but I also got upset when I saw Leroy with you. To tell you the truth, when you first said you had plans for Tuesday night, I worried those plans might include Leroy."

Karen groaned and shook her head. "Will Henderson, what part of 'I love you' don't you understand?"

"I know you love me, but I still struggle with jealousy whenever I see Leroy talking to you."

She made little circles with her thumb across his knuckles. "Leroy's a friend, but you're my *best* friend."

Will swallowed around the lump in his throat. "You're my best friend, too."

CHAPTER 7

A lump formed in Frank Henderson's throat as he stared at the calendar on his bedroom wall. Today was his son's twenty-second birthday, only Frank wouldn't be celebrating the occasion with him. Frank didn't know where his son was, how he was doing, or what kind of a man he'd become. He hadn't seen Will in nearly sixteen years.

As a deep moan escaped Frank's lips, he sank to the edge of his bed. A flood of memories cascaded over him, dragging him back in time. . .back to the night he decided to leave Will. . . .

"Did you get Will tucked into bed?" Mark asked when Frank entered the Stoltzfuses' kitchen. Mark and his wife, Regina, sat at the table, drinking coffee and eating cookies.

Frank nodded. "He's out like a light. I think he fell asleep as soon as his head hit the pillow."

Regina motioned to the coffeepot sitting on the gas-operated stove. "Would you like some coffee?"

"That sounds good."

She started to get up, but Frank shook his head. "Don't trouble yourself; I can get it." He filled a mug with coffee and took a seat at the table. "I can't begin to tell you how much I appreciate your letting us stay with you during the holidays. It would have been a cold, lonely Christmas for Will if we'd spent it on the road."

Regina smiled, her dark eyes revealing the depth of her caring spirit. "It's been our pleasure having the two of you here."

Mark nodded his blond head in agreement. "Since Regina and I aren't able to have children of our own, having a child in the house on Christmas has been a lot of fun."

Frank took a swig of coffee, hoping to push down the lump that had lodged in his throat. "There's. . .uh. . . something I'd like to discuss with you."

"What's that?" Mark leaned forward.

Frank paused and took another drink. "My wife, Patty, and her folks are dead, and I've had no contact with my own family since I was a teenager. So I have no one I can leave Will with while I'm on the road making deliveries in my truck."

"Isn't that why he travels with you?" asked Regina.

"Yeah, that's how it's been since Patty died. But the thing is, Will turned six two months ago, and if I keep hauling him around in my truck, how's he ever gonna attend school?"

"Have you considered doing something else for a living?" Mark questioned.

Frank nodded. "That's what I'm hoping to do. I need something that will bring in enough money for me to make my truck payment and provide for Will."

"Have you thought of hiring someone to stay at home with Will while you're on the road?" Regina asked.

"I don't have a home anymore. A few months ago, our landlord upped the rent, and I couldn't pay what he was asking. So Will and I have been sleeping in the back of my truck ever since." Frank slowly shook his head. "Even if I did have a home, until I met you, I didn't know anyone I would trust enough to take care of my boy."

Regina passed Frank the plate of cookies. "What are you saying?"

Frank shifted in his chair, searching for the right words. "I'm saying—well, I was wondering if you might keep Will— just until I'm able to find another job."

Regina looked at Mark then back at Frank. "Have you spoken with Will about this?"

"No, but I thought if you agreed to the arrangement, I'd leave a note that you could read to Will so he'll understand things a little better."

Deep wrinkles formed across

Mark's forehead. "Why leave him a note? Why not tell him to his face?"

"If I told Will what I planned to do, he'd beg to go with me, and I don't think I'd have the heart to say no." Frank took another drink from his mug. "It would be better if I wrote Will a note and explained things to him."

"When would you leave?"

"Early tomorrow morning, before Will wakes up." Frank drew in a ragged breath. "This hasn't been an easy decision for me, and I'll understand if you say no." He touched his chest. "I feel in my heart that you'd be good to my son, and I promise to send money as often as I can to help with his expenses."

Regina tapped her fingernails along the edge of the table, and Mark pulled his fingers through the end of his full beard. Finally Mark turned to Regina and said, "Well, what do you think?"

She nodded her head slowly. "I think taking care of Will until his dad returns is something God would want us to do."

Mark smiled. "I think so, too."

"Frank, aren't you coming down to breakfast? I called several times."

Frank's memories faded as his wife's voice invaded his thoughts. He lifted his head and looked up at her. "I didn't hear you."

Megan sat beside him on the bed. "What's wrong, Frank? You look so solemn. Are you upset about something?"

Frank pointed to the calendar across the room. "Today is Will's birthday, and I don't even know where he is. He's twenty-two years old, and I've only spent six of those years with him."

She leaned closer, her soft brown hair brushing his cheek. "I know that must hurt."

"You know what hurts the most? That I wasn't able to explain to Will why I never returned. In the note I left for Regina to read to him, I said I'd come back after I found another job." Frank moaned. "He must have grown up believing I abandoned him. He probably hates my guts."

"Frank, I'm sure he doesn't hate you."

"How do you know that? Think about it, Megan: If your dad left you with people you barely knew when you were only six years old and you never heard from him again, what would you think?"

"I'm sure I would have been very upset and probably felt as if I'd been abandoned, but I don't think I would have hated my father."

"That's easy for you to say. You weren't abused as a child."

Megan's mouth dropped open. "You. . .you abused Will?"

"No, I was abused by my dad."

"You were?"

He nodded.

"You never mentioned that before."

Frank ground his teeth together as he struggled with an image from the past. "Every time that man came home drunk, he smacked me around. I hated him for the abuse, and I hated my mother for not trying to stop him."

"Maybe she did. Maybe he wouldn't listen to her."

"She just stood there and let it happen." Frank grimaced. "He smacked her around plenty, too, and she never did a thing about it."

"Maybe she was too afraid. Maybe—"

"She was afraid, all right, but her fears weren't for me."

Megan took Frank's hand and gave his fingers a gentle squeeze. "I understand your anger and pain, but hating your parents is wrong. You need to forgive them instead of—"

"You don't know what it was like for me growing up with that man as my father!"

"No, I don't, but my father favored my sister. For a long time, I resented Beth for being his favorite and I felt angry at both of them. When I accepted Jesus as my Savior, I was able to release my pain and find forgiveness in my heart toward my father and my sister."

"I'm not sure I believe any of that feel-good religious stuff."

Megan reached for the Bible sitting on the nightstand by her side of the bed. "Let me read something to you, Frank." She opened the Bible and flipped through several pages. "John 8:32 says, 'And ye shall know the truth, and the truth shall make you free.' "

Frank shook his head. "I don't get it."

"When you accept Christ as your Savior

and ask Him to forgive your sins, you'll understand His truths and be able to forgive others. Wouldn't you like to do that, Frank? Wouldn't you like to—"

Frank jumped to his feet. "I need to eat breakfast so I can get to work. That's what I need to do."

Megan opened her mouth as if to say something more, but he held up his hand. "I don't want to talk about this anymore. I've got a trucking business to run, and it won't get done with me sitting here moaning about my past or listening to you quote Bible verses. The past is in the past. What's done is done. There's nothing I can do about it!"

"I'm glad you invited us to join you and Karen tonight," Mama Regina said, leaning over the buggy seat and tapping Will on the shoulder.

He glanced back at her and smiled. "I should have thought to invite you and Papa Mark in the first place. I don't know what I was thinking, leaving the two of you out of my birthday supper."

Papa Mark chuckled. "You were thinking

like a man in love. You wanted to spend your birthday alone with your future wife."

"Karen and I will have plenty of time to be alone after we're married." Will pulled back on the reins a bit to keep his horse from trotting too fast, although he was anxious to get to the Yoders' place to pick up Karen.

They rode the rest of the way in silence, and Will spent the time counting his blessings and enjoying the sights and sounds of the pleasant fall evening. Soon winter would be upon them, and then there would be sleigh rides in the snow, ice skating on the neighbor's pond, and sledding on the hill behind his folks' place. Will looked forward to becoming a father someday and taking his children outside to play in the snow, the way Papa Mark had done many times when Will was a boy. He remembered the time when Papa Mark decided to try out the sled he'd bought for Will's birthday. He'd said he wanted to give it a trial run and had ended up nearly hitting a tree. Instead, he'd landed in the frozen waters of the creek behind their house.

Will smiled as he pictured Papa Mark sitting in front of the fireplace with one of

Mama Regina's quilts wrapped around his shoulders and his teeth chattering so bad Will could hear them click. That was the last time Papa Mark had ridden Will's sled.

I thank God for Papa Mark and Mama Regina, Will thought. *Without their love and care, who knows where I'd be right now? They're my real parents in every sense of the word—not that man who called himself my dad then walked away and never came back. If Pop really loved me, then he would have at least written some letters letting me know where he was.*

Will clamped his teeth together so hard that his jaw began to ache. *I've got to quit thinking about the past and keep my thoughts on the future. That's all that counts—the future Karen and I will have together once we're married.*

Karen grabbed Will's birthday present and hurried out of her bedroom. When she got downstairs, she spotted Will in the hallway talking to Mom. The way he smiled when he saw Karen warmed her heart. A dimpled smile and twinkling blue eyes—that was the Will she'd fallen in love with.

"Are you ready?" he asked.

Karen nodded. "I just need to get my shawl and outer bonnet." She hurried into the kitchen and returned moments later, wearing the items.

They said good-bye to Karen's mother and went out the door.

"I don't know about you," Will said as they headed for his buggy, "but I'm sure lookin' forward to eating at Das Dutchman tonight. They have some real tasty choices on their menu."

Karen hoped Will wouldn't be disappointed when he discovered they weren't going to Das Dutchman, after all.

"So what'd you get me?" Will asked, motioning to the small box wrapped in green tissue paper that Karen held.

"You'll have to wait and see."

"You're not going to make me open it at the restaurant in front of a bunch of strangers, I hope."

"Of course not. You can open it after we've eaten—in the privacy of the buggy, if you like."

He grinned at her. "Maybe I'll wait until

we've dropped my folks off after supper and I've brought you back home. Then I can ask for a birthday kiss to go with the gift."

Karen felt the heat of a blush cascade over her cheeks. She hated how easily she blushed.

"I didn't mean to embarrass you." Will leaned close, and his warm breath tickled her ear, causing her to shiver. "I just wanted you to know that I'm looking forward to a little time alone with my soon-to-be bride."

She looked up at him and smiled. "I'm looking forward to that, as well."

Will had just guided his horse and buggy down the Yoders' driveway and was preparing to turn in the direction of Das Dutchman when Mama Regina tapped him on the shoulder. "I need to go home for a minute, Will."

"How come?"

"I forgot my pocketbook."

"Can't you go to supper without it? I'm hungry."

"My money's in the pocketbook, and I'll need it to pay for our meal."

Will glanced over his shoulder. "I figured Papa Mark would pay for our meal."

Papa Mark's face turned red as a radish. "Well, uh. . .your mamm insisted that she pay for supper, so I. . .uh. . .left my money at home."

"It's no big deal," Will said. "I'll take care of the check."

"No, you can't do that!" Mama Regina's voice rose. "It wouldn't be right for you to pay for your own birthday supper."

Will looked over at Karen, figuring she might offer to pay for the meal, but she stared straight ahead with a placid look on her face.

"How about this: I'll pay for our meals, and you can pay me back after we get home."

"No way!" his folks said in unison.

"Our place isn't that far from here, and it won't take long for your mamm to get her purse," Papa Mark insisted.

Will grunted. "Oh, all right." His folks could be pretty determined when they made up their minds about something. Clucking to his horse and giving the left rein a little tug, Will turned in the direction of home.

When they reached the house, Will

stopped the horse close to the porch so Mama Regina wouldn't have far to walk. Then he climbed down from the buggy and went around to the passenger's side to help her out.

"Would you mind going in after my purse?" she asked, making no move to leave her seat. "I think I left it on the kitchen counter."

"Jah, sure." Will figured he'd probably be quicker than she would, anyway, and he was eager to get to the restaurant.

He took the porch steps two at a time. When he opened the door and moved toward the kitchen, several people jumped out of the shadows. "Surprise! Happy birthday, Will!" they shouted.

CHAPTER 8

Will jumped back and bumped the wall with his elbow. "Yeow!"

Someone lit a gas lantern, flooding the room with light. There stood several of Will's friends: David Graber with his girlfriend, Amelia; Norman Yutzy with his girlfriend, Emma Sue; and Harley Kauffman with his wife, Luanne.

Karen, Mama Regina, and Papa Mark entered the house, wearing smiles that stretched from ear to ear.

"No wonder you wanted me to come inside and get your purse," Will said to Mama Regina.

She grinned. "Karen and I have been working on this little surprise for a couple of weeks."

Will looked over at Karen. "So we're not going out to supper?"

She shook her head. "Not tonight, anyway. Everyone brought food, so we'll eat supper here. Then we'll have cake and ice cream." She leaned closer to Will. "I hope you're not disappointed."

"He'd better not be," David said. "It wasn't easy to keep this secret."

"That's right. Finding a place to hide our horses and buggies was no small task," Norman said with a chuckle.

"Where did you put them?" Will asked.

"Left 'em over at Aaron Chupp's place, and then we walked over here."

"We were glad it wasn't raining," Luanne put in.

Will scratched his head. "So you snuck over here while we were at the Yoders' place picking up Karen?"

"That's correct," Harley said with a nod. "We had it timed just right, too."

"I guess you did."

"Let's go into the living room where we

can sit and visit awhile before we set out the food," Mama Regina suggested.

Will had just taken a seat on the sofa next to Karen when a knock sounded on the front door.

"I wonder who that could be," Papa Mark said with a sly smile. He looked over at Will and winked. "Why don't you answer it?"

Will hurried across the room and opened the door. His friend Nathan Chupp stood on the porch. Nathan and his family had moved to Ohio when Nathan and Will were teenagers, and Will hadn't seen Nathan for two years.

"Well, don't just stand there with your mouth hanging open," Nathan said with a grin. "Are you gonna invite me in to join your party?"

"Jah, of course. I. . .I'm just so surprised to see you." Will stepped aside. "I mean, I didn't know you were back in the area, and I sure didn't expect you'd be here to help celebrate my birthday."

"Aunt Susanna and Uncle Aaron have been kind of lonely since my cousin Sarah and her family moved to Illinois a few months ago. So I thought I'd come back to Middlebury and cheer 'em up for a bit."

Nathan entered the hallway and thumped Will on the back. "Figured while I was here, I may as well help you celebrate your twenty-second birthday."

"I'm glad you did. How long are you here for?"

Nathan shrugged. "Awhile, I guess."

"What about your job in Ohio?"

"Things are slow in the tree-cutting business right now, so my boss said he has no problem with me being gone a few weeks."

"And how are your folks doing?"

"Real well. They moved to Sarasota, Florida, a few months ago, and they seem to like it. The warmer weather helps my daed's arthritis."

"What about your sister? Is she still living in Ohio?" Will asked.

Nathan nodded. "Alice and her husband, James, like it there, so I'm sure they'll stay."

"How about you? Do you like it better in Ohio than here in Indiana?"

Nathan shrugged. "I like Ohio well enough, but there are some things I miss about living here." He thumped Will's back again. "I especially miss pickin' on you."

Will chuckled. "You think you might stick around for Karen's and my wedding?"

"I'd like that, but if I have to go back before then, I'll be sure to return for the wedding."

Will motioned to the living room. "Come join the others. I'm sure everyone will be glad to see you."

Nathan nodded. "I'm lookin' forward to seeing some of our friends again, too."

They were almost to the living room when the door swung open, and in walked Karen's parents and her sister, Cindy.

"Happy birthday, Will," Alvin said, clasping Will's shoulder.

"Danki. I'm glad you folks could come over."

"We wouldn't have missed your party for anything," Hannah said with a friendly smile. "After all, you'll soon be part of our family."

As Megan sat across the kitchen table from Frank, she felt concern. He hadn't said more than a few words since he'd returned home from work. No doubt he was still brooding about his son's birthday.

Megan had been married to Frank for ten years, and they'd been blessed with two beautiful girls, but something had always seemed to be missing in Frank's life. She felt sorry for him when he sank into depression on his son's birthday every year, but it upset her when it lingered through the holidays.

When Frank had brought up his son's birthday that morning, Megan thought he might open up and discuss his feelings, but he'd hurried off to work instead. She wanted to get him to talk about the way he felt—but not in front of the girls.

She glanced over at Carrie—their brown-eyed, dark-haired, eight-year-old daughter, who had just finished her plate of spaghetti. Red-headed, freckle-faced Kim, who had recently turned five, was still dawdling with hers. Frank, who'd been staring vacantly across the room, had only eaten a few bites.

Megan turned to Carrie and said, "Would you please take Kim to the bathroom and help her wash up?"

Carrie started to get up, but Kim frowned and pointed to her plate. "I'm not done, Mommy."

Megan pursed her lips. "You're just playing with your food, so it looks like you're done to me."

Kim scooped some spaghetti onto her fork and popped it into her mouth. "Is dat better?"

"Don't talk with your mouth full," Frank scolded. It was the first time he'd spoken since they'd sat down to supper.

Kim's chin trembled. "S—sorry, Daddy."

He reached over and patted the top of her head. "Just finish your meal and wash up like your mother said."

"Okay."

"Can I be excused?" Carrie asked, looking at Megan.

Megan nodded. "But when your sister is done, you'll need to see that she gets her hands and face washed."

"All right, Mommy." Carrie picked up her dishes, placed them in the sink, and scampered out of the room. A few minutes later, Kim did the same.

Megan turned to Frank. "I think we need to talk."

"About what?"

"About the mood you've been in all day."

He stared at her. "How would you know what kind of mood I've been in? I've been at work most of the day."

"That's true, but you were in a depressed state this morning, and ever since you came home from work, you've been in a sour mood."

He shrugged.

"If you'd talk about it, you might feel better."

"There's nothing to talk about."

Megan touched his arm. "Yes, there is, Frank. I'm pretty sure you're still fretting about your son's birthday. Don't you care how your gloomy moods affect me and the girls? Don't you care how it affects you?"

"I can't help it, Megan. Losing my first wife when she got hit by a car was hard enough to deal with, but at least that was no fault of mine." He pressed his fingers against the side of his head. "Losing Will nearly a year later isn't something I can forget, because that was my fault."

"It wasn't your fault, and I'm not saying you should forget about it. I'm just saying you can't let it consume your thoughts. It's not fair to any of us."

"I know, and I'll try to do better."

"You've told me a few things about having to leave your son behind, but there are so many details I don't know. I think it might help if you talk about it. Maybe sharing the details will help heal some of your emotional wounds."

Frank's fingers grazed the back of his wavy red hair. "If I knew where Will was and had the assurance that he was okay, I could quit brooding about the past."

"Maybe you should look for him."

"I've tried that, and where did it get me?" He grunted. "I wish I'd never gone to Regina and Mark's house with Will. I wish I'd never read that letter Patty received from Regina Stoltzfus."

"Didn't you tell me that Patty's folks used to live near Regina and that Patty's mother had written to Regina?"

"That's true, and after Patty's mother died, Regina started writing to Patty. In one of her letters, she told Patty that she was welcome to visit anytime. She also said if there was anything they could do for her, she shouldn't hesitate to ask."

"I didn't realize that. Some of the things you've told me have been rather sketchy."

"I didn't think you'd be interested in a blow-by-blow account of things."

"But I am interested, Frank. Please continue with your story."

He drew in a deep breath and sighed. "While Will and I were driving through Lancaster County a few days before Christmas, I decided to stop at Mark and Regina Stoltzfus's place to say hello. When I explained who I was and told them about Patty's death, they invited me and Will into their home to spend Christmas." Frank paused and took a drink of water. "I was amazed at how kind Mark and Regina were to us and how they lavished Will with so much attention. Then on Christmas night after Will went to bed, I made a regrettable decision."

"What was that?"

"I spoke with Regina and Mark, asking if they would keep Will until I could find a job that would keep me closer to home. Since both of Patty's parents were dead and I'd cut myself off from my family after I left home, I had no one to leave Will with." He grunted. "Not that I'd have left him with anyone in my dysfunctional family."

Megan opened her mouth to comment, but he rushed on.

"When Mark and Regina agreed to the arrangement, I left a note for Regina to read to Will, explaining things and saying that I'd return as soon as I could. Little did I know that two days later I would be involved in a terrible accident. As you know, the injuries I sustained in that accident put me in the hospital and kept me from returning for my boy for almost two years. If I'd known I couldn't get back to Will within a short time, I never would have left him with Regina and Mark."

"But if you'd taken Will with you, you still might have had the accident, and Will could have been seriously injured, or worse," Megan said.

"You're right, but even so, I don't think I'll ever get over the fact that once I was well enough to return to Lancaster County, I discovered Mark and Regina Stoltzfus had moved and taken my boy."

"There must have been a good reason for them moving, Frank. What I don't understand is why they didn't leave word with a neighbor or someone who could tell you where they'd moved."

"It's never made any sense to me, either. The only conclusion I could come to is that Mark and Regina moved on purpose so they could raise Will as their son. So they'd never have to see me again."

Megan gasped. "Do you really think that's why they moved?"

He nodded. "What other reason would there be for them not leaving word so I could find Will when I returned?"

"I. . .I don't know."

"When I went back to their farm and discovered someone else was living there, neither the English couple who'd bought the farm nor any of the neighbors knew where Mark and Regina had moved."

"I can only imagine how defeated you must have felt." Megan gave Frank's shoulder a gentle squeeze. "I'm still amazed that you were able to rise above your circumstances and establish your own trucking business."

"That didn't happen overnight, Megan. I spent a couple of years wallowing in self-pity, barely able to hold on to my job."

"But you did finally make something of yourself, and that's what counts."

He clasped her hand. "Meeting you

changed my life. If you hadn't been working at that truck stop where I stopped to eat supper, I'd probably still be trying to drown my sorrows. You gave me the strength to go on. You gave me the courage to start up my own business." He leaned his head on her shoulder. "I promise I'll try to be in a better mood this holiday season—for you and for the girls."

"Did you enjoy your birthday party?" Karen asked as she and Will headed toward her place in his buggy.

He nodded. "I don't know how you and Mama Regina pulled it off, but it sure was a surprise."

"We women have our ways," she said with a giggle.

"I especially liked the pocket watch you gave me. That was thoughtful."

"I know you lost your old pocket watch not long ago, and since I don't want you to be late for our wedding, I figured I'd better buy you a new one."

He reached across the seat and took hold of her hand. "Speaking of the wedding, are you sure you don't mind us living at my folks' place after we're married?"

She shook her head. "Not at all. Since you help your daed with the dairy cows and sometimes help your mamm in the health food store, it'll be easier for you to keep doing that with us living close by."

"That's true, and since my folks' bedroom is downstairs, we'll have the whole upstairs to ourselves. It'll almost be like having a place of our own."

She smiled. They rode in companionable silence the rest of the way home, and Karen enjoyed the familiar *clippety-clop* of the horse's hooves against the pavement as the buggy rocked gently from side to side. She loved being with Will like this and was pleased that he was in such a pleasant mood. The things that had been bothering him last week were obviously no longer on his mind.

Karen rested her head on Will's shoulder and closed her eyes, sending up a silent prayer. *Dear Lord, thank You for the fun evening Will and I shared with our friends. Help us remember to talk about our feelings when we're upset or concerned about something. And help me be the kind of wife Will needs. Amen.*

When Will turned the horse and buggy up the lane leading to Karen's house, she lifted her head from his shoulder and sighed. "I wish our evening didn't have to end so soon, and—"

Will stopped the horse, pulled Karen close, and halted her words with a kiss so sweet she felt as if she could melt right into his arms.

"I've been waiting all evening to do that," he whispered against her ear.

"I've been hoping you would."

He nuzzled the top of her head with his chin. "I wish December would hurry up and get here. I can hardly wait to make you my wife."

"And I can't wait for you to be my husband. Happy birthday, Will."

CHAPTER 9

As Frank headed down the road in one of his delivery trucks toward East Earl, Pennsylvania, he thought about the business he'd established ten years ago. Things had gone well for him in that regard. He had several drivers but was shorthanded this week because a couple of men were sick. That meant Frank had to make some runs himself. But that was okay; he rather enjoyed being behind the wheel of a semi, although he wouldn't want to drive full-time anymore.

Frank clicked on the radio and sang along with the country-western song blaring through the speakers. It was one of his all-time favorites—"On the Road Again."

His thoughts turned to the discussion he'd had with Megan a few nights ago. He had promised her that he'd be in a good mood during the holidays. He hoped he could keep that promise. In order to do it, however, he would need to focus on Megan and the girls and not allow himself to think about the son he'd left with Regina and Mark Stoltzfus.

By the time Frank had turned onto the highway leading to East Earl, he'd convinced himself that he could put his thoughts about Will on hold throughout the holidays and stay in a pleasant mood for his family.

He'd only gone a few miles when he spotted a buggy tipped on its side along the shoulder of the road. The horse that had been pulling the buggy lay on its side, too, and it wasn't moving. A car parked in front of the buggy had a dent in one fender.

Frank pulled over and reached for his cell phone. He was about to call 911 when he heard sirens in the distance. Apparently someone had already called for help.

Frank hopped out of his truck and raced across the street. "Is anyone hurt?" he called to the middle-aged man standing beside the car.

"I'm fine. The Amish man who was driving the buggy went to one of the nearby farms for help. He was shaken up a bit, and he's got some bumps and bruises, but I think he'll be okay." The man pointed first to the buggy and then to the horse. "I'm afraid the buggy will require some work, but that poor animal's not so lucky."

Frank slowly shook his head. "That's a shame."

The man nodded. "I feel really bad about hitting the horse and buggy, but I didn't see the buggy going down the hill until it was too late."

The sirens grew closer, and Frank glanced at his watch. "I've got a delivery to make, so unless you need my help, I'd better be on my way."

"No problem. Help will be here soon."

Frank sprinted across the street and climbed into his truck. As he pulled onto the road, his forehead beaded with sweat. Every time he saw an Amish buggy, he thought of Will and wondered how he was doing. Was he still living with Regina and Mark? Did they live somewhere in Pennsylvania, or had they moved to another state? Had Will joined the Amish church? Could he be married by now? These questions haunted Frank, no matter how hard he tried to push them out of his mind. Regrettably they were questions he'd probably never have answers for.

"I wish I didn't have to get my wisdom teeth pulled this morning," Karen said to her mother as they sat in the waiting room at the oral surgeon's office.

Mom reached over and took hold of Karen's hand. "Are you nervous about the procedure or worried about the pain you might have afterward?"

"A little of both, but I'm mostly worried about not being able to help in our store." Karen sighed. "I'll probably be stuck at home taking pain pills and rinsing my mouth for the next couple of days, and I won't be much help to anyone but myself."

Mom gently squeezed Karen's fingers. "It's okay. Your daed, Cindy, and Mavis can manage things in the store."

Karen rolled her eyes. "My little sister's not much help to anyone these days. It seems like she's always got her mind on some *kall* instead of the job at hand."

Mom chuckled. "That's true, but it's normal for a girl Cindy's age to be thinking about fellows."

"Not when she's thinking about the *wrong* fellow."

Deep wrinkles formed in Mom's forehead. "What fellow does Cindy have her eye on?"

"Leroy Eash."

Mom's mouth fell open. "Has she told you she has an interest in Leroy?"

Karen nodded. "You should have seen the way she looked at him when he stopped by our house the other day. If it was obvious to me, I'm sure Leroy must have noticed it, too."

"I'd better have a talk with Cindy."

"I already did. I reminded her that's Leroy's too old for her and said she shouldn't be thinking about him in a romantic sort of way."

Mom pursed her lips. "The age difference might be okay if Cindy was older, but since she's not, it's good that you discouraged her. I'll talk to her about the matter, too. If she doesn't listen, then I'll mention it to your daed and let him take things from there."

A middle-aged woman entered the room and called Karen's name.

"Guess it's now or never," Karen said as she rose from her seat.

Mom gave her a reassuring smile. "I'll be praying that everything goes well."

When Will entered the makeshift shop he'd set up in their storage shed, he noticed that the door was ajar. He figured Papa Mark must have gotten something from the shed earlier and forgotten to close the door.

He lit the lantern hanging overhead, as well as the small propane-operated stove. He rubbed his hands briskly to warm them up and was about to grab his hammer and a can of nails when he heard a strange squeaking noise. He tipped his head and listened. There it was again.

He followed the sound to the back of the shed and halted when he came to a wooden box full of rags. There lay Sandy with five squealing puppies nestled against her body.

"Well, what do you know?" Will leaned closer to the box for a better look. "I guess you didn't like the bed I made for you in the barn, huh, girl?"

Sandy grunted as she opened her eyes and looked up at him.

Will patted the top of her head. "Go on back to sleep; I won't disturb you or your sleeping pups." He grabbed his tools and some pieces of wood, figuring he could work in the barn. He'd just stepped outside when he spotted his friend Nathan coming from the store.

"Wie geht's, Will?" Nathan asked.

"I'm doing okay. How about you?"

"Can't complain. I stopped at your mamm's store to see if you were working, and she said you were either in the shed or the barn."

Will motioned to the shed. "I was going to do some work in there, but I discovered that my cocker spaniel snuck in and had her hundlin there. I figured I'd better head out to the barn to work so I wouldn't disturb Sandy and her brood."

"How many pups did she have?"

"Five in all. Would you like to see 'em?"

"Maybe some other time. I'm on my way to Goshen to do some shopping at Wal-Mart and wondered if you'd like to go along."

"I appreciate the offer, but I think I'd better pass." Will lifted his tool pouch. "I'm heading to the barn to work on a birdhouse I plan to give Karen for Christmas. When I'm done, I'm going over to Karen's house to see how she's doing."

"What's wrong with Karen? Is she grank?" Nathan asked as he followed Will to the barn.

Will shook his head. "She's not sick. She was supposed to have her wisdom teeth pulled this morning. If it goes anything like it did when my mamm had hers out a few years ago, Karen probably won't feel like herself for the next couple of days."

"Karen's got youth on her side, so I'm sure it won't be near as bad as what your mamm went through."

"Are you saying Mama Regina's old?" Will asked as he placed the wood and tools on the workbench inside the barn door.

" 'Course not. That isn't what I meant at all."

"What did you mean?"

"I meant that Karen's young and—"

Will held up his hand. "That's okay. No need to explain. I guess I'm a bit oversensitive where Mama Regina's concerned."

"How come?"

"You know the story, Nathan. If Mama Regina and Papa Mark hadn't taken me in and raised me like a son, I'd have probably been hauled off to some orphanage or put in a foster home."

"I'd never thought about that possibility. I can see why Mark and Regina are so special to you."

Will nodded and picked up his hammer and a nail. He positioned it over one of the pieces of wood and brought down the hammer. "Yeow!" He pulled his thumb back, and the hammer thudded to the floor.

"You'd better watch what you're doin', *dummkopp*." Nathan bent to pick up the hammer. "A few more misses like that, and you won't have a thumb left."

"I was watching. I just missed the nail, that's all." Will squinted at Nathan. "And what's up with the dunce remark? I thought you were my *gut* friend."

"I was only kidding, and I am your good friend." Nathan placed the hammer on the workbench and thumped Will on the back. "Which is why I've decided to stay here in Indiana—at least until after your wedding."

"Really? You're not going back to Ohio for Thanksgiving?"

"Nope. I may not go back for Christmas or New Year's, either. I may decide to stay here permanently."

"That'd be great, Nathan." Will's face broke into a wide smile. "Now I know for sure that you'll be here as one of my witnesses."

"At your wedding?"

Will gave his friend a playful swat on the arm. "Of course, at my wedding. What else would I want you to be my witness for?"

Nathan motioned to Will's throbbing thumb. "I thought maybe you wanted me to witness you smacking your thumb a few more times."

Will grunted. "I'll take that to mean you like being with me."

"Of course." Nathan moved toward the door. "I'd better get going."

Will picked up his hammer. "See you soon."

CHAPTER 10

When Frank entered his house and smelled
the distinctive aroma of stuffed peppers
coming from the kitchen, his stomach rumbled. It felt good to be home, and he was
more than ready to eat supper.

"Daddy!" Kim squealed as she wrapped
her arms around his legs. "I missed you,
Daddy!"

"I missed you, too." Frank bent down
and scooped the little girl into his arms.
"Where's your big sister?"

"She's in the kitchen settin' the table."

Frank kissed the top of Kim's curly

head. "How come you're not in there help-ing her?"

" 'Cause I'm in here with you."

He smiled and set the child on the floor. "Where's your mother? Is she in the kitchen, too?"

Kim nodded. "Mommy made hot dogs for me and Carrie." She crinkled her nose. "That's 'cause we don't like green pep-pers."

Frank grimaced. Megan was always pacifying the kids. He thought they ought to learn to eat real people food, but he wouldn't make an issue of it tonight. He was too tired to argue about anything. He just wanted to relax and enjoy his meal then spend the rest of the evening sprawled out on the couch watching his favorite game show on TV.

Frank took Kim's hand and headed for the kitchen, where he found Megan mak-ing a tossed green salad while Carrie filled the glasses on the table with water.

"Be careful with that pitcher," Frank ad-monished. "And don't fill the glasses too full."

Megan whirled around, a frown marring

her forehead. "Is that any way to greet your daughter?"

"Sorry," Frank mumbled. He waited until Carrie was finished with the water then bent down and kissed her cheek. "Did you have a good day at school?"

She nodded. "We got to draw pictures of our favorite zoo animal. I drew a monkey, and Teacher said my picture was really good."

"That's nice, honey." Frank snatched a pickle from the jar on the counter and took a bite. "How soon until supper's ready, Megan?"

Her frowned deepened. "Is that all I get—'How soon until supper's ready'?"

"Sorry. It's been a long day, and I'm hungry enough to eat a horse."

Kim's eyes widened. "You wouldn't really eat a horse, would ya, Daddy?"

He ruffled her hair. "It's just an expression, pumpkin."

She stared up at him and blinked a couple of times. "What's a 'spression?"

"It's 'expression,' and it means a way of saying something." Frank turned to give Megan a hug. "How was your day?"

"It was fine. I—"

"You'll never guess what I saw on my way to East Earl this morning."

"What'd you see, Daddy?" The question came from Carrie.

"I saw an Amish buggy turned on its side, and the horse pulling the buggy was on the ground."

Carrie gasped, and Kim's mouth fell open. "Was it dead?" they asked in unison.

"It seemed to be. I stopped to see if I could help, but the emergency vehicles were on the way, so I didn't hang around long."

"Was anyone hurt, Daddy?" Carrie questioned.

"From what I was told, the driver of the buggy was shaken up pretty good, but he wasn't seriously hurt." Frank slowly shook his head. "He sure could have been, though. I've heard of some buggy accidents that left—"

Megan nudged Frank's arm. "Could we please talk about something else? I don't think this is a good topic of conversation for the girls."

He shrugged. "It's a fact of life, and the girls shouldn't be sheltered from the truth."

Megan shot Frank an icy stare as she handed him the bowl of salad. "Would you please put this on the table? It's time to eat."

"Yeah, sure." Frank placed the bowl on the table and went to the refrigerator to get the salad dressing. He'd just taken a seat when Megan placed the hot dogs and stuffed peppers on the table. He swallowed the temptation to talk to her about the unhealthy way she fed the girls.

When Megan sat down, she looked over at Kim and said, "Would you like to ask the blessing tonight?"

Kim nodded and bowed her head. "Dear God, thanks for the yummy hot dogs and please keep all the horses in the world safe. Amen."

Frank bit the side of his cheek to keep from laughing. Most kids had a soft spot for animals, and Kim was certainly no exception.

He grimaced as a rush of memories flooded his mind—memories of when Will was a little guy, seeking answers to countless questions and often begging for a dog. But Frank couldn't give Will a dog because they were always on the road. To his way of thinking, it wasn't practical to have a pet unless he could give it a good home. A boy needed a home, too—a place his father would return to each evening after work.

"Frank, did you hear what I said?"

He jerked his head in Megan's direction. "What was that?"

"Would you please pass the salad?"

"Yeah, sure." He handed her the salad, as well as the bottle of dressing.

"How much longer do you think you'll be on the road driving one of your trucks?" Megan asked.

"That depends on how long Mitch and Ray are out sick." He grabbed the salt-shaker and sprinkled some on his salad.

"Do you have to use so much salt? It's not good for your blood pressure."

Frank gripped his fork so tightly that his fingers started to throb. Megan was worried about him eating too much salt, yet she fed the kids hot dogs four times a week. Where was the logic in that?

"My insurance policy's paid up," he muttered as he forked some salad into his mouth. "If I die from eating too much salt, your financial needs will be met."

"Frank!" Megan pursed her lips and gave him her "You shouldn't talk like that in front of the girls" look.

Frank crammed another forkful of salad into his mouth. Fine, then—he would eat the rest of his meal in silence!

As Megan watched Frank, she noticed how red his face had become. He was obviously upset about something, and she figured it wasn't just her mentioning that he had used too much salt on his salad. More than likely, seeing the results of that Amish buggy accident today had brought back memories of his son. He'd probably been stewing about his past most of the day.

When Frank finished eating, he put his dishes in the sink and headed for the living room.

Megan turned to the girls and said, "When you're done eating, I'd like you to go upstairs and get ready for bed."

"Can't we play awhile?" Carrie whined.

"After you're in your pajamas, you can

play for half an hour. Oh, and be sure to say good night to your daddy before you go upstairs."

As Megan did the dishes, she rehearsed what she wanted to say to Frank when she joined him in the living room. She had come up with an idea she wanted to share and hoped he would be open to it.

When she entered the living room a short time later, she found him lying on the couch, watching TV. "Mind if I join you?"

"Be my guest." Frank shifted his feet, making room for her to sit on the other end of the couch. "This new game show is really good. The contestants are expected to—"

"Frank, we need to talk."

"Yeah, okay. As soon as there's a commercial."

"I'd like to talk to you now, if you don't mind."

Deep wrinkles formed in his forehead. "What's so important that it can't wait until commercial time?"

"Our lives—that's what's important."

He muted the volume on the TV. "What about our lives?"

"I think this whole fixation you have with

Amish people and their buggies and horses needs to stop."

"I don't have a fixation with the Amish."

"Yes, you do. Ever since we moved to Pennsylvania, all you've done is look at Amish buggies, talk about Amish people, and brood over the loss of your boy."

Frank pulled himself to a sitting position and swung his legs over the couch. "What would you have me do—forget I ever had a son named Will?"

"Of course not, but you don't know where Will is, and you have a wife and two beautiful daughters who need your love and attention." Megan sighed. "Just a few weeks ago, you promised you'd keep your focus on me and the girls."

"I am keeping my focus on you. I just can't think about you every waking minute." He grimaced and thumped the side of his head. "No matter how hard I try, I can't stop thinking about Will. Every time I see an Amish buggy or a young Amish man, I'm reminded that my son is out there somewhere, and short of a miracle, I'll never see him again."

"Then I think we should move."

"What?"

"I think we should move someplace where there are no Amish communities."

His lips compressed as he folded his arms. "I can't believe you said that, Megan. In case you've forgotten, my business is here."

"I know, but you can relocate."

He shook his head. "I am not relocating!"

CHAPTER 11

Karen stretched her legs to the end of the sofa as she snuggled beneath the quilt Mom had draped over her. Despite the pain Karen had in her mouth, it felt kind of nice to be pampered a bit.

"Is there anything I can bring you?" Mom asked. "Maybe some juice or a bowl of Jell-O?"

Karen shook her head. "I'm still full from the oatmeal I had for breakfast."

"Do you need another pain pill?"

"No, I'm fine."

Mom patted Karen's feet. "If you need anything, just give a ring."

Karen looked at the little bell Mom had placed on the table near the sofa. "How are you going to hear me ring that if you're working in the store?"

"I won't be working there today. Cindy and your daed can manage without me, and Mavis plans to work a few hours this afternoon."

"But you didn't work in the store yesterday because you went with me to the oral surgeon's, and since I won't be up to helping for a few more days—"

Mom held up her hand. "Don't worry about it. I wouldn't feel right about leaving you in the house alone. What if you started bleeding real bad or needed me for something?"

Karen was tempted to argue further but didn't have the strength for it. Besides, it would be nice to know Mom was in the house. "Danki," she said as she relaxed against the pillow Mom had placed under her head.

"You're welcome." Mom moved toward the door. "I'll be in the kitchen doing the dishes. Don't forget to ring the bell if you need me."

When Mom left the room, Karen took

her Bible from the coffee table and turned to Psalms. Her gaze came to rest on Psalm 146:5: "Happy is he that hath the God of Jacob for his help, whose hope is in the LORD his God."

She closed her eyes. *Thank You, Lord, for the reminder that You are my help. Please give me the patience to rest while I heal."*

A knock at the back door ended Karen's prayer.

"I'll get it," Mom called from the kitchen.

A few seconds later, Leroy stepped into the living room. "Wie geht's?" he asked as he approached Karen.

"I've been better, but I think I'll live."

"That's good to hear." Leroy smiled as he took a seat in the chair across from her. "I was over at your folks' store, and Cindy said you'd had your wisdom teeth pulled yesterday. So I decided to stop in and see how you're doing."

"Except for the swelling and some pain, I'm getting along okay."

Leroy touched his left cheek and grimaced. "When I had one of my wisdom teeth pulled a few years ago, I ended up with a dry socket. Sure hope that doesn't happen to you, because I think the pain of it was worse than the aftermath of getting the tooth pulled."

"I'm being careful to do everything the dentist said, so hopefully it won't."

The chair squeaked as Leroy began to rock. "How are things going with your wedding plans? Have you got your invitation list made out yet?"

"I've been working on mine. Hopefully Will has his about ready, too."

"Speaking of Will, I figured he'd be here right now, hovering over you like a lovesick *hundli*."

"Will's not a lovesick puppy."

"Jah, okay. Whatever you say."

"My mamm said Will came by to see me yesterday afternoon while I was sleeping, and he left me a plant." Karen motioned to the Christmas cactus sitting on the small table across the room. "I'm sure he'll be over again sometime today."

Leroy gave Karen a wide grin and winked at her. "I hope you know when I said Will was a lovesick puppy, I was just trying to give you a hard time."

"The way you did when we were *kinner*?"

"Right."

Karen thought about the way Leroy had tormented her during their growing-up years—putting cold snow down her back in the wintertime, passing her notes in school that got both of them in trouble with their teacher, hiding her bike in the bushes so she'd be late getting home from school, and generally making a nuisance of himself. Yet despite Leroy's crazy, irritating ways, Karen had begun courting him as soon as she'd turned sixteen. They'd never been really serious about each other—at least not in a romantic way. But they had spent many fun times together, and since she felt comfortable with Leroy, she'd been content to be courted by him—until Will had caught her eye at a singing one night and asked if he could give her a ride home in his buggy. Since Leroy hadn't been able to attend the singing due to a bout with the flu, Karen hadn't hesitated to accept Will's offer. From that night on, she knew she could never have a serious relationship with Leroy. The day Karen told Leroy that she wanted to break up with him, she had been pleased that he'd taken it so well. Leroy had even suggested that he and Karen should still be friends.

Another knock sounded on the door. A few seconds later, Will stepped into the room holding a paper sack. He took one look at Leroy and halted; then he looked over at Karen with a questioning look. "I didn't realize you had company." He set the paper sack on the coffee table. "Maybe I should leave your mamm's vitamins and come back later."

Leroy jumped up. "Don't leave on my account. I need to get back to work, anyway." He smiled and winked at Karen. "Take care of yourself now, ya hear?"

She nodded. "I will. See you later, Leroy."

As soon as Leroy left the room, Will took a seat on the sofa beside Karen. "I came by yesterday, but your mamm said you were sleeping."

"I know. I'm sorry I missed you. I think the pain medicine knocked me right out." She motioned to the plant. "Danki for the Christmas cactus. It has some real pretty blooms on it already."

"You're welcome. I'm glad you like it."

He reached for her hand. "How are you feeling? Are you in much pain?"

She shook her head. "It's not bad. Of course, I did have a pain pill with my breakfast this morning."

He studied her intently. "You look pretty good. There isn't as much swelling as I thought there would be."

She touched the side of her face. "I do have a black-and-blue mark right here, though."

"It's not that noticeable, and it'll go away soon, I expect."

"That's what my mamm said, too."

Will let go of her hand. "I'm curious about something."

"What's that?"

"I'm wondering why every time I come over to see you, Leroy is here."

"I've told you before, Leroy's just a friend. And he's not here every time you come over."

"Sure seems like it."

"I've also told you many times that you have no reason to be jealous of Leroy. We've known each other since we were bopplin. When we were toddlers, we used to play in the sandbox together. Once, Leroy tried to get me to eat some sand. I said I would if he ate some first."

"What happened?"

"Leroy ate some sand."

"Guess that proves he's not so *schmaert,* after all."

"Leroy didn't know any better; he was just a little *buwe*." Karen wrinkled her nose. "I hate to admit it, but I tried some, too."

"How'd it taste?"

She grimaced. "It was pretty awful."

"Are you warm enough?" Will asked, changing the subject. "It seems kind of chilly in here to me."

She patted the quilt covering the lower half of her body. "I'm plenty warm, but if you're cold, maybe you should throw another log onto the fire."

"Okay." Will moved over to the wood box, threw two logs into the fireplace, and stoked the fire until it crackled nicely, sending plenty of warmth into the room.

"Guess what?" Will asked as he sat beside Karen again.

"What?"

"Sandy had five hundlin sometime

during the night, and she found her way into the storage shed to give birth."

"I'll bet the puppies are cute. I'm anxious to see them."

Will shrugged. "Right now they don't look so cute, but in a few days, I'm sure they will. That's how it always is with newborn pups."

Karen's mother entered the room and smiled at Will. "Would you like something to drink? Maybe some coffee, tea, or hot chocolate?"

"Hot chocolate would be nice."

Hannah turned to Karen. "What would you like?"

"A glass of water will be fine for me, Mom."

"I'll be back soon." Hannah left the room and returned a few minutes later, carrying a snack tray, which she set on the table near the sofa. "The cookies and hot chocolate are for Will, and the water and applesauce are for you," she said, smiling at Karen.

"Danki, Mom."

Will grabbed a cookie and bit into it. "Mmm. . .peanut butter's my favorite."

Karen poked Will in the ribs. "I think all cookies are your favorite."

He finished the cookie and took a drink from his mug. "You're right—I like cookies and most any dessert."

"Talking about desserts," Hannah said, "it won't be long before my daughters and I will begin baking pies for Thanks-giving. Then there will be preparations for your wedding, and after that, we'll have Christmas goodies to bake."

Will thumped his stomach and groaned. "By the time the new year rolls around, I'll have eaten so much I'll have to go on a diet."

Hannah chuckled. "What's your favorite holiday dessert, Will?"

"Without a doubt, it's White Christmas Pie. Mama Regina fixes that every year at Christmas. Sometimes she serves it for Thanksgiving, too."

"I'll have to get the recipe from her," Karen said. "That way I can make it for you after we're married."

"Speaking of Mama Regina," Will said, "she wanted me to let you know that she's thinking of you and praying for a speedy recovery. Oh, and I almost forgot," he added, reaching for the paper sack he'd set on the coffee table and turning to Hannah.

"Here are the vitamins and shampoo you wanted."

"Danki," Hannah said as she took the sack. "How much do I owe you?"

Will shrugged. "I don't know. Guess you can settle up with my mamm the next time you drop by the store."

"I'll do that. And now I'd better get back to the kitchen and check on the cookies I have in the oven." Hannah scooted out of the room.

Will finished his refreshments and visited with Karen until he noticed her eyelids drooping. Then he set his cup on the table and stood. "You look tired. I'd better go so you can rest."

"So soon?" She yawned. "It seems like you just got here."

He leaned over and kissed her forehead. "I'll check on you again tomorrow."

"Okay." She yawned again. "Danki for coming over."

"You're welcome." Will picked up the tray and slipped out of the room. When he entered the kitchen, he placed the tray on the table. "I just wanted you to know that I'm leaving now, Hannah."

"You didn't stay very long."

"Karen's sleepy, so I figured it was best to let her rest." He motioned to the tray. "Danki for the refreshments."

"You're welcome. Would you like to take a few cookies to eat on your drive home?"

"The offer's tempting, but I'd better not eat anything more. Mama Regina won't like it if she fixes a big noon meal and I'm not able to eat any of it."

Hannah chuckled. "We mothers do like our families to eat what we put on the table."

"I'll be back to see Karen again soon," Will said as he turned toward the door.

"Good-bye, Will."

Will stepped outside, and as he headed for the hitching rail on the other side of the barn, he began to whistle. When he rounded the corner of the barn, he halted. His horse and buggy were gone!

"If Leroy let my horse go as some kind of a prank, he's going to be in big trouble!" Will glanced around and whistled for Ben, but he saw no sign of the horse.

Just then a van came up the driveway. A middle-aged English man got out and headed toward Will. "A horse and buggy with no driver came tearing down this driveway a few minutes ago. It plowed right into my van and scared me and my wife half to death! Would you happen to know who owns that rig?"

"I think it's mine." Will's heartbeat picked up speed as he imagined the worst. "Is—is my horse hurt? Did he do any damage to your van?"

The man shook his head. "Except for a trail of mucous left from the horse's nose, my van's fine. I wasn't able to check the horse over, though. He went tearing down the road, whipping the empty buggy from side to side."

Will groaned. "I'd better see if I can catch him."

"If you'd like to get in my van, we can probably get to your horse faster than you can on foot."

"Thanks, I appreciate the help." Will climbed into the backseat of the van, and they pulled onto the road.

A short time later, Will spotted Ben running full speed ahead, with the buggy zig-zagging back and forth like a snake slithering through the grass.

"I'll try to pass the buggy and pull in

front of the horse to slow it down," the English man said.

"Be careful, Lew." The man's wife stiff-
ened as she braced her hands against
the dashboard.

Lew accelerated and whipped into the
other lane. As he was about to pass the
buggy, Will's horse veered to the right.
Bang!—the buggy smacked into the side
of the van.

The woman screamed as Lew pulled
the van in front of the horse and rammed
on the brakes. He and Will jumped out,
and Will raced around to grab Ben's bridle.

"What's the damage?" Will called to the
Englisher.

"Looks like your buggy has a few dents
in it, and my van a nice big ding in the rear
door, as well as some ugly scratch marks."

"I'm sorry about all this," Will apologized.
"If you have something I can write my
name and address on, you can contact
me. I'll be happy to pay for the damages
done to your vehicle."

Lew went back to the van and returned
with a notepad and pen. "Do you think you

can get your buggy home okay, or will you need a tow?"

"The buggy's not totaled, and my horse seems to be okay, so I think I can manage on my own." Will led Ben to the side of the road and made sure the harness, bridle, and reins were secure. Then he climbed into the buggy and started for home. He wasn't thrilled about having to pay to fix his buggy, as well as the Englisher's van, but at least no one had been hurt. In buggy accidents involving other vehicles, that was not always the case.

CHAPTER 12

That Sunday, Will swung his legs out from under the covers on his bed and sat up. He had to help Papa Mark milk the cows before they left for church. Milking twice a day was part of running a dairy farm, even on their day of rest.

He hurried to get dressed and headed downstairs, where he found Mama Regina scurrying around the kitchen.

"Did you sleep well, son?" she asked.

He yawned and stretched his arms over his head. "As well as could be expected, I guess."

"Are you still fretting over that bill the

English man brought by yesterday for the damage your horse and buggy did to his van?"

"I can't say I'm thrilled about having to pay for the repairs, but that's not what kept me awake."

"What, then?"

"I'm irritated with Leroy because I think he released Ben from the hitching rail."

Mama Regina's eyebrows lifted high on her forehead. "Do you really believe Leroy would do something like that?"

Will shrugged. "He's been a thorn in my side ever since we moved to Indiana. I wouldn't put anything past that *narrish* fellow."

She clicked her tongue. "Come now, Will; Leroy's not crazy. He may be a bit of a character, but I don't think he's a thorn in your side, either."

"Jah, he is. You should see the way he hangs around the Yoders' place all the time, hovering over Karen and talking her ear off." Will grunted. "Even though he and Karen aren't a couple anymore, I think he wishes they were."

"It's you Karen agreed to marry." Mama Regina poured coffee into a thermos and handed it to Will. "You need to keep that in mind."

"But what if Leroy talks her out of marrying me?"

"I'm sure he doesn't have that much influence over Karen. It's you she loves." She patted Will's back. "Now set your worries aside and take that coffee out to the milking barn. Your daed's out there now waiting for you."

"I'd better hurry, then." Will grabbed his jacket and rushed out the door.

As Megan waited in the kitchen for Frank and the girls to come down for breakfast, her gaze came to rest on the Amish newspaper a friend had given her.

Flipping through the pages, she discovered the classified section. "Hmm. . .I wonder. . ."

"You wonder what?" Frank asked when he stepped into the room.

"Look at this." Megan pointed to the paper. "There are some interesting want ads and notices in the classified section of this Amish newspaper."

He meandered across the room and

poured himself a cup of coffee. "Like what?"

"Under the notice section, there's an ad from someone searching for a friend who moved from Nevada to Ohio to learn more about the Amish communities there."

"That's interesting, but don't you think you ought to get breakfast started? I'm hungry, and I'm sure the girls will be, too."

"I thought this was supposed to be your Sunday to fix breakfast."

He drank some coffee and flopped into a seat at the table. "After driving a truck all week, I'm really bushed this morning. Would you mind making breakfast?"

"Since you asked so nicely, I'd be happy to fix breakfast." Megan motioned to the newspaper again. "I'd like to discuss something with you first, though. I think you should run an ad in *The Budget*. I'm surprised one of us hasn't thought of it before."

His eyebrows lifted. "Why would I want to run an ad in *The Budget*? I don't have anything to sell that would interest the Amish."

"Maybe not, but you do have a son you haven't been able to find."

He drummed his fingers along the edge of the table. "Are you suggesting I place an ad asking if anyone knows my son or the Amish couple I left him with who used to live in Lancaster County, Pennsylvania?"

"That's exactly what I think you should do."

He shook his head. "I think it would be a waste of money."

"How come?"

"Because when I was able to return to Lancaster County after my accident, no one I spoke with knew where Will and the Stoltzfus couple had gone."

"But if you ran an ad in *The Budget*, you'd be doing something that might lead to your son. Wouldn't that be better than moping around here every holiday season, making everyone in the family feel miserable?"

"I'm not moping around or trying to make anyone miserable. I'm having a cup of coffee while I wait for my breakfast. After I'm done eating, I'm going to stretch out on the couch and watch TV."

"I was hoping you might go to church with me and the girls this morning."

"Not interested." Frank pushed away from the table. "I think I'll go upstairs and see if the girls are awake."

"What about the ad for *The Budget*?"

He shook his head. "I really don't think it's worth the effort."

At eight thirty, Will pulled his horse and buggy up to the Grabers' place, where church was being held. Several black buggies were parked in a row near the box-shaped wagon that had been used to transport the wooden benches from the Bontragers' place, where they'd had their last church meeting. The first person Will spotted was Leroy, dressed in his Sunday white shirt, black pants, matching vest, and *mutza* coat.

"How'd you get those dents in your buggy?" Leroy asked as Will began to unhitch his horse.

"My horse got loose from the hitching rail when I was visiting Karen last week, and he ran into a van out on the road. Then as we went to chase after the horse, the buggy sideswiped the man's van." Will glared at Leroy. "You wouldn't know any-thing about that, would you?"

Leroy's dark eyebrows drew together. "Huh?"

"Did you let my horse go?"

"Of course not. Why would I do some-thing like that?"

"You tell me."

"Don't be lecherich, Will."

"I'm not being ridiculous. You've always liked to get my goat, and I figured you—"

"Well, you figured wrong! It's too bad about your horse breaking free, but I had absolutely nothing to do with it." Leroy grabbed his horse's bridle and led him to the rope that had been stretched between several posts in the barnyard.

Will figured there wasn't much more to be said without making a scene, so he fol-lowed with his horse. Maybe Leroy was telling the truth. Ben might have gotten tired of waiting and broken free on his own. He had been pretty unpredictable lately. Since Will had no proof that Leroy had done it, he guessed he'd better give him the benefit of the doubt.

As soon as Will had his horse tied to the

rope, he headed for the new addition the Grabers had built onto their house for church and other large gatherings. He was almost to the porch when he spotted Karen's folks coming up the walkway with Karen's sister, Cindy, trailing behind. "Where's Karen?" Will asked, stepping up to Cindy.

"She woke up with a lot of pain in her jaw, so she stayed home in bed."

Will winced. "I'm sorry to hear that. When I was over the other day, she seemed to be getting along fairly well."

"That's what we thought, too," Hannah interjected. "I'm pretty sure Karen has a dry socket, so we'll have to see the dentist sometime tomorrow."

"I could take her if you like," Will offered.

Hannah smiled. "I appreciate the offer, but I'd rather go with Karen myself. That way I can ask the dentist a few questions."

"Maybe when church is over, I'll go over to see Karen. I'd feel better if I knew how she was doing."

"She might be sleeping," Karen's father, Alvin, replied. "Maybe you should wait until late this afternoon."

Will nodded. As much as he wanted to see Karen, he wouldn't go against her father's wishes.

"Where are your folks?" Hannah asked. "Aren't they with you today?"

"They came in their own buggy and left home before I did, so I'm guessing Mama Regina's in the kitchen visiting with the women, and Papa Mark's probably in the yard someplace talking to the men. Since I was planning to take Karen for a buggy ride after church, I brought my own rig today. I wanted to show her my dog's puppies today, too."

"I'm sorry your plans were ruined," Hannah said. "Karen felt bad about not being able to come to church this morning, and I know she was looking forward to spending time with you afterward."

Alvin thumped Will on the back. "I'm sure there'll be plenty of other times for you and Karen to go buggy riding."

"Jah."

Will spotted Bishop Miller and the other ministers leading a group of older men to the addition. He followed, along with several others, and when he stepped onto the porch, he removed his black hat and placed it on a bench near the door where other men's hats lay. Then he entered the house and found a place on a backless wooden bench beside his friend Nathan.

"I haven't seen you for a few days," Nathan said. "How are things going?"

"Not so good." Will began telling Nathan the story of how his horse had gotten loose but had to stop talking when the bishop announced the opening of the service.

Harley Kauffman, the song leader, announced the page number of a hymn and asked David Graber to lead it. The people opened their *Ausbund* hymnals to the appropriate place. As they began to sing, the ministers left to meet in another room so they could decide who would take which parts of the service and discuss church business.

The congregation finished the first hymn and began the second. It took almost fifteen minutes to sing the four verses of the praise song, and Will's mind began to wander as he thought about Karen. He was anxious to check on her and see how she was doing.

During the second verse of the next song, the ministers returned to the room and took their seats. The singing stopped at the end of the verse. Will pulled his attention to the side of the room where Perry Hochstetler, a visiting minister, stood. Perry spoke for half an hour; then everyone knelt for silent prayer. After that came the scripture reading from Deacon Mast, and then Bishop Miller delivered the main sermon.

Will's mind continued to wander as he thought about his encounter with Leroy. He knew it was wrong to nurse a grudge or feel jealous of someone, but he couldn't seem to help himself where Leroy was concerned.

By the time church was over, Will was struggling with his emotions so much that his face was beaded with sweat. When the men and boys exited the house by rows, he hurried outside for some much-needed fresh air. He was tempted to get his horse and buggy and head over to see Karen but remembered that her father had said she was probably sleeping.

"Let's find a place to sit, and you can tell me the rest of that horse story you began before church started," Nathan said.

Will nodded and motioned to the barn.

"Why don't we go in there and get out of this chilly air?"

"Sounds good to me."

"How are those hundlin of yours doing?" Nathan asked as they began walking.

"Real well. They're cute little pups. I don't think I'll have any trouble finding homes for them after they're weaned."

"If I knew for sure that I'd be staying in Indiana, I might buy one from you."

"You could always take the pup back to Ohio."

"That's true, but I'll have to wait and see how it goes."

They were almost to the barn when David Graber came running across the yard, waving his arms and hollering. "There's a horse hung up on the hitching rope, and I think it's dead!"

Everyone in the yard dashed toward the line of horses, including Will and Nathan. When Will reached the rope, he screeched to a stop and gasped. His horse was hung up on the rope!

CHAPTER 13

I'm sure sorry about this," Elam Graber said to Will as they watched his lifeless horse being loaded into the dead animal truck for removal on Monday morning.

Will slowly shook his head. "I still can't figure out how Ben got hung up on that rope. He's been pretty spooky lately, so I guess it's possible that he was trying to break free."

"There's gonna be a horse auction in Topeka on Saturday. If you're lookin' to buy another horse right away, that might be a good place to go."

"That's what I'll probably do, but I'm not

happy about having to buy a horse right now. I just got a bill from that English fellow whose van my horse and buggy ran into the other day, and I've got some repairs to have done on my buggy, as well." Will shrugged. "At least I can borrow one of my daed's driving horses until I'm able to get a new one."

"I'm sure he's got an extra buggy that you can use while yours is being repaired."

"Jah. Well, guess I'd better get going," Will said as the truck pulled out of the Grabers' driveway. "I've got a couple of errands to run, and then I want to stop by the Yoders' and see how Karen's doing. After everything that happened with my horse yesterday, I wasn't able to make it over there like I'd planned."

"Sometimes those wisdom teeth can sure cause trouble. I remember when I had mine out that it took nearly a month until I felt well enough to eat a decent meal." Elam patted his oversized belly. "Thought I might starve to death, drinkin' liquids and eatin' nothing but soft foods for so long."

Will moved toward Bob, Papa Mark's horse, waiting patiently at the hitching rail with his buggy. Elam was quite the talker, and Will knew if he didn't get going he probably wouldn't make it over to Karen's house today, either. "Danki for seeing that my horse got hauled away this morning and for paying the pick-up fee."

Elam nodded. "No problem. It was the least I could do, seeing as it was my rope that strangled your horse to death."

Will released Bob from the hitching rail, climbed into his buggy, and gave Elam a friendly wave. It was time to see Karen.

"I'm glad I went to see the oral surgeon this morning," Karen said as she and her mother entered the house.

Mom nodded. "It's good that we know it's a dry socket causing all the pain. Now that the doctor has begun treatment, you should feel better soon."

"I hope so." Karen hung her jacket on a wall peg near the kitchen door. "I'm getting bored sitting around the house all day when there's so much to be done."

"Cindy, Mavis, and your daed have been managing fine in the store, and whatever needs to be done around here can be done by me." Mom smiled. "It's important for you to rest and let your mouth heal."

Karen nodded. "Maybe I can use this time to finish sewing my wedding dress. That won't take much effort."

"That's a good idea. You can always stop sewing if you get tired." Mom stepped into the kitchen. "Are you hungry? I could fix you a bite to eat."

"Maybe something to drink."

"Cold or warm?"

"How about some warm apple cider?"

"That sounds good. I may have some, too." Mom soon had a kettle of cider on the stove. She added some spice, and before long, the whole room smelled like warm apples and cinnamon. "If you'd like to relax in the living room, I'll bring it in to you when it's ready," she said, glancing over her shoulder at Karen.

"Okay." Karen was almost to the living room when a knock sounded on the door.

When she opened it, Will stood on the porch, holding an African violet. "This is for you." His genuine smile drew her attention to the deep dimples in his cheeks. "I picked it up at the Millers' greenhouse on my way over here."

Karen took the lacy purple plant. "That was thoughtful of you, Will, but you already brought me a plant after I first had my wisdom teeth removed. I sure didn't expect another."

"I know how much you like flowers, so I figured it might help cheer you up," he said, following her into the living room.

"Danki, I appreciate it."

"So how are you feeling? Did you see the dentist this morning?"

"Jah." She set the plant on the table near the sofa and took a seat.

Will hung his jacket on the back of the rocking chair and sat beside her. "What'd he say?"

"I have a dry socket, which is just what Mom suspected."

"What'd he do about that?"

"He put medicine in the socket, and I'm supposed to go back to have it looked at in a few days." Karen touched the side of her face. "After only one treatment, I'm noticing less pain."

"That's good to hear."

"How are those hundlin of yours getting along?" Karen asked. "I'm sorry I haven't been able to see them yet."

"The puppies are doing well—growing like little weeds." He smiled. "As soon as you have some free time and are feeling better, you'll need to see them."

"I'm looking forward to that." Karen touched Will's arm. "When Mom and Dad got home from church yesterday, they told me about your horse getting hung up on the hitching rope. I'm sorry Ben died. I know you had a fondness for him."

The sparkle in Will's blue eyes faded. "I did until a few days ago—when the critter broke free of the hitching rail here and smacked into that Englisher's van. Maybe it's a good thing Ben's gone, because he's sure cost me a lot of money. I'm planning to go to the horse auction in Topeka on Saturday to buy a new one."

"Maybe you'll get a good deal and find a better horse."

"I hope that's the case."

Karen gave his arm a gentle squeeze. "Things are bound to go better for both of us soon."

"Once we're married, I think everything will be better."

"Speaking of getting married, I was wondering if you've been able to get your list done so we can send out our invitations soon."

"Mama Regina worked on the list the other night. I should have thought to bring it with me today. I'll bring it the next time I come over." Will's forehead wrinkled. "Since most of Mama Regina's and Papa Mark's relatives are either dead or live in some other state, our list is mostly friends." He grunted. "And we sure can't invite my real daed, since I have no idea where he lives or even if he's still alive."

"I'm sorry about that, Will."

He pulled her into his arms and gave her a hug. "It's okay. You, Mama Regina, and Papa Mark are the only family I need."

As Frank approached the village of Paradise on his return trip from Philadelphia, where he'd made a delivery, he spotted a young Amish man with red hair walking toward a convenience store. Frank's heart gave a lurch. The man looked like Will. Or at least the way Frank imagined Will might look at age twenty-two. Could this young man actually be Will? Should he stop and ask?

He turned on his blinker and pulled into

the parking lot. By the time he reached the store, the redheaded Amish man had already gone inside.

Frank entered the store and glanced around. He walked briskly up the first aisle. No sign of the Amish man there. He turned the corner, started down the next aisle, and halted when he spotted the young man in front of the ice cream freezer.

Frank's heart pounded as he stepped up to him. "Are you buying ice cream on a cold day like this?"

The young man nodded, his blue eyes twinkling like fireflies on a hot summer day. Frank swallowed hard as his heart continued to thump in his chest. Will had blue eyes like that. Will had freckles on his nose, too.

"I really like ice cream." The young man reached into the freezer and plucked out a box of ice cream bars. "Fact is, I could eat ice cream most any time of the year."

Frank gnawed on his lower lip as he contemplated what to say next. He couldn't come right out and ask if this Amish man was his long-lost son. That would be too bold, and the man might think Frank was crazy.

The man stepped aside. "Are you getting ice cream, too?"

"Uh. . .no. . .I. . ." Frank reached in and grabbed one of the single bars. "Maybe I will have one."

The young man started to move away, and Frank figured if he was going to say anything more, it had better be now. "Are you from around here?"

"I live down the road apiece. My dad owns a buggy shop on Churchtown Road."

"What's your dad's name?"

"Leon Fisher."

"Then I guess your name's not Will."

"My name's Joseph. Do I look like someone named Will?"

Frank couldn't hide the disappointment he felt. "I haven't seen Will in a good many years, but you do look the way I think he would look now."

Joseph rubbed his chin thoughtfully. "Well, I'd best pay for this and get back to the buggy shop before my dad comes lookin' for me."

"It was nice talking to you." Frank put the ice cream bar back in the freezer and left the store. His hands shook, and his legs felt like two sticks of rubber. He knew he needed to get a grip on himself. He couldn't go around asking every Amish man with red hair if his name was Will. He couldn't keep looking for his son under every Amish man's hat.

As he climbed into his truck, he spotted Joseph exiting the store. When the young Amish man got to his buggy, he pulled an ice cream bar from the paper sack he held, opened it, and took a bite.

An image of Will popped into Frank's mind, and he thought about the last time he and his son had shared ice cream together. It was the day Frank had decided to take Will to see Mark and Regina Stoltzfus.

He leaned his head against the back of his seat, closed his eyes, and let the memory wash over him. . . .

"I'm hungry, Pop. Can we stop and get somethin' to eat?"

Frank reached across the seat of his truck and thumped Will lightly on the knee. "What have you got there, boy, a hollow leg?"

Will's forehead crinkled as he stared at his knee. "I—I don't think it's hollow. I think there's a bone in my leg, Pop. Yeah, that's the reason I can walk."

Frank chuckled. "Of course you've got a bone in your leg. When I asked if your leg was hollow, I was trying to say that you eat so much you must be putting all that food someplace besides your stomach."

"Nope. I only put it here." Will patted his stomach then pointed to a fast-food store up ahead. "Can we stop there and get some ice cream?"

"Okay." Even though Frank was anxious to get to his destination, he couldn't say no to the expectant look on his son's face.

"Mama liked ice cream, didn't she, Pop?"

Frank's throat constricted as he slowly nodded. He missed Patty so much.

"Mama's never comin' back, isn't that right?"

"You're right, Will; she's not."

"I wish she didn't have to die."

"I wish she didn't, either." Frank hoped he was doing the right thing by

going to the Stoltzfuses'. The letter from Regina Stoltzfus to Patty had said if Patty ever needed anything, she should ask. Frank hoped that offer from Regina included him and Will, and he hoped it really meant anything. . . .

A horn honked, and Frank's eyes snapped open. His heart thumped against his chest when he realized how close a car had come to hitting the young Amish man's buggy as it pulled onto the road.

If Will's still living with Mark and Regina, then he probably drives a horse and buggy. I hope he's careful and doesn't pull in front of any cars. I hope he knows how much I love him.

Frank put the key in the ignition and started his truck. *I wish I'd never gone to the Stoltzfuses' that day with Will. I wish I had bought us some ice cream and headed down the road in the opposite direction.*

Megan shifted on the sofa, trying to find a comfortable position. She glanced at the

clock on the mantel above the fireplace.
Frank was late getting home again. She
would be glad when all his men were back
to work and he didn't have to be on the
road so much. It wasn't fair to the girls to
have their daddy come home after they
were in bed. It wasn't fair that she had to
spend her evenings alone, either.

She grabbed the remote and turned on
the TV. After flipping through several chan-
nels, she realized nothing held her interest. All she could think about was Frank
and how much she missed him.

She turned off the TV and picked up a
notepad and pen from the coffee table. *I
think I'll work on my Christmas list. Let's
see now. Carrie told me this morning that
she wants a pair of Rollerblades, and Kim
said she would like a baby doll. Then both
girls made it perfectly clear that they would
like to have a puppy. The Rollerblades
and baby doll are doable, but I'm not sure
Frank will agree to the idea of us having a
dog.*

Megan stuck the end of the pen between her lips. *I wonder what I should get
Frank for Christmas. He doesn't need any*

new clothes. He's got every DVD that's been recently released. He doesn't have any hobbies. . . .

Her gaze came to rest on the Amish newspaper she'd left lying on the coffee table. *If I could help Frank find his son, that would probably be the best Christmas present he's ever received.*

CHAPTER 14

Will's nose twitched as he pulled his horse and buggy into the parking lot where the horse auction would be held in Topeka. Even though the horses hadn't been brought out yet, he could smell the pungent odor of manure and horseflesh. "I appreciate you coming to the auction with me," Will said to Nathan as they climbed out of his buggy. "It's always nice to get a second opinion when it comes to buying a horse."

Nathan nodded as Will tied the horse he'd borrowed from Papa Mark to the hitching rail. "If I stick around the area much longer, it might be me looking for a horse to buy. I can't borrow Uncle Aaron's horse and buggy forever, you know."

"Do you really think you might not go back to Ohio?" Will asked as they started walking toward the horse auction barn.

"There's a good possibility that I'll stay, since I do like it here." Nathan smiled. "I think Aunt Susanna and Uncle Aaron kind of like having me around, too."

"I'm sure they do."

Nathan nudged Will's arm. "The first horse is coming in. Guess we'd better quit yakking."

Will pulled his attention to the front of the arena. The first horse up for bid was a light brown American saddlebred pacer. Will wasn't interested in that one. A few more horses were auctioned off, and Will waited patiently. Finally an American stan-dardbred trotter was brought in—sleek and black, with a white blaze on his fore-head. Will knew that a trotter held its head up high as it trotted with one foot in front of the other, in sort of a prancing style. He wasn't as concerned about speed, however, as he was about the look and dependability of a horse. No more unpredictable, skittish horses for him. He liked the way the trotter held his head as it pranced around the arena, looking impressive and sure of itself. Will really wanted that horse.

The bid started at $1,000, and Will quickly upped it to $1,500. Someone else bid $1,750, and Will jumped in with $2,000. The next bid came in at $2,500, and Will's face heated up. Apparently someone else wanted this horse as much as he did. He upped the bid again—this time to $3,000.

The person bidding against Will raised the bid to $3,500. Will glanced to the left to see who had made the bid, and his mouth dropped open. It was Leroy Eash!

Will ground his teeth together. *I need that horse more than Leroy does. His horse isn't dead.*

He bid once more. This time for $3,700.

Leroy went again—$3,800.

Will clenched his fingers and gave another bid. He held his breath and waited. No further bids. Leroy sat motionless.

The auctioneer's hand came up, and he pointed at Will. "Sold for $4,000!"

Nathan nudged Will with his elbow. "You got the horse, but you paid a lot more for it than I ever would."

Will grimaced. "I paid more than I'd planned to pay, too."

"Then why'd you keep bidding?"

"Because I wanted the horse, and because. . ." Will's voice trailed off. If he was being completely honest, he'd have to admit that part of the reason he'd kept bidding was to keep Leroy from getting the horse. "I have a hunch Leroy ran the bid up on purpose," he mumbled.

"Why would he do that?"

"To get a rise out of me." Will turned and was about to leave the auction barn when he bumped into Mary Jane. "What are you doing here?" he asked. "I figured you'd be working at the health food store today."

She shook her head. "It's my day off, so I came here with my daed to watch him bid on a new horse."

"Hmm, guess Papa Mark must be helping Mama Regina in the store, then. When we did our milking this morning, he never mentioned what he'd be doing today, but I figured he might putter around in the barn."

Nathan cleared his throat a couple of times and poked Will's arm. "Looks like Leroy has his eye on some other horse now, because he's bidding on another trotter."

Will waited to see what would happen. Would Leroy find someone else to bid against? Would he make the other bidder run the bid up high, the way he'd done with Will?

A couple of bids came in on the trotter, but Leroy ended up getting it for two thousand dollars—half as much as Will's new horse had cost him.

Nathan's nose twitched as he sniffed the air. "I smell hot dogs roasting. Should the three of us get something to eat?" he asked with an eager expression.

Will shrugged. "I'm not really hungry yet. If you don't mind, I'd like to get my horse and head out of here. I'm sure Mama Regina left something in the refrigerator that we can have for lunch, so let's wait to eat until we get back to my place."

Nathan pointed to a nearby hot dog

stand. "Are you sure you don't want a hot dog? They really smell good."

"You can get one if you like and eat it on the way home," Will said.

Nathan looked over at Mary Jane. "How about you? Would you like a hot dog?"

She smiled and shook her head. "I'd better not. Dad's taking me out to lunch after we leave here, so I don't want to fill up on anything before then."

"Oh, okay."

Will moved quickly out of the barn. "Are you coming, Nathan?"

"Jah, sure, I'm right behind you."

Karen finished putting some new kettles out and went to the front of the store, where her mother sat behind the counter going over some paperwork. "Do you need my help with anything here?" she asked.

"Not right now, but I'd appreciate it if you went over to the house and got the thermos of coffee I left sitting on the counter after lunch."

"Sure, I can do that." Karen slipped into her jacket and left the store. It felt good to be able to work again. She was almost to the house when a horse and buggy rumbled up the driveway. She didn't recognize the horse, but when the buggy came to a stop and Will stepped down, she realized he must have gotten a new horse.

"I went to the auction this morning," Will said as he approached Karen. "Paid more than I should have, but I think I got myself a good driving horse. What do you think?"

"He's a nice-looking animal. How does he drive?"

"Real well. Not too fast, not too slow. He trots along just the way I like."

"How much did you pay for him?" she asked.

"Four thousand dollars."

Karen gasped. "Could you afford that much, Will?"

"I had the money, but I wasn't planning to go that high with my bid." He grunted. "It's Leroy's fault I had to pay so much for the horse."

"How can it be Leroy's fault?"

"He bid against me."

"Why didn't you stop bidding and let him have the horse before the price got so high?"

Will's forehead creased. "I wanted the horse, and I didn't think Leroy needed it, so—"

"So you kept bidding just to keep Leroy from getting it?"

He shrugged. "At first, but then after it was all said and done and the price had gone up to four thousand dollars, I realized he'd taken the bid up high just to make me pay top dollar."

Karen slowly shook her head. "I can't imagine Leroy doing something like that, but even if he did, I don't see why you thought you had to keep upping the bid. You're not a schoolboy trying to beat Leroy at some game, Will. You're a grown man and ought to be more sensible about the way you spend your money, don't you think?"

Will's face flamed. "What I think is that I got myself a nice, dependable horse."

"Well, good. I'm glad."

Just then another buggy rolled in, with a chestnut-colored gelding pulling it.

Will grunted. "Oh great, it's Leroy. He probably came over here to brag about the horse he got for a fair price, while he made me pay too much for mine."

Karen clutched Will's arm. "Please don't start anything with Leroy. I really doubt that he ran the bid up just to irritate you."

"Why are you sticking up for him?"

"I'm not. I just don't think you're seeing things as clearly as you should be."

Leroy sauntered over to them, ending their conversation and grinning at Karen. "What do you think of the horse I got at the auction in Topeka? Isn't he a winner?"

"The horse is very nice-looking."

"You're right; he sure is. He's a trotter, and he pulls my buggy real well, too. I think I'm gonna be happy with him for a long time." Leroy looked over at Will and smiled. "I'd say you got yourself a good-lookin' horse today, too."

Will frowned. "Did you run the bidding up on the black trotter so I'd have to pay top dollar?"

"No way! I really wanted that horse."

"Then why'd you stop bidding on it?"

"Because I'd gone as high as I could afford."

"Humph! I doubt you even needed a new horse."

"I did so. I—"

Karen stepped between the two men. "I've got better things to do than stand here listening to the two of you bicker. If you'll excuse me, there's something I need to do for my mamm." She hurried into the house.

Leroy's eyebrows drew together as he glared at Will. "Now look what you've done!"

"What are you talking about?"

"Karen's obviously upset, and I think—"

"I don't care what you think!" Will swung around and headed for his horse and buggy.

"Where are you going?" Leroy called.

"I'm taking my expensive horse home to his new stall in my daed's barn!" Will untied the horse and stepped into the buggy.

I hope Karen doesn't believe Leroy's story about needing a new horse, Will fumed as he headed for home. He grimaced. *Maybe I shouldn't have said anything. Karen might have thought I was making an issue of Leroy getting me to up the bid like that.*

By the time Will reached home, he was so worked up, he was sweating. As soon as he put his horse and buggy away, he headed straight for the woodpile. He hoped chopping a few cords of wood might help him work out some of his frustrations.

Will picked up the hatchet and swung it with all his might. He liked feeling his muscles work. He liked watching the pile of wood grow. What he didn't like was Leroy bragging about the horse he'd bought for a reasonable price. More than that, he didn't like Leroy hanging around Karen.

He positioned another piece of wood on the chopping block. *Whack!*—the wood split in two as his ax came down. *Maybe Karen would be better off with someone like Leroy. Can I ever get over the bitterness and pain of my past to secure my future with Karen? Maybe I'm not cut out to be a husband or father. Will I eventually destroy my family, the way Pop did? Is there a chance there won't be a December wedding, after all?*

Will gritted his teeth and set another hunk of wood in place. *What am I thinking? It would break my heart if Karen chose Leroy or any other man over me.*

What I need to do is find a way to keep Leroy from hanging around Karen so much.

A slow smile spread across Will's face. *I know exactly what I should do. I just have to figure out the best way to do it.*

CHAPTER 15

Are you planning to be home from work by dinnertime tonight?" Megan asked as she followed Frank out to his truck on Monday morning.

"As long as all my guys are back working today, I shouldn't have to make any deliveries. If that's the case, I'll be home on time." He kissed her and was about to climb into his truck when he turned back around. "To tell you the truth, I kind of enjoyed driving a big rig again—especially when some of my deliveries took me through Amish country. Did I tell you about the young Amish man with red hair I saw last week?"

"I don't remember you mentioning that."

"I know this probably sounds foolish, but when I first saw him, I thought he might be Will."

"Did you talk to him?"

"Yeah, I found out his name is Joseph Fisher and his dad owns a buggy shop on Churchtown Road." Frank pulled his fingers through his hair. "I've got to get over the idea that every red-haired Amish man I see might be Will."

Megan touched his arm. "Maybe you won't have to keep wondering where your son is."

"What do you mean?"

"On Saturday I placed an ad with *The Budget*."

His eyebrows arched upward. "You did what?"

"I put an ad in the notice section of *The Budget*, telling your story about leaving Will with an Amish couple in Lancaster County and asking anyone who knows Will or the Amish couple to contact you."

"I can't believe you'd do something like

that without asking me." Frank grimaced. "If you called the ad in two days ago, how come you're just now telling me about it?"

"I probably should have told you sooner, but you worked Saturday, and on Sunday, you slept half of the day, so I didn't think about it until now."

He grunted. "You probably wasted our money. I doubt that anyone will respond to that ad."

"You never know. The Amish couple you left Will with might subscribe to *The Budget*. If they do, they're likely to read the notice and hopefully contact you."

"I won't get my hopes up," Frank said as he climbed into his truck. "If Regina and Mark Stoltzfus moved from Lancaster County so they could have my boy, even if they do read the notice, I don't think they'll respond."

Karen had just left the dry goods store and was preparing to go to Shipshewana when Will showed up.

"Wie geht's?" he called as he stepped down from his buggy.

"I'm doing fine. So much better now that

I have no pain and I'm finally about to get my wedding dress made." She smiled. "I'm also back working in the store."

"Glad to hear it." He joined her outside the buggy shed. "Are you going somewhere?"

She nodded. "I'm meeting my friend Vonda Nissley for lunch. Then I have another appointment with the oral surgeon."

Will's eyebrows puckered. "I was hoping I could take you to lunch today and then over to my place to see Sandy's hundlin."

"I'm sorry, Will. Maybe we can make it another day this week." She hated to disappoint him. He seemed in a good mood today—better than the last time he'd dropped by to show her his new horse.

Will opened the buggy shed door and pushed her buggy outside. "Would you like me to get your horse and hitch it to the buggy?"

"Sure, if you don't mind."

"Don't mind at all."

"How's your new horse working out?" Karen asked as she followed him to the barn.

"So far so good. Of course I haven't had him long enough to know for sure."

"Have you given him a name yet?"

Will nodded. "Since he's got a white blaze on his forehead, I decided to call him Blazer."

"Seems like a good name to me."

"What restaurant will you and Vonda be having lunch at today?" Will asked as he hitched Karen's horse to her buggy.

"The Blue Gate in Shipshewana. We're supposed to meet at 12:30, so I'd best be on my way."

Will helped Karen into the buggy and gave her hand a gentle squeeze. "I'll see you soon."

She nodded and got the horse moving. In the side mirror, she saw Will climb into his buggy. When he got to the end of the driveway, he turned in the opposite direction of the way she was heading.

Maybe I should have invited him to join Vonda and me for lunch. She sighed. *But I guess it's too late for that.*

Regina looked up as Mark entered the store. "I spoke with Bishop Miller a few minutes ago," Mark announced, "and he said the Kings' harness shop burned to the ground last night."

Regina gasped. "That's terrible! What happened, do you know?"

"I guess a propane tank blew up, and the whole place caught on fire. The bishop said there's going to be a work frolic in a few days to rebuild the harness shop."

"Will you be going to the frolic?"

Mark nodded. "I'm sure our son will want to help out, too."

Regina smiled. "Will's always been willing to help others in their time of need. He's turned into a real fine man. Remember when we first met him? He was so polite, but I've never seen a six-year-old boy who could put away as many cookies as Will did that day."

"He's always had a pretty good appetite."

Regina grabbed her jacket from the wall peg near the door. "Speaking of appetites, why don't you come over to the house with me while I fix some lunch?"

"Is that a hint that I should help you fix it?"

"Only if you want to. I mostly thought we could visit."

Mark chuckled. "Jah, okay."

"What brings you by our place today?" Leroy asked when Will stepped into the Eashes' blacksmith shop. "Is that new horse of yours in need of some shoes?"

Will shook his head. "I was on my way to Shipshewana for lunch and thought I'd drop by and see if you'd like to join me."

Leroy quirked an eyebrow. "You want me to go to Ship-shewana with you for lunch?"

"Jah."

"Mind if I ask why? I mean, you and I have never been that close."

"Well, I. . .uh. . .thought maybe we ought to try to mend some fences between us—for Karen's sake, you know."

"I suppose that would be a good idea."

"So are you free to join me for lunch?"

Leroy glanced at his brother Gerald. "Do you think you and Dad can get along without me for a few hours? Will wants to treat me to lunch."

Will grimaced. He hadn't actually planned to treat Leroy, but if that's what it took to get him to go, he'd gladly pay the bill.

"Jah, sure, you go ahead," Gerald said. "Dad should be back from lunch most anytime, and I can manage on my own until he shows up."

"Great! I'll see you later, then." Leroy grabbed his jacket and followed Will out the door.

"Before we head out, there's something I'd like to say," Leroy said as he climbed into Will's buggy.

"What's that?"

"I hope you don't still think I ran the bid up on that horse just to make you pay a big price."

Will shrugged.

"I told you the other day that I really wanted that horse. I just couldn't go any higher than I did."

"Jah, okay." Will gathered up the reins and directed the horse onto County Road 8. "Blazer's a fine horse. I can see why you wanted him."

"I did want him, but I like the horse I got, so I have no complaints."

"I'm curious to know something," Will said.

"What's that?"

"How come you wanted a new horse? Was there something wrong with the one you had?"

"Tinker's a good horse, but he's getting up in years and isn't as fast as I'd like him to be. So I gave him to my mamm, and she's real pleased, because she likes a slower, more easygoing buggy horse."

"I see."

"Changing the subject," Leroy said, "which restaurant do you plan to go to for lunch?"

"The Blue Gate. They have some pretty good Dutch-style meals."

Leroy smacked his lips. "That's true. The desserts they have are pretty tasty, too."

As they continued to travel toward Shipshewana, they talked about the chilly November weather, their new horses, Papa Mark's dairy cows, Sandy's puppies, and the blacksmith shop Leroy ran with his father and older brother. By the time they arrived at their destination, Will had decided that Leroy wasn't such a bad fellow when he wasn't hovering around Karen. If Leroy had a girlfriend of his own, he and Will might even become friends.

When they stepped into The Blue Gate Restaurant, Will glanced around to see if he could spot Karen or Vonda. He didn't see them in the lobby and figured they might be at a table already.

When the hostess came and led them to the dining room, Will spotted Karen and Vonda sitting in a booth. "Can we sit over there?" he asked, motioning to the booth where they sat. "We know those women."

The hostess nodded and led them across the room. As they approached the booth, Karen looked up and smiled. "Will, what are you doing here?"

"Leroy and I came for lunch. If you don't mind, we'd like to join you."

Karen glanced over at Vonda, whose face turned crimson as she shrugged. Dark eyed and dark haired, Vonda was an attractive young woman, and Will thought her good looks would turn most any man's head. The only thing that detracted from Vonda's beauty was her shyness. Will hoped Leroy might see past that if he got to know Vonda better.

"We've already placed our orders, and we'll have to leave by one thirty so I can be at my appointment on time, but you're welcome to join us." Karen slid across the seat, and Will slipped in beside her. That left the seat beside Vonda for Leroy.

A young Mennonite waitress came to take Will's and Leroy's orders, and Karen's and Vonda's food arrived a few minutes later. The four of them bowed their heads for silent prayer, and then Karen and Vonda started eating.

"How's your turkey sandwich?" Leroy asked, looking at Karen.

She smiled. "It's good. Turkey's one of my favorite meats. On Thanksgiving, I always eat more of it than I should, though, and then I'm miserable the rest of the day."

"Speaking of Thanksgiving," Will put in, "Mama Regina's already planning her menu." He glanced over at Vonda, who hadn't said a word since he and Leroy had sat down. "What's your favorite Thanksgiving food?"

"Pumpkin pie, I guess."

"How about you, Leroy?" Will asked.

"Let's see now. . .turkey, stuffing, mashed

potatoes, yams, and apple pie." Leroy grinned at Karen again. "Remember that time when we were kinner and our mamms made mincemeat pie, but we thought it was apple with raisins?"

"Jah, and what a surprise we got when we took our first bite."

Leroy chuckled. "It was the first and last time I ever ate mincemeat pie."

"Leroy," Will interjected, "why don't you tell Vonda about your new horse?"

"Huh?" Leroy blinked a couple of times.

"Why don't you tell Vonda about your new horse?"

Leroy's face colored slightly, and he reached for his glass of water. "There's not much to tell, and I—I doubt she'd be interested."

"What about your new horse?" Karen asked before Vonda could respond.

As Leroy listed the many attributes of his trotter, Will gritted his teeth. Things weren't going the way he'd hoped. Karen and Leroy were talking, and Will had managed to get in a few words; Vonda seemed more interested in her turkey sandwich than in Leroy, though. For that matter, Leroy hadn't shown any interest

in Vonda. Will was beginning to think inviting Leroy to join him for lunch had been
a mistake.

*Maybe Vonda's not the right woman for
Leroy,* Will thought. *I'd better come up
with someone else. Maybe I can get Leroy and Mary Jane together. As far as I
know, she doesn't have a boyfriend.*

CHAPTER 16

When Will and his folks arrived at the Kings' place for the work frolic, Will and Papa Mark joined the men, who'd already begun framing the new harness shop. Mama Regina headed to the house to help the women make coffee and prepare snacks. Will hadn't seen any sign of Karen's buggy, so he figured the Yoders might not have arrived.

He spotted Leroy's rig, though, and noticed Leroy and his youngest brother, Owen, carrying some lumber across the yard toward the work site. Then he saw Dan Lambright's rig pull in and was relieved to see Mary Jane and her mother step down from the buggy. Now he needed to figure out some way to get Leroy and Mary Jane talking.

"How's it going, Will?" Leroy asked as he set the lumber down near the place were Will stood.

"It's going okay. How are things with you?"

"Real good. I'm sure liking that horse I got at the auction. How's your horse working out?"

"Just fine. Blazer's a good buggy horse and doesn't get skittish the way Ben used to do."

"I've never liked a skittish horse," Leroy said. "It's dangerous enough to be on the roads without having to worry about a horse that can't be trusted." He glanced across the yard. "I see Karen and her family have just arrived. Maybe I'll head over there and say hello before I haul more wood."

Will ground his teeth together. He was getting ready to follow Leroy when Nathan and Harley walked up to him.

"I heard you got a new horse," Harley said.

Will nodded. "Got him at the auction in Topeka last Saturday."

"What kind did you get?"

"A beautiful black trotter."

"He's a real nice one, too," Nathan put in. "I was with Will when he got the horse."

"My buggy horse is getting old and kind of slow, and I'd like to get a new one," Harley said with a wistful expression. "Guess that's not gonna happen for a while, though. At least not until Luanne has her boppli and I've paid the hospital bills."

"I didn't know your wife was expecting a baby," Will said.

"She's due in April. I'm sure I mentioned it to you."

"Guess I must have forgotten," Will mumbled. Truth was, he'd been so consumed with thoughts of Karen and Leroy that he hadn't paid much attention to anything else.

Harley thumped Will on the back. "I bet it won't be long until you're a daed yourself."

Will blinked a couple of times. "Huh?"

"You and Karen will be getting married in December, right?"

"That's the plan."

"Then by this time next year, you could be a daed."

Will nodded slowly. He wanted to have children, but the thought scared him a bit. What if he didn't measure up? What if he turned out to be like Pop, who had cared so little about his son that he'd run off and left him with people he barely knew?

"Will, could you bring some of that lumber over here?" Papa Mark hollered from across the yard. "We're ready to begin building the side walls."

"Okay," Will called in response.

"Guess we'd better get busy," Nathan said. "We should be able to get the harness shop pretty well done in a day if everyone does his part."

Will glanced in the direction of the field where the buggies were parked. He caught sight of Karen walking across the yard with Leroy at her side.

I've got to put a stop to this.

"Where's that lumber?" Papa Mark shouted.

"I'm coming!" Will bent down and grabbed some wood. "Yeow!" He dropped the wood and stared at the one-inch sliver embedded in his thumb.

"Looks like a pretty nasty splinter," Nathan said. "Guess you should have been wearing gloves."

Will nodded. "That's what I get for not paying attention to what I'm doing."

"You'd better go up to the house and see about getting that splinter removed."

Will glanced at the wood lying near his feet.

"Don't worry about that. I'll haul it over to your daed," Nathan said as he slipped on a pair of leather gloves.

"Danki." Will sprinted across the lawn to the back door and nearly collided with Mary Jane, who was on her way out.

"I—I'm sorry," he mumbled. "Guess I wasn't watching where I was going."

"That's okay, no harm done. Were you looking for something to eat or drink?"

He held up his hand. "I've got a sliver and came to the house to get something to take it out."

"I'll take care of it for you." Mary Jane pointed to a chair on the back porch. "Have a seat, and I'll run inside and see what I can find."

Will lowered himself into the chair as Mary Jane went into the house. A few minutes later, she was back with a first aid kit. "I've got what we need," she said, sitting beside Will.

She took his hand, and Will winced when she poked a needle under the sliver. "Ouch, that sure hurts!"

"Hold still. If you move around, it'll hurt a lot more." Mary Jane continued to probe until the sliver was finally free. Then she poured some antiseptic on it and applied a bandage. "There you go. Good as new."

"Danki," Will said as the throbbing subsided.

"You're welcome."

Just then Karen stepped onto the porch. "What's wrong, Will? Why are you wearing a bandage on your hand?"

"I picked up a nasty sliver. Mary Jane got it out for me, though."

Karen pursed her lips as she looked at Will; then she glanced over at Mary Jane and frowned. "I figured you'd be in the house helping the other women get coffee and refreshments going."

"I was, but I was coming outside to see

if anyone needed coffee, when I bumped into Will and he told me about the sliver."

Karen looked back at Will. "How'd you get a sliver in your hand? Were you wearing gloves?"

Will shook his head. "Forgot to put my gloves on before I picked up some wood." He glanced toward the work site and noticed Leroy heading that way. At least the irritating fellow wasn't with Karen anymore. "I'd better get back to work, but I'll see you during the noon meal if not before." Will smiled at Karen and rose from the chair. He was disappointed when she didn't smile in return.

Did Leroy say something to make Karen upset with me? Will was about to ask when Karen pushed past him and stepped into the house.

Will looked over at Mary Jane to see what her reaction was to Karen's strange behavior, but Mary Jane sat staring across the yard.

"If you're going out to see who wants coffee, you can walk out with me," Will said. He figured if Mary Jane came out to the work site, she might end up talking to

Leroy. At least that would be a start at getting them together.

Will and Mary Jane headed across the yard and stopped when they reached the spot where Leroy was working.

"Mary Jane would like to know if you'd like some coffee," Will said.

"Is that so?" Leroy asked with barely a glance in Mary Jane's direction.

Will nodded. "She was kind enough to take a sliver from my hand, too."

"That's nice."

Mary Jane nudged Leroy's arm. "Do you want some coffee?"

He shook his head. "Not right now. I need to get to work." He lifted a can of nails. "Are you planning to help now, Will?"

"Jah, sure." Will smiled at Mary Jane. "Why don't you bring a pot of coffee out, anyway? I'm sure some of the men would like a cup."

"Okay."

When Mary Jane headed back to the house, Will grabbed a hammer and faced Leroy again. "Mary's Jane real nice, don't you think?"

Leroy shrugged.

"She looks pretty good in the face, too, don't you agree?"

Leroy squinted as he stared at Will. "Is there something going on between you and Mary Jane?"

"Huh?"

"I said—"

"I heard your question. What I don't understand is why you asked it."

"You said she took a splinter from your hand, and she kept smiling at you the whole time she was standing beside us."

"I never saw her smiling at me, and there's nothing going on between us."

"Sure looked like it to me." Leroy grunted. "I saw her visiting with you at the auction the other day, and you two looked pretty cozy."

"She came there with her daed, and we were only talking."

Leroy shrugged. "Whatever you say."

Will clenched his fists until his fingers dug into his palms. Things weren't working out the way he'd planned at all.

Karen stood at the kitchen window, watching Mary Jane walk back to the house. *I shouldn't have let her walk out there with Will. I should have gone with them.*

In all the time Karen and Will had been seeing each other, she'd never felt jealous. But seeing the way Mary Jane had looked at Will when he talked about how she'd removed his sliver made Karen wonder if Mary Jane might be interested in him.

Come to think of it, when she'd talked with Leroy earlier, he'd mentioned seeing Mary Jane at the horse auction talking to Will.

Now that I think about it, whenever I've seen Will working in his mamm's health food store, Mary Jane's always acted real friendly toward him. Surely Will doesn't have an interest in Mary Jane, or he wouldn't have asked me to marry him. Maybe he's been acting so friendly toward her in order to make me jealous. He might be doing it to get back at me because he's jealous of my friendship with Leroy.

Mary Jane entered the kitchen a few minutes later and removed the coffeepot from the stove. "Some of the men are ready for coffee," she said to Doris King, who was cutting up brownies.

"I'm sure they'd like some of these to go with the coffee," Doris replied. She looked over at Karen and smiled. "When Mary Jane goes out with the coffee, why don't you take the brownies to the men?"

Karen nodded.

"How about if I go along?" Cindy asked. "Someone will have to carry the Styrofoam cups so the men will have something to drink their coffee in."

Doris nodded. "You can take out some hot apple cider, as well as the cups."

Karen and Cindy slipped into their jackets; grabbed the brownies, hot cider, and cups; and followed Mary Jane out the back door.

"There aren't as many here today as I thought there would be," Mary Jane said as they crossed the yard.

"There seems to be enough to get the job done." Karen pointed to the building, which was quickly going up. "At this rate, the harness shop might be done by the end of the day."

When they reached the work site, they set the refreshments on the makeshift table.

"I'll let one of the workers know the

snacks are ready." Mary Jane headed right for Will. "There's coffee, hot cider, and brownies waiting on the table."

He smiled. "Great. I'll let the others know."

"How does your hand feel?" Mary Jane asked. "Does it still hurt?"

"Not so much."

Karen frowned as she watched the interaction between Will and Mary Jane. It seemed obvious that Mary Jane thought of Will as more than a friend. "Would you like me to bring you a cup of coffee?" Karen asked, stepping up to Will.

"That'd be nice." Will looked over at Mary Jane. "I think Leroy might need a break. Why don't you see if he'd like something to eat or drink?"

"I'll ask him," Cindy said before Mary Jane had a chance to respond. She grabbed the container of brownies and hurried off toward the side of the shop where Leroy worked.

Karen poured coffee into a Styrofoam cup and handed it to Will.

He smiled. "Danki."

Karen figured Mary Jane would either take some coffee to the other men or head back to the house, but she just stood beside Will, wearing a silly-looking smile.

Karen was about to suggest that Mary Jane offer coffee to the men, when a pigeon flew off the barn roof and landed on Will's head.

Mary Jane gasped, and Will jumped. "What in the world?" He reached up, grabbed hold of the pigeon, then tossed it into the air.

Karen pointed to Will's zipple cap. "Looks like that pigeon left something behind for you to remember him by."

Will jerked the cap off his head and stared at the droppings. "Why does everything always happen to me?"

Karen bit back a smile. *That's what you get for flirting with Mary Jane.*

CHAPTER 17

Clippety-clop, clippety-clop. . . Will's horse moved along at a steady pace as Will headed down the road in his buggy. He'd been running errands for Papa Mark all morning and figured he might as well stop at Das Dutchman for lunch. That would save Mama Regina from having to fix him anything when he got home.

Will pulled up to the hitching rail in the restaurant parking lot and secured Blazer. "I shouldn't be gone too long," he said, patting the horse's flank. "I'll reward your patience with a juicy apple after we get home."

Blazer whinnied and nuzzled Will's hand with his nose. Will gave the horse a few more pats and headed for the restaurant.

As he entered the building on the bakery side, the yeasty smell of warm bread and rolls greeted him, and his stomach rumbled. Maybe he would pick up a few baked goods before he went home.

Will made his way to the restaurant side of the building and spotted a revolving rack full of books. Many of them were about the Amish and Mennonite way of life. He stopped and picked up one of the books, noting that it had been written by a man who used to be Amish and was now a college professor.

I wonder what I'd be doing for a living if I had remained living in the English world with Pop. He might have an English girlfriend or already be married. No doubt he would be living in some fancy house with a TV and all kinds of electrical appliances. Would he live near Pop? Would they spend time together, the way he and Papa Mark did as they worked side by side?

Will's lips compressed as he stared at the book. *Where are you, Pop? Do you ever think of me? Are you alive or dead?*

"Excuse me, sir, but are you planning to buy that book?"

Will jerked at the sound of a woman's voice. He turned to see a middle-aged woman with faded brown hair standing beside him. "I. . .uh. . .no." He put the book back on the rack. "I was just looking."

She tipped her head and gave him a curious stare. "Were you wondering what these books might have to say about you and your people?"

He shrugged in reply.

"I find the Amish way of life so interesting," the woman said. "I think I've read most of the books that have been written about the Plain People." She plucked the book Will had been looking at off the rack. "All except this one, that is."

"Feel free to buy it. I'm here for lunch, not to buy any books." Will smiled and walked away. When he entered the restaurant, he spotted Karen sitting at a table across the room. This was an unexpected surprise.

He was about to head that way when he realized someone sat in the chair across from her. He craned his neck for a better look and groaned. It was Leroy!

So much for trying to mend any fences with that fellow, he fumed. *If I weren't Amish, I would probably march right over there and punch Leroy in the nose for trying to take my girlfriend.* Will grimaced. *Maybe I should go over to their table and demand that Leroy stop bothering Karen.* He shook his head. *No, that would embarrass her. It would be better if I speak to Leroy alone. But since that's not going to happen right now, the best thing I can do is head for home. I'll deal with this matter when the time is right.*

Karen turned her head and caught a glimpse of Will leaving the restaurant. At least she thought it was him. But if it had been Will, why hadn't she seen him sooner, and why hadn't he seen her and come over to the table?

She was tempted to see if she could catch up to the man, but Leroy put a stop to that when he leaned closer and said, "I just can't figure out why I feel so tongue-tied whenever I'm around Vonda. You saw the way things were when Will and I met you and Vonda at The Blue Gate Restaurant last week. She never said more than a few words the whole time we were sitting at the table." Leroy shook his head. "I'm sure she doesn't like me."

"That's lecherich. I've never heard her say anything negative about you."

"Really?" he asked with a hopeful expression. "What *has* she said about me?"

"Nothing specific."

Leroy frowned. "I was afraid of that."

Karen reached for her glass of water and took a drink. "I'm sure you must realize that Vonda's quite shy."

"She doesn't seem shy around you."

"That's because we're friends. Vonda's only shy with people she doesn't know well. Since she and her family moved to Indiana less than a year ago, she hasn't made a lot of close friends."

"Without letting anyone else know, could you put in a good word for me with Vonda?" Leroy's expression was so solemn that Karen didn't have the heart to say no.

"I suppose I could, but I think it would be a good idea if you made some effort to get to know her better on your own."

He shrugged his broad shoulders. "I'm

not sure how I'm supposed to do that with her being so shy and all."

"You could start by trying to engage her in conversation when you're both at some social function," Karen suggested. "After you get her talking, maybe you could invite her to go for a buggy ride or out to lunch."

Leroy's voice lowered to a whisper. "Do you think I might have a chance with her?"

"I can't answer that, but you'll never know unless you try."

Just then Karen's mother returned to the table from the restroom. She looked at Leroy, blinked a couple of times, and gave Karen a questioning look.

"Leroy was having lunch at the counter and spotted me," Karen explained.

"Oh, I see."

Leroy's face turned red as he pushed his chair away from the table and stood. "I didn't realize Karen was here with anyone, or I wouldn't have bothered her."

"You weren't a bother," Karen said with a shake of her head.

"I probably need to get back to the blacksmith shop, anyway." Leroy smiled at Karen. "Danki for listening. . .and for the good advice."

"You're welcome. Have a good after-noon."

"You, too." Leroy gave Karen's mother a quick nod and strode off toward the cash register.

"What did he want?" Mom asked.

"He just wanted to talk to me about a few things."

"Do you think it's a good idea for you and Leroy to be so friendly when you're on the verge of marrying Will? I mean, some-one might get the wrong impression when they see the two of you together."

Karen sighed. "Will's already gotten the wrong impression. He thinks Leroy is in-terested in me."

"Well, you used to go out with Leroy. I can see why Will might be jealous."

"But we broke up a long time ago, and I was never really serious about Leroy in a romantic sort of way. We're just good friends, same as we have been since we were kinner."

"Even so, Leroy's attention could be misconstrued."

"But the other day, you said a little jeal-ousy isn't such a bad thing."

"I know what I said, but after seeing the

way Leroy looked at you just now, I've changed my mind. I can see why Will might be jealous, and I feel for him."

"I don't think Leroy looked at me in any special way. I also don't think Will has any more reason to be jealous of me and Leroy than I do of him and Mary Jane."

Mom's forehead wrinkled. "What's that supposed to mean?"

"Mary Jane hangs around Will every chance she gets. Whenever I've been in the health food store when Will's been working there, Mary Jane's always smiling and talking his ear off."

Mom smiled. "Of course she would be talking to him. Mary Jane works at the health food store, so it's only natural that she would talk to the owner's son. I'm sure she's not romantically interested in Will. They're just friends, same as you and Leroy."

"I hope you're right, because I'm feeling kind of anxious about the way things are between me and Will right now."

Mom reached across the table and patted Karen's hand. "Remember what the Bible says about worry. In 1 Peter 5:7, we are reminded to cast all our cares on the Lord because He cares for us."

Karen nodded. "Jah, I know, but sometimes it's not so easy to remember."

"With your wedding day only a month away, you're probably feeling a bit over-anxious and so is Will. Most brides and grooms feel that way right before they're married. I know your daed and I sure did. We almost called off the wedding because we were both feeling so naerfich, which of course led to a big misunderstanding."

Karen had no idea her folks had almost called off their wedding. "What was the misunderstanding about?"

"You know, it happened so long ago that I can't remember all the details. The point is, tension happens and nerves can be on edge when a couple's wedding day approaches. That's why you and Will need to discuss your feelings. If you air things out between you now, you'll have fewer problems with communication once you're married."

Karen considered Mom's advice. Maybe she was right. Talking about their concerns might do wonders for both of them.

"Is it all right if we stop by the Stoltz-fuses' on our way home so I can talk to Will?" Karen asked. "I'd like to see those puppies his dog had not long ago, too."

"Could it wait until this evening? Mavis can't work this afternoon, so I'm going to need your help in the store for the rest of the day."

"But Cindy's working today. Can't you do without my help for an hour or so this afternoon?"

"Normally I could, but your daed has an appointment with the chiropractor at three o'clock, and Cindy's going with him because her neck's been hurting."

Karen shrugged. "I guess if Cindy and Dad need to see the chiropractor this afternoon, then I'll wait until after supper to see Will. I want to get some things resolved between us before we have a misunderstanding that could ruin our plans to get married."

As Will helped Papa Mark herd the cows from the pasture to the milking barn, he continued to fume over seeing Leroy at Das Dutchman with Karen. He'd been so upset when he left the restaurant that he'd forgotten all about getting any baked goods to bring home. He just couldn't figure out why Leroy hung around Karen so much if he had no interest in her, romantically.

"You seem preoccupied," Papa Mark said as they approached the milking barn. "Is something bothering you?"

A dark gray cat darted out of the barn, and another cat followed. The first cat zipped under one of the cows. As Papa Mark bent down to shoo away the cat, the cow let out a raucous *moo* and kicked out her back leg.

Papa Mark groaned and dropped to the ground in a heap.

Will gasped and rushed forward. "Are you okay?"

Papa Mark lay quiet and unmoving.

Will's heart pounded in his chest. He had to get help for Papa Mark!

CHAPTER 18

Regina sat in the hospital waiting room, feeling done in and discouraged. She stood up and began to pace. *I wish Will was here. I feel so alone.*

Will had said he would come as soon as the milking was done, and she knew that job couldn't wait. But it had been hard to come to the hospital without him and wait by herself while Mark was being examined. When Will had come to the house and told her about the accident, Regina had rushed to the phone shed to call for help.

She walked to the window and peered out at the night sky. How thankful she felt that her husband was still alive. Many weren't so fortunate. Just last year, Owen Kauffman, one of the minister's sons, had been killed when an unruly horse had kicked him in the head. Last fall, Silas Bontrager had broken his neck when he'd fallen from the hayloft in his barn.

Life was full of uncertainties and tragedies, and Regina had learned a long time ago that the best way to deal with life was to take one day at a time and trust God in all things.

"I came as soon as I heard the news. How's Mark doing? Is he going to be okay?" Susanna Chupp asked.

Regina whirled around. She'd been in such deep thought that she hadn't heard anyone come into the room. "Mark suffered a concussion, but the doctor thinks he should be okay in a few weeks." She clasped her friend's hand. "How'd you know we were here?"

"Aaron heard the sirens blaring, and when he saw the ambulance go up your driveway, he and Nathan went right over.

They got there soon after the ambulance took Mark away, and when Will told them what had happened with the cow, Nathan stayed to help with the milking." Susanna drew in a quick breath. "Then Aaron came home and called our English neighbors to give me a ride to the hospital. He figured you'd be here alone and might appreciate some company."

"Jah, I sure do. Danki for coming, Susanna."

"Of course. That's what friends are for—to support one another during times of need."

Tears welled in Regina's eyes. "Mark was unconscious for several minutes after the cow kicked him, and I was afraid he might not make it."

Susanna motioned to the chairs behind them. "Shall we sit awhile?"

"If Nathan's helping with the milking, it shouldn't be long until Will is able to get a ride to the hospital," Regina said as she took a seat beside her friend.

"Jah, I'm sure he'll be here soon."

"The doctor said Mark won't be able to do any of his chores for a few weeks, so it's going to put a hardship on us for a while."

Susanna gave Regina's arm a gentle squeeze. "Once the word gets out about Mark's accident, you'll have plenty of help."

"I appreciate your coming over to help me," Will said as he and Nathan left the milking barn.

"No problem. Glad I could do it, even though you did most of the work and had to talk me through my part of the procedure." Nathan motioned to the phone shed in front of the health food store. "You'd better call for a ride and get to the hospital so you can see how your daed's doing."

Will nodded. "I was really scared when that cow knocked him unconscious, but I felt better when the ambulance got here and he started coming around. I don't know what Mama Regina would do if anything happened to Papa Mark."

Nathan clasped Will's shoulder. "If something happened to your daed, I know you'd miss him, too."

Will moved toward the phone shed. "You're right about that. Papa Mark has been like a real daed to me."

"It's always hard to lose a loved one." Nathan pointed to the driveway. "Looks like a buggy's coming in. The word must be out about your daed's accident already."

Will halted and waited to see who it was. When the horse and buggy stopped, Karen stepped down.

"You must have heard the news," Will said as he rushed up to her.

Karen's eyebrows furrowed. "What news?"

"Papa Mark was kicked by one of our cows and was taken by ambulance to the hospital in Goshen."

Karen gasped. "Ach, that's *baremlich*!"

"It is terrible," Nathan agreed.

"How'd it happen?" Karen asked.

Will grimaced. "One of our barn cats was chasing another cat, and it ran under the cow. Papa Mark bent down to shoo the cat away, and the cow kicked him in the head."

"Is he going to be all right?"

"I hope so. He was unconscious for a

spell but came awake before the ambulance took him to the hospital."

"Did your mamm go with him?"

"Jah. I told Mama Regina I would join her there as soon as I got the milking done." Will motioned to Nathan. "Thanks to my good friend's help, I was able to get it done quicker than I could have on my own."

Nathan smiled. "That's what friends are for."

Will nodded and turned to face Karen. "If you hadn't heard the news, what prompted you to come over here this evening?"

"I wanted to talk to you about some things."

"What things?"

Her cheeks colored slightly. "It's not important. I mean, what I had to say can wait for another time."

Will wondered if what Karen wanted to talk about had anything to do with the lunch she'd shared with Leroy today. He hoped she hadn't changed her mind about marrying him because of something Leroy had said.

"Will you be heading to the hospital soon?" Karen asked.

"I was getting ready to call for a ride when you showed up."

"I'd like to go along if you don't mind."

"Of course I don't mind. I'd appreciate the company."

"I'd like to go, too," Nathan put in. "My aunt's probably there with your mamm by now. She and I can get a ride together when she's ready to head for home."

When Will entered the hospital waiting room with Karen and Nathan, he spotted Mama Regina sitting in a chair by Susanna. Her face looked pale as goat's milk, and her shoulders trembled.

"How's Papa Mark? Is he going to be okay?" Will asked as he dropped into the seat on the other side of her.

She reached for his hand. "Your daed suffered a severe concussion, but the doctor thinks he'll be all right. He won't be able to do any work for a few weeks, however."

"That's okay," Will said. "Nathan's agreed to help with the milking until Papa Mark's well enough to resume his duties, and I can help in the store when I'm not busy with other things."

Regina patted Will's arm. "I'll see if Mary Jane can work full-time for the next couple of weeks. Even though you and your daed have helped me when things have gotten busy, I think we women can manage just fine on our own."

"If you need some help, I'll see if my folks can spare me for a few days," Karen said as she and Nathan took seats in the chairs opposite them. "Since there are five of us working in the dry goods store most of the time and we're not always super busy, I'm sure they can get along without my help for a few days or even weeks."

Mama Regina smiled. "That's nice of you, Karen. I'll keep your offer in mind if Mary Jane and I get too busy to handle things on our own."

"I wonder if Will and I should postpone our wedding because of this," Karen said.

Mama Regina spoke before Will had a chance to respond. "That won't be necessary. Mark should be fine in a few weeks, and then things will be back to normal."

A nurse entered the room and stepped up to Mama Regina. "We've finished running the rest of our tests on your husband, so you and your family are welcome to see him now."

"Thank you." Mama Regina rose from her chair, and Will joined her.

Mama Regina looked over at Susanna. "Don't feel that you have to sit out here and wait. I appreciate your coming to be with me, but I'm sure you have things to do at home."

"I don't mind staying if you need me," Susanna replied.

"I'll be fine now that Will is here."

Susanna glanced at Nathan. "Would you call Bob Simmons for a ride? He brought me to the hospital so I could be with Regina, and I'm sure he'll come back here to get us."

"I'll do that right now." Nathan started for the door but turned back around. "I'll be over at your place by four thirty tomorrow morning, Will."

"Danki." Will turned to Karen and smiled. "Feel free to ride with the Chupps if you need to go home."

"I'd rather stay with you." Karen reached

for a magazine. "I'll be here waiting while you and your mamm go in to see your daed."

Will nodded and hurried from the room.

CHAPTER 19

Mary Jane's brother Dan stopped by while I was in the milking barn," Will said to Mama Regina when he came into the kitchen for breakfast three days later.

"Was he offering his help?"

Will shook his head. "I've got Nathan's help, so I'm getting along okay. The reason Dan dropped by was to let us know that Mary Jane came down with the flu last night, so she won't be able to help at the store today."

"I'm sorry to hear Mary Jane's sick. Home in bed is where she needs to be, though."

"But who's going to mind the store? Since Papa Mark came home from the hospital yesterday afternoon, I figured you'd want to stay close to him all day."

Mama Regina pursed her lips. "I guess I could see if Karen's available. She did say the other day that I should let her know if I needed any help."

"That's a good idea. Do you want me to run over there now and see if she can help out?"

"Going over to ask is probably a good idea, since we can't be sure when someone from the Yoder family will check their answering machine. But it might be best if you wait until after breakfast and devotions to go there, don't you think?"

Will nodded. "I guess I should give Karen time to eat."

"You need to have your breakfast, too." Mama Regina motioned to the stove. "Speaking of which, the pot of oatmeal I've got cooking is almost ready, so if you'd like to wash up, I should have breakfast on by the time you're done."

"What about Papa Mark? Will he be joining us at the table?"

"He was still sleeping when I left our

room, so I think I'll let him sleep. I can take a tray to him after we're done." Mama Regina tapped Will on the shoulder. "Run along now and get washed up."

When Karen stepped into the kitchen, she caught a whiff of warm cinnamon rolls, fresh from the oven. Her stomach growled in response to the wonderful aroma. "Where's Mom?" she asked Cindy, who was busy setting the table.

"She went to the chicken coop to get a few more eggs for breakfast, and Dad's still in the barn doing his chores."

"There's no need for her to do up any eggs on my account." Karen leaned over the plate of cinnamon rolls and drew in a deep breath. "A few of these delicious rolls will be all I need this morning."

Cindy shook her head. "If you're gonna marry a man whose mother runs a health food store, don't you think you ought to start eating healthier?"

Karen smiled. "I'll start eating healthy after Will and I get married. This morning, I'm going to enjoy the delicious cinnamon rolls Mom made, and I'm not even going to worry about whether they're healthy or not."

"Dan Lambright likes cinnamon rolls real well, too."

"Mary Jane's little brother?"

Cindy wrinkled her nose as she glared at Karen. "Dan is not 'little.' He's seventeen years old, for goodness' sake."

"You don't have to get so huffy. It was only my way of asking if you were talking about Mary Jane's younger brother."

Cindy's face softened. "Dan is Mary Jane's youngest brother, and he's also very good-looking."

"Since when have you taken such an interest in Dan?"

"Since I went to the last young people's function and he asked if I'd like a ride home in his buggy."

"Hmm. . ." Karen's forehead creased in thought. She'd had so many other things on her mind lately that she hadn't realized her sister had been brought home from the last young people's gathering by a potential suitor. She smiled. *This is a good thing. If Cindy has taken an interest in Dan, it must mean she's given up on her quest to attract Leroy's attention.*

Cindy nudged Karen's arm. "What's so funny? How come you're grinning like that?"

"Oh, nothing. I was just thinking, is all."

A knock sounded at the back door, and Karen went to answer it. Will stood on the porch.

"Is everything okay?" she asked. "Your daed's not worse, I hope."

Will shook his head. "Papa Mark's doing fairly well. He came home from the hospital yesterday afternoon."

"That's good to hear."

"The reason I came over is because Mary Jane is sick with the flu and Mama Regina was wondering if you could work in the health food store today."

"I think so, but I'll have to check with Mom and Dad, just to be sure they don't need my help in our store here."

"And she hasn't had her breakfast yet," Cindy called from the kitchen.

Karen grimaced. "That little sister of mine has a bad habit of listening in on other people's conversations."

Will chuckled. "Guess maybe I was blessed to be an only child."

"Would you like to come in and have a

cup of coffee and some cinnamon rolls?" Karen asked.

"Sounds good, but I'd better pass. The milk truck will be at our place within the hour, so I need to get back as soon as possible."

"Then let me run out to the chicken coop and see what Mom has to say. If she has no problem with me helping in your mamm's store today, I'll ride back to your place with you." Karen grabbed her shawl from the wall peg. "While I'm out there, why don't you go in the kitchen where it's warmer?"

"Okay." Will slipped past Karen and headed in that direction.

A musty smell greeted Karen when she stepped into the chicken coop. She found her mother bent over a fat red hen and was relieved to see that Herman, their mean old rooster, was nowhere in sight.

"How's it going in here?" Karen asked. "Did you find enough eggs for breakfast?"

Mom frowned. "Only four eggs, so far. With the weather turning colder, the chickens aren't laying as much."

"That's usually how it goes."

"Did you need something?" Mom asked.

"Jah. I came to ask if you would mind if I worked in Regina's health food store today."

"I thought she had Mary Jane Lambright working for her."

"She does, but Will just dropped by and said that Mary Jane has the flu." Karen glanced at the door. "He's waiting in the house for my answer, so if it's okay with you, I'll ride over to his place with him."

Mom nodded. "It sounds like you're needed at the health food store more than you are here. I'm sure we can manage without you today."

"If Mary Jane doesn't get over the flu right away, I might be needed more than just today."

"Let's take one day at a time."

"Okay." Karen hugged her mother and hurried back to the house. When she stepped into the kitchen, she found Will sitting at the table across from Cindy, eating a cinnamon roll.

"I thought you didn't want any cinnamon rolls," she teased.

Will grinned up at her. "They smelled so good I changed my mind."

She snickered. "They have that effect on me, too."

"So what did your mamm say?"

"She can get by without my help today." Karen moved over to the counter where the cinnamon rolls sat. "I'll grab a few of these, and we can be on our way."

"Great. Maybe during our lunch break today, we can sneak into the shed and take a look at Sandy's pups."

She smiled. "I'd like that, Will."

As Will and Karen headed down the road in his buggy, Will glanced over at her and said, "There's something I need to ask you."

"What's that?"

"I was at Das Dutchman the other day and saw you and Leroy having lunch together."

Karen's mouth fell open. "You were at Das Dutchman?"

He nodded.

"I thought I saw you there. Why didn't you come over to my table?"

"Because when I saw you with Leroy, I figured—"

"I was having lunch with my mamm. She'd gone to the ladies' room. Leroy had been eating lunch at the counter and stopped by our table."

"What did he want?"

"He wanted to discuss something with me."

"Like what?"

"I really can't say."

"Why not?"

"Leroy asked me not to."

"Oh, so now we're keeping secrets?" A muscle on the side of Will's neck quivered.

"I'm not keeping secrets. I just don't think it would be right to repeat what Leroy said when he asked me not to." She wrinkled her nose. "Besides, telling what Leroy said would be like gossiping."

"If you're not willing to tell me, then how do you expect me to believe there's nothing going on between you and Leroy?"

"Don't you trust me, Will?"

"If you're not going to be honest, then how can I trust you?"

"If you have to ask that question, then I guess you can't."

Will's knuckles turned white as he gripped the reins.

She reached across the seat and touched his arm. "Please believe me—Leroy's only a friend. It's you I love."

The muscles in Will's face relaxed some. "I love you, too." Maybe he had been wrong for pressing Karen to tell him what Leroy had said. Maybe he needed to be more trusting.

"There's something I'd like to say, Will."

"What's that?"

"I've had some concerns about you and Mary Jane."

"What kind of concerns?"

"Well, I noticed you talking with her on the day of the work frolic, and she seemed awfully friendly, so I wondered if maybe the two of you—"

"Don't tell me you thought something was going on between me and Mary Jane."

She nodded. "Leroy said he saw you and Mary Jane together at the horse auction in Topeka."

"That's right; Mary was there with her daed. When Nathan and I were getting ready to leave the auction barn, we ran into her, so we talked a few minutes. That's all there was to it."

"I know it's silly of me, but I felt jealous when Leroy said he'd seen you with her, and then when I saw the way she kept smiling at you the other day at the frolic, I started to worry."

"Well, you've got nothing to worry about. Mary Jane is just a friend who works at the store for my mamm. The reason I was talking to her the day of the work frolic was because I was trying to get her and Leroy together."

Karen's eyebrows shot up. "What?"

"I had hoped if I could get Leroy interested in someone else, he would stay away from you." Will grunted. "But I didn't have much luck. Leroy didn't seem any more interested in Mary Jane than he did in Vonda when we had lunch with you in Shipshewana the other day. Mary Jane didn't seem interested in Leroy, either."

"Maybe that's because Mary Jane's interested in you."

Will shook his head vigorously. "No, she's not! If anyone's interested in anyone, it's Leroy. He's interested in you."

"He is not!"

"Jah, well, I don't like him hanging around

you all the time. It's putting a strain on our relationship."

"I wish you'd quit worrying about Leroy. I shouldn't have to keep telling you that I only think of him as a friend." Karen placed her hand on Will's arm. "You know what my mamm thinks?"

"What's that?"

"She thinks the reason things have been strained between you and me lately is because we're having prewedding jitters."

"She could be right. Any idea what we can do about it?"

"Maybe we need to focus on each other rather than on what's going on around us. And if it will make you feel any better, I'll try to discourage Leroy from hanging around me so much."

"That would help a lot, and I'll try not to be so jealous."

She smiled. "Okay. I'll work on that issue, too."

CHAPTER 20

Will was on his way out of the health food store with some empty boxes Mama Regina had asked him to dispose of when Nathan showed up.

"I didn't expect to see you here," Nathan said, stepping into the store. "Figured you'd be out in the barn waiting for me to help with the afternoon milking."

"I'll be heading there soon." Will's eyebrows drew together. "If you figured I'd be in the barn, then what are you doing here?"

Nathan's face turned red as a radish. "Well, I was. . .uh. . ."

"Were you lookin' to buy some vitamins for your aunt?" Will asked as he shifted the boxes in his arms.

"No, I. . .uh. . ." Nathan glanced around. "Is Mary Jane working today?"

Will shook his head. "She's home sick with the flu."

"Really? You didn't mention that this morning when we were doing the milking."

"Didn't know about it until after we were done. Mary Jane's brother Dan dropped by and gave me the news." Will nodded toward the back of the store. "Karen's taking Mary Jane's place today, and I've helped out this afternoon some, too."

"That's really too bad."

"Too bad I've been helping out?"

"No, no. It's too bad Mary Jane's got the flu."

Will scratched his head. "Why the sudden interest in Mary Jane's health?"

The color in Nathan's face deepened. "Well, uh. . ."

Will punched Nathan playfully on the arm. "You're sure big on the word *uh* this afternoon. Have you got some kind of interest in Mary Jane that I should know about?"

"Jah, actually, I do. She's one of the reasons I've decided to stay in Indiana."

Will smiled. No wonder Mary Jane showed no interest in Leroy. She was probably as smitten with Nathan as he obviously was with her. He thumped Nathan on the back. "And here I thought you were sticking around because you and I are such good friends."

"That's part of it, too."

"Well, if you're planning to stay on for good, then you'll need to find a full-time job. Once Papa Mark is able to resume his duties, I won't need your help with the milking anymore."

Nathan nodded. "That's okay. I just came from an interview at the trailer factory, and I'm supposed to begin working there in two weeks."

"That's great!"

Karen stepped around the corner. "Oh, it's you, Nathan. I was in the back room and thought I heard Will talking to someone out here. I was afraid I'd missed a customer."

"Nope, it's just me and my good friend Nathan."

Nathan smiled at Karen. "Will said you were filling in for Mary Jane today."

Karen nodded. "Thankfully Will's been able to help me some, and Regina came over to check on things a couple of times, too." She made an arc with her arm. "Working in the health food store is a lot different from working in my folks' dry goods store. There's so much I don't know about vitamins and such."

"I think you've caught on pretty well." Will winked at Karen. "If you were given the chance to work here a few more days, you'd know all you need to know."

She shook her head. "I doubt that very much."

"Have you had the chance to see Sandy's hundlin?" Nathan asked.

"Jah. Will took me out to the shed to see them during our lunch break." Karen smiled. "They're sure cute little things. Will shouldn't have any trouble finding them good homes once they're old enough to be weaned."

"I'm sure he won't. I may even buy one myself."

Will looked at the boxes he held. "If you

two want to keep on yakking, that's up to you, but I'd better get these boxes taken out like Mama Regina asked me to. Then I'll need to get the cows rounded up so we can begin the afternoon milking." He glanced at Karen. "Do you think you can manage things on your own here until closing time?"

She nodded. "Jah, I'll be fine."

"Don't forget about coming over to the house for supper. After we've eaten, I'll drive you home."

"I won't forget."

Will looked over at Nathan. "You're welcome to eat with us, too."

"I appreciate the offer, but Uncle Aaron's got a bad cold, so after I finish helping you with the milking, I'd better get home and do his evening chores." Nathan grinned. "Besides, I promised Aunt Susanna I'd eat supper with them tonight. She's fixing baked pork chops, and that's one of my favorite meat dishes."

Will chuckled. "As I recall, most foods are your favorite."

Nathan shook his head. "No way! I've never liked spinach, no matter how it's prepared."

"Jah, well, enough of this talk about food." Will gave Karen a wide smile and moved toward the door. "See you up at the house when I'm done with the milking."

"It was nice of you to invite me to stay for supper," Karen said as she set dishes and silverware on the table in Regina's kitchen.

Regina lifted the lid on the pot of simmering stew and smiled. "Since you worked so hard in my store today, the least I can do is feed you supper. Besides, I figured my son might enjoy spending the evening with his future wife."

"It'll be nice for me, as well."

Regina moved across the room. "I hope you don't think I'm overstepping my bounds, but I've sensed something's not quite right in the way Will's been acting lately. I'm wondering if everything's as it should be between the two of you."

"We have had a few misunderstandings, but I think it's because we're both feeling a bit naerfich about our upcoming wedding."

Regina nodded. "That does often happen right before a couple gets married, although Mark and I somehow got through that time without any misunderstandings."

"Maybe that's because you're both so easygoing."

"Most of the time, but we do have our moments."

"Some of Will's and my problems stem from jealousy."

"Jealousy of what?"

"Leroy and Mary Jane."

Regina's eyebrows lifted. "I don't understand."

"Will has gotten jealous whenever he's seen me talking to Leroy, and I've felt jealous when I've seen him and Mary Jane together." Karen sighed. "It's really silly, though, because Leroy and I are only friends. I've told Will several times that he has nothing to be jealous about."

"Nor do you," Regina said. "Not only is Mary Jane just a friend of Will's; she's taken an interest in Nathan."

"She has?"

Regina nodded. "Nathan looks for any excuse to visit the health food store, and it didn't take me long to figure out that he has a definite interest in Mary Jane." She chuck-led. "Each time Nathan leaves the store, Mary Jane comments on how nice he is or how she thinks he's the best-looking Amish man she's ever met. I wouldn't be a bit sur-prised if they start courting real soon. You never know—there just might be another wedding on the horizon."

Karen smiled. "Will and I had a good talk this morning, and we've agreed to try to keep our focus on each other and set our jealous feelings aside."

"That's good to hear."

Just then Mark stepped into the room. He looked tired, and a deep purple bruise accentuated his slightly swollen forehead.

"How are you feeling this evening?" Re-gina asked after he'd taken a seat at the table.

"I'm feeling hungry."

She snickered. "I meant, how's your head feel?"

"Oh, that. It feels like a woodpecker thought my head was a tree, but I think I'll live." He grinned at Karen. "Danki for help-ing out in the store so my *fraa* could be here hovering over me most of the day."

"I wasn't hovering. I was making sure

you didn't do anything you weren't supposed to do." Regina opened a cupboard door, took out a small bottle, and handed it to him. "I was also making sure you took some Arnica tablets several times during the day."

"What's Arnica used for?" Karen asked.

"It's a homeopathic remedy that's used for bruising, pain, and the swelling that accompanies many injuries," Regina explained. "Arnica lotion can also be rubbed directly on the bruise."

"I can see there's much a person needs to know if they're going to run a health food store," Karen said. "I always thought it was just about selling vitamins, herbs, and healthy food products."

"A lot is involved," Regina agreed. "My folks owned a health food store when I was a girl, and since I got to work there on the days I wasn't in school, I learned quite a lot. Then after I graduated eighth grade, I worked in the store full-time and learned even more."

"Would you be willing to teach me about running a health food store?" Karen asked.

"Jah, sure. After you and Will are married, you can work in the store as much as you like. I'd be happy to teach you whatever you need to know."

"I'd like that."

Mark popped two Arnica tablets into his mouth and glanced at the back door. "I wonder what's taking Will so long. He and Nathan ought to be done with the milking by now."

Regina placed her hand on his shoulder. "Don't get any ideas about going out to the barn. You're supposed to stay in the house and rest until the doctor says otherwise."

"I know, I know." Mark touched his forehead and winced. "As long as my head continues to hurt, you don't have to worry about me going back to work."

The back door squeaked open, and Will stepped into the room. "Brr. It's mighty cold out," he said, rubbing his arms.

"Did everything go all right with the milking?" Mark asked.

"It went fine."

"Did you invite Nathan to join us for supper like I asked you to?" Regina questioned.

"I did, but he said his uncle isn't feeling

well, so he thought he ought to get home and do the evening chores."

"What's wrong with Aaron?" Regina's eyebrows furrowed. "When Susanna was at the hospital with me, she didn't say anything about her husband being sick. I hope it's nothing serious."

"He's only got a cold. Nathan said he woke up with it this morning."

"You should have sent Nathan over to the health food store to get some vitamin C and Echinacea for his uncle."

"Nathan and I were both in the health food store before we did the milking, but I didn't think of suggesting anything that his uncle might take. If I don't forget, I'll mention the vitamin and herbs when Nathan comes tomorrow morning to help with the milking." Will looked over at Karen and smiled. "Did you manage okay at the store after I left to milk the cows?"

She nodded. "There weren't too many customers, so I did just fine."

"That's good to hear."

"Oh, I almost forgot. Mary Jane's mother came by the house this afternoon," Regina said. "She wanted to let me know that Mary

Jane's still down with the flu and won't be here tomorrow, either."

"I can help again," Karen was quick to say. "I talked to Mom on the phone during lunch, and she said they can get by without me for the rest of the week if you need my help here."

"It would be much appreciated." Regina ladled the stew into a serving bowl and placed it on the table. "Shall we eat?"

Mark nodded. "I thought you'd never ask."

"Daddy, Kim's bothering me!"

Frank groaned as he rose from the couch. He'd spent the entire evening refereeing petty squabbles between his daughters when all he'd wanted to do was relax and watch a little TV.

"That's what I get for agreeing to watch the girls while Megan went to her Bible study," he mumbled as he climbed the stairs leading to their bedrooms.

He spotted Kim at the top of the stairs, scuttling across the hardwood floor. Carrie was right behind Kim, poking her in the back.

Frank reached out and grabbed Carrie by the arm, and Kim disappeared into her room. "I thought I told you to get ready for bed! Don't you ever listen to anything I say?" The emotions surging through him defied explanation.

Carrie's dark eyes filled with tears, and her lower lip trembled. "Y–you're hurtin' me, Daddy."

He let go of her arm and shook his finger in her face. "I told you and Kim to brush your teeth and get ready for bed half an hour ago, and you're not even in your pajamas yet!"

Carrie's shoulders shook as she buried her face in her hands.

"Don't start crying on me now." He smacked his hands together, and she jumped. "Go to your room and get ready for bed!"

"Please don't yell anymore," Carrie whimpered. "I'll be good; I promise." She slunk off to her room, sniffling all the way.

With an exasperated grunt, Frank tromped down the stairs. As he flopped onto the couch, an image from the past rose in his mind. . . .

"I didn't mean to do it, Pop. I just wanted to—"

Smack! Frank felt the sting of his father's hand as it connected with his face. "Don't talk back to me, boy!"

Frank darted behind the sofa and cowered. Pop had been drinking again, and that always spelled trouble.

"Come out of there and face me like a man!"

Knowing he would be in bigger trouble if he didn't obey, Frank stood on shaky legs and inched his way out from behind the sofa.

Smack! Smack! Smack! Several more blows came, this time to Frank's face, arms, and the small of his back.

Frank cried out and held his arms in front of his face, hoping to shield himself from the next blow.

Smack! It came with such force that it sent Frank flying across the room. He bounced against the wall and dropped to the floor with a thud.

"Get up, you stupid boy! You're worthless, you know that?"

Frank's stomach churned as the bitter taste of bile rose in his throat. Why didn't Mama come to his rescue? Why didn't she tell Pop to stop this madness?

"Please don't hit me no more," Frank whimpered. "I'll be a good boy; I promise I will."

"I know you'll be good, because I'm gonna make sure you're good." Pop's mouth twisted as he grabbed Will's ear and jerked him to his feet. He was obviously proud of himself for being able to control his unruly son.

He backhanded Frank again and pushed him onto the sofa. "You need to learn a good lesson; that's what you need!"

I hate you, Pop! *Frank cried silently.* I hate you, and I hate Mama, too!

Tears streamed down Frank's face as his thoughts returned to the present. He'd spent most of his childhood hating and living in fear of his father. When Frank's mother had died of cancer soon after his seventeenth birthday, Frank had left home and struck out on his own, never to return. He'd seen his dad's obituary in the paper a few years later but felt no sorrow that Pop was gone. He'd vowed never to be like his dad, but seeing how Carrie had reacted to his display of temper made Frank realize that if he wasn't careful to keep a lid on his temper, he could end up following in his dad's footsteps.

Frank didn't want his girls to live in fear the way he had as a child. In the six years he'd raised Will, he'd never struck the boy. But tonight, standing in the hallway with Carrie, he'd had to fight for control.

He felt remorse for making Carrie fearful in his presence, and the pain of his harsh words washed over him like a wave of fire. He needed to apologize and make things right between them. And he needed to do it now.

Frank rose from the couch and headed upstairs. He found Carrie in her room, dressed in her pajamas, sprawled out on her bed, sobbing like her little heart would break in two.

He sat beside her and took hold of her hand. "I'm sorry, Carrie. I didn't mean to yell like that."

"I—I'm sorry, Daddy." She sniffed a couple of times. "I should've listened when you told me to get ready for bed."

Frank gathered the child in his arms. "I love you, sweetie."

"I love you, too."

As Frank rocked his daughter back and forth, his thoughts went to Will. *Did Regina and Mark Stoltzfus comfort my boy over the years, the way I'm doing with Carrie right now? Maybe Will was better off growing up with the Amish couple as his parents than he would have been if he'd stayed with me.*

When Megan entered the living room, she found Frank slouched on the sofa with his head resting in his hands. The TV was off. Something must be wrong.

She took a seat on the end of the sofa. "What's the matter, Frank? Are you feeling all right?"

He lifted his head and looked at her with a vacant stare.

A feeling of trepidation crept up her spine. Something *was* wrong. She touched his leg. "What is it, Frank?"

He blinked a couple of times, as though coming out of a trance. "Don't ever ask me to watch the girls again. I can't be trusted."

Megan's heart leaped into her throat. "Did something happen to Carrie or Kim?"

He shook his head. "No, but it could have."

"You're scaring me, Frank. What happened while I was gone?"

"I told them several times to get ready for bed, but they kept playing and fussing at each other." He paused and drew in a quick breath. "When I went upstairs to check on things, I. . .I almost hit Carrie."

"You mean you wanted to give her a spanking?"

"No, I wanted to slap her face or shake some sense into her head." His shoulders slumped, and he buried his face in hands.

Megan knelt on the floor in front of him. "You're not the only parent who's ever felt like slapping his child. And sometimes, when an act of disobedience has occurred, a correctly applied spanking might be necessary."

"I realize that, but I'm afraid I might not be able to control my temper if I dole out any kind of corporal punishment." He groaned. "I'm afraid I'll become an abusive father, like my dad was to me."

"But you didn't hit Carrie. You stopped yourself before you lost control of your temper. That counts for something."

He sat up straight, slowly shaking his head.

Megan's heart filled with compassion for Frank. She knew from the things he'd told her that his dad had been abusive and had a drinking problem, but until this moment, she hadn't realized how much it had affected Frank.

"I hated my dad when I was a boy, and I hate him now for making me question my ability to be a good father to our girls." Deep lines etched Frank's forehead, and his clenched jaw revealed the extent of his anger and resentment.

Megan took hold of his hand. "You've got to stop hating your father. You need to find forgiveness in your heart for what he did to you."

"I can't."

"Yes, you can."

He shook his head. "I can't forgive my dad because I'm no better than he was."

"You mean because you were tempted to hit Carrie tonight?"

"That's only part of it." Frank's hand trembled as he reached up to rub his forehead. "I was a lousy father to Will, too. If I live to be one hundred, I'll never forgive myself for leaving him with that Amish couple."

Megan reached for her Bible on the coffee table. "I want to read something to you." She opened the Bible to Romans 3:23. " 'For all have sinned, and come short of the glory of God,' " she read. "Not one of us is without sin, Frank."

"I—I suppose you're right about that."

"But there's a way we can be released from the oppression of our sins." Megan flipped over to 1 John 1:9. " 'If we confess our sins, he is faithful and just to forgive us our sins, and to cleanse us from all unrighteousness.' "

"If I could only find my son, I might feel released from my guilt and sin."

"No, Frank. You need to ask the Lord to

forgive your sins, and He will release you from your guilty feelings. Then you need to forgive your father and forgive yourself, regardless of whether you ever find Will or not. It's the only way you'll find peace in your heart. It's the only way you'll be able to be the kind of father our girls need you to be."

Tears pooled in Frank's eyes. "I—I don't know how to pray, Megan. Would you help me say what needs to be said?"

She nodded and motioned him to join her on the floor. Kneeling in front of the sofa together, Megan led her husband in a prayer of repentance and forgiveness.

CHAPTER 21

As Frank sat at the kitchen table two weeks later, he picked up his Bible to read a few verses of scripture before it was time to eat supper. The girls were in the living room playing with their dolls, and Megan had gone to the basement to check on the clothes in the dryer.

Frank picked up his coffee mug and took a drink; then he opened the Bible and turned to the passage he'd been studying, John 8:32: "And ye shall know the truth, and the truth shall make you free."

The truth of God's Word and His plan of salvation: That's what made me free, Frank mused. Ever since he'd given his heart to the Lord and confessed his sins, he'd felt a sense of peace that went beyond all understanding. He was a new creature in Christ—saved by the blood of the Lamb. The hate he had felt for his father was gone. The self-recrimination he'd been living with for the past sixteen years had been replaced with a sense of peace. The future was God's. Will, wherever he might be, was in God's hands. If it was meant for Frank to see his son again, then it would happen in God's time, in God's way.

I need to keep my focus on Megan and the girls and try to be the best husband and father I can be. Frank took another drink of coffee. *When I'm not working, we need to do more things together as a family—and that includes going to church.*

"I put the last load of clothes in the dryer, so I'm ready to start supper now," Megan said as she stepped into the room.

"No hurry. I'm not really hungry yet, anyway." Frank looked at her and smiled. "I've been thinking about some things we can do with the girls this coming year."

"Such as?"

"Maybe a trip to see Niagara Falls this summer."

"That would be fun."

"I also thought it would be good for us to take them camping—maybe do a little fishing, too."

Megan nodded. "When I was a girl, my folks used to take me and my sister camping every summer." She moved across the room and picked up the pieces of mail that had been stacked on the counter. "I've been so busy today I haven't had a chance to go through the mail. Since you're not in a hurry to eat, maybe I'll go through it now." Megan pulled out the chair across from him and took a seat.

As Frank continued to read his Bible, Megan thumbed through the mail. Suddenly she let out a squeal.

Startled, he jumped. "What's wrong? Did you see a mouse or something?"

"It's here, Frank! The copy of *The Budget* with your ad in it is here." She leaned across the table and handed the newspaper to him.

Frank scanned the paper until he found the notice section. His heartbeat picked up speed as he read the notice aloud: " 'I'm looking for my son, Will, whom I left with an Amish couple, Mark and Regina Stoltzfus, 16 years ago. The Stoltzfuses lived in Lancaster County, Pennsylvania, but have since moved. Anyone having knowledge of their whereabouts, please contact Frank Henderson, 555-230-9110.' "

He let the paper fall to the table and looked over at Megan. "Do you think it's possible that one of the Stoltzfuses or even Will might read this notice and contact me?"

Megan smiled. "With God, all things are possible."

"Will, could you find me a pitchfork?" Papa Mark asked as he entered one of the horses' stalls. "There doesn't seem to be one in here."

"Jah, sure." Will found a pitchfork leaning against a bale of hay not far from the horse he was feeding and handed it to Papa Mark.

"Danki, son."

"You're welcome."

"Sure does feel good to be back working again. I missed getting dirty and sweaty every day."

Will chuckled. He was glad Papa Mark was doing better and could do most of his chores again. Besides the fact that Papa Mark was happier when he busy, having him working again meant Will had a little more free time. He'd been so busy these past few weeks that it had been difficult to find time to be with Karen. She'd only helped at the health food store a couple of days, just until Mary Jane had returned to work and Papa Mark had convinced Mama Regina that he didn't need her hovering over him all day.

When Karen and I get married, I'll want to spend every free moment with her, Will thought. *And if she hovers, I think it'll make me feel loved.* He smiled to himself as he opened a fresh bale of hay. *I'll bet that's how Papa Mark felt when he and Mama Regina were first married.*

"It was nice of your friend Nathan to help out while I was recuperating," Papa Mark said.

Will nodded. "He's been a big help to his uncle since he came back to Indiana, too."

"You think he'll stick around?"

"Jah. Now that he's working at the trailer

factory, he has an even better reason to stay permanently."

"I'm sure his aunt and uncle are happy about that."

"From what I understand, Mary Jane is, as well."

Papa Mark forked another bunch of hay. "Mind if ask you a question, Will?"

"Don't mind at all."

"I'm wondering if you're happy, son. I mean, you don't have any regrets about joining the Amish faith, do you?"

Will's forehead wrinkled. "Of course not. I like being Amish."

"Me and your mamm are glad you came to live with us."

"I'm glad, too. I just wish. . ." Will's voice trailed off.

"What do you wish?"

"Oh, nothing." Will pulled the bale of hay apart and headed for the next stall. He wasn't about to admit, not even to himself, that he wished he at least knew if Pop was still alive.

Regina reached for her cup of coffee as she read the latest issue of *The Budget*. It was interesting to read about the things that went on in other Amish communities around the country—trips people had taken, visitors who had come to their house, accidents that had occurred, sicknesses in the family, weddings they'd attended, and the births of children and grandchildren.

She read several articles that had been written by various scribes in Ohio, Pennsylvania, Illinois, and Indiana; then she turned to the ad and notice pages. Skipping the ones that held no interest, her gaze came to rest on one particular notice, printed in bold type with a box around it. *"I'm looking for my son, Will, whom I left with an Amish couple, Mark and Regina Stoltzfus, 16 years ago. The Stoltzfuses lived in Lancaster County, Pennsylvania, but have since moved. Anyone having knowledge of their whereabouts, please contact Frank Henderson, 555-230-9110."*

Regina gasped, and fear closed in on her like a vise. After all these years, Will's father was trying to contact him!

Her hands shook as she let the paper fall to the table. *Should I show this to Will?* It would be the right thing to do, but what if

Will contacted his father and then decided to leave the Amish faith and go English? If Frank came back into Will's life now, they might lose Will forever. And what of Will's plans to marry Karen? Would news of Frank's father disrupt Will and Karen's wedding?

Regina sat still for several minutes, staring into her cup, trying to decide what to do. Finally she rose from her chair, picked up the newspaper, and placed it inside one of the kitchen drawers. She would wait and talk to Mark before she said anything to Will.

When Karen entered the kitchen to help with supper, she found her mother sitting at the table, reading *The Budget*. Suddenly Mom's face paled, and she gasped.

Karen's heart pounded against her rib cage. "What's wrong, Mom?"

"*Kumme*, look at this." Mom's eyes widened as she pointed to the newspaper.

Karen came over to the table. "What is it?" she asked, leaning over Mom's shoulder.

"You need to read this notice."

As Karen read the notice, her palms grew sweaty and her mouth went dry. "Ach, Mom, Will's real daed must have put that ad in *The Budget*. After all these years without making any contact with Will, he's looking for him."

"I wonder if Will knows about this."

Karen pulled out a chair and sank into it. "I. . .I don't know."

"Are you going to ask him about it?"

Karen contemplated her mother's question. She had thought several times how nice it would be if Will's real father could be at their wedding, but now her mind was filled with doubts. If Will read the notice and met his father, what kind of impact would it have on him? Would it affect his plans to marry her? If Will were reunited with his father, would he decide to leave the Amish faith and be English again?

CHAPTER 22

"Can I speak to you a minute, Regina?" Mark asked as he entered the health food store the following morning.

She turned from stocking shelves and smiled. "Jah, sure. Mary Jane's up front waiting on Susanna Chupp, so I have time to talk."

Mark's eyebrows furrowed. "I've been thinking about that notice you read in *The Budget* that was put there by Will's daed."

Regina motioned to the front of the store, and her voice dropped to a whisper. "Let's keep our voices down. I don't want anyone to hear this conversation."

Mark moved closer to Regina. "I think we need to tell Will about that notice before he reads it himself or hears about it from someone else."

"You're right, but I can't help but be worried about his reaction. What if Will gets together with his daed and decides to leave the Amish faith and go English?" Regina blinked against the tears clinging to her eyelashes. "I don't think I could stand it if we lost Will now."

Mark patted her arm. "I don't think we'll lose him, but I do think he needs to be told."

Regina nodded. "We'll tell him at supper tonight."

When the bell above the door of the dry goods store jingled, Karen went to see who had come in.

She started down the aisle and almost bumped into Susanna Chupp. "Oh, I wondered who'd come into the store."

"I'm getting low on kerosene and thought I'd better stop by and get some."

"Were you in town shopping?"

Susanna shook her head. "I went to

Regina's store to get some vitamins." She squinted at Karen over the top of her glasses as she tipped her head. "I heard some distressful news while I was there and wondered if you'd heard it, too."

"What news is that?"

"I heard Regina and Mark talking about Will and his real daed."

"What about them?"

"I guess Will's daed put an ad in *The Budget*, trying to contact Will." Susanna paused and moistened her lips. "I heard them say that Will's planning to leave the Amish faith and go English."

Karen's breath caught in her throat, and she grabbed the edge of the counter to keep from falling over. Apparently Will had read the notice in *The Budget* just as she had done last night. Had he already made contact with his father? Had their reunion caused Will to decide he wanted to go English? If so, there would be no wedding next month, because despite Karen's love for Will, she could never leave the Amish faith and hoped he wouldn't ask her to.

"You look kind of pale." Susanna touched Karen's arm. "Are you feeling grank?"

"I'm not sick. What you said about Will just took me by surprise." Karen swallowed around the lump in her throat and blinked back tears that threatened to spill over.

"Then you didn't know?"

Karen shook her head.

"Oh dear. I'm sorry for being the one to tell you. It should have come from Will, not me."

Karen's brain felt foggy. Her body felt numb. This couldn't be true. It had to be a mistake. Surely Will wouldn't decide to leave the Amish faith without talking to her about it. She needed to speak to him right away!

Will had just finished washing the floor in the milking barn when Karen stepped through the open door. Her eyes were wide, and her cheeks were crimson, probably from the cold.

"I'm surprised to see you," he said. "Aren't you needed at your folks' store today?"

"I was working there this morning, but I needed to speak with you. So I went next door and asked Mavis to help Cindy while I was gone, and she was more than willing."

"Aren't your folks working today?"

Karen shook her head. "They both had dental appointments, and then they had some errands to run in Shipshewana."

Will motioned to a couple of wooden stools. "Should we take a seat?"

"Jah, sure." Karen sat on one of the stools, and he took the other. She folded her hands in her lap and looked at him expectantly.

"What was it you wanted to talk to me about?"

"I'm sure you must know."

He scratched his head. "If I knew, I wouldn't have asked."

She drew in a deep breath and sighed. "Susanna Chupp came into our store awhile ago, and she told me something very disturbing."

"What'd she tell you?"

"She said. . ." Karen paused, and he noticed tears clinging to her lashes.

"What is it, Karen? What's got you so upset?"

"Susanna said you've been in touch with your real daed and that you're planning to leave the Amish faith and go English."

Will's mouth dropped open, and a tremor

shot through his body. "That's lecherich! I haven't heard from Pop since he walked out on me nearly sixteen years ago. And I'm certainly not planning to leave the Amish faith."

"Then you don't know about the notice in *The Budget*?"

"What notice?"

"The one from your real daed."

Will shook his head, partly in response to her question and partly to clear his mind. "What did this notice in *The Budget* say, and what makes you think it was from my daed?"

Papa Mark cleared his throat loudly.

Will turned his gaze from Karen to Papa Mark. "I didn't know you'd come into the barn. How long have you been standing there?"

"I came in to see if you needed any help cleaning things up and heard the last part of your conversation." He motioned to the door. "I think you need to come into the house with me, Will."

"What for?"

"There's something your mamm and I want to speak to you about. She's in the house now, starting lunch."

Will looked at Karen then back at Papa Mark. "Is this about some notice that's supposedly in *The Budget*?"

Papa Mark nodded. "Let's go inside so we can look at the paper together." He smiled at Karen. "You're welcome to come with us, of course."

She looked at Will, as if seeking his approval.

He nodded and reached for her hand.

When the three of them entered the kitchen, Will spotted Mama Regina in front of the counter, cutting slices of ham.

She turned and smiled when she saw Karen. "What a nice surprise. Would you like to join us for lunch, Karen?"

Before Karen could respond, Papa Mark stepped forward and said, "You'd better get out *The Budget* and show it to Will."

Mama Regina's eyebrows pulled together. "I thought we were going to wait until supper."

Papa Mark shook his head. "Since Karen's already told Will a few things, I think it's best that we show him the newspaper now."

Mama Regina hesitated; then she scurried across the room, removed a copy of

The Budget from a drawer, and placed it on the table.

"What's this all about?" Will asked, following her across the room.

Mama Regina flipped through the pages. "Right here," she said, touching one section of the paper. "This is the part you need to read."

Will leaned over and read the notice. His heart pounded so hard it seemed to echo in his ears. A feeling of helplessness and confusion swept over him as he stared at the page in disbelief. "It can't be. It just can't be," he muttered, shaking his head. "After all these years with no word from Pop, I was sure he must be dead."

Will shuddered. There were times when he had secretly hoped his father might be dead. At least it would have accounted for his not coming back. But there were other times when Will felt a strong need to know that his father was alive.

"Your daed is obviously not dead," Karen said, stepping up to Will. "This notice in *The Budget* means he's looking for you."

As Will tried to let everything sink in, a stark realization hit him with the force of a tornado. He had thought he'd put the past behind and was ready to make a future with Karen. He'd thought if he just knew Pop was alive, it would be enough for him. But now, after reading this notice, he realized he still hadn't come to grips with his past or forgiven his dad for abandoning him. He knew, too, that even though he was curious to know where Pop had been all these years, he couldn't deal with the thought of seeing him again.

He turned to face Mama Regina. "How long have you known about this notice?"

"I read it last night."

"Why didn't you say something to me about it then?"

She dropped her gaze to the floor. "I wasn't sure how you would take it. I was afraid you might. . ." Her voice trailed off, and when she looked at Will, tears filled her eyes. "Are you going to call your daed?"

He sank into a chair and let his head fall forward into his hands. "I'm not sure what I should do. I need time to think."

CHAPTER 23

When Will stepped into the kitchen the following morning, Regina touched his arm. "Have you thought any more about that notice in *The Budget* from your daed?"

He gave a quick nod.

"What did you decide to do about it?"

"Nothing."

"You're not going to contact him?"

He shook his head and reached into the cupboard for a mug. "Is there still some coffee left?"

"I made a fresh pot after you and your daed went out to do the milking." Regina got the coffeepot. "Do you mind telling me why you don't plan to contact your daed?" she asked as she poured coffee into Will's mug.

"For a long time after Pop left, I longed to see him. But then when I realized he wasn't coming back, I came to think of you and Papa Mark as my parents." He shrugged. "So after all these years have gone by, what's the point in me seeing Pop again? If he'd wanted to get in touch with me, he'd have done so sooner, don't you think?"

Regina took a seat at the table and motioned for Will to do the same. "What I think is that you're being offered an opportunity to meet with your daed and find out why he never returned to our home in Pennsylvania. I'll admit I had some misgivings about this at first, but after thinking it over, I believe you need to contact him and find out where he's been all this time, don't you?"

A muscle on the side of Will's neck quivered as he stared into his mug. "Right now, I only want two things: to marry Karen and to forget I ever had a daed named Frank Henderson."

"But you've said many times that you

wished you knew where he was and that you'd like to ask him some questions."

"I know, but I've changed my mind."

She took a drink of coffee as she mulled things over. She set the mug down and decided to try again. "I think maybe you should reconsider, Will. I really don't think you'll ever put the past to rest until you've talked to your daed and heard why he left and never returned."

Will grunted. "Any man who would abandon his own child doesn't deserve to be anyone's daed!" He pushed his chair away from the table and stood. "I'd better go back to the barn and see how Papa Mark's doing with that cow. Maybe you should wait on breakfast until we both come in."

"Jah, okay." Regina knew that to say more would be futile. As soon as Will left the room, she opened the drawer where she'd put *The Budget* and took it out. She found Frank's notice then copied down the phone number. *If Will's not going to contact his daed, then I will.*

🌿

"What are you doing out here again?" Papa Mark asked when Will stepped into the barn. "I told you I could handle this. There was no reason for you to come out in the cold again."

Will squatted beside the cow Papa Mark was working on. "The reason I came back has nothing to do with me thinking you couldn't handle this cow."

"What is the reason?"

"Mama Regina was giving me her thoughts on that notice in *The Budget*, and I didn't want to talk about it anymore."

"I see."

"She thinks I ought to contact Pop and find out why he left and never came back."

"What do you think, Will?"

"I think if Pop ever cared anything about me, he would have left a note like he told Mama Regina he was going to." Will grunted. "And I think he shouldn't have waited until now to try to contact me."

Papa Mark nodded. "I have to agree with both of those things, but your daed is trying to find you now, so don't you think you ought to find out what he has to say?"

"I don't care what he has to say."

"Are you sure about that?"

"Jah."

"You're a man now, Will, and you have the right to make your own decisions. However, I think you might need to mull things over a bit before you make a final decision on this."

Will gave no reply.

"I just want to say one more thing."

"What's that?"

"I believe that God has a reason for bringing people into our lives at certain times. He had a reason for bringing you into our lives when you were a boy, and maybe He has a reason for bringing your real daed back into your life now."

Will shrugged.

"Enough said. Would you please get me some antiseptic?"

Will nodded, glad for the change of subject.

"Can I talk to you about something?" Karen asked her mother.

"Of course." Mom motioned to the kitchen table. "Would you like to sit while we talk?"

"What about breakfast?"

"There's no hurry. Your daed's still outside doing his chores, and Cindy hasn't come downstairs yet."

"Okay." Karen pulled out a chair and sat down.

"What'd you want to talk to me about?" Mom asked.

"It's about Will and that notice we read in *The Budget* from his real daed."

"You mentioned last night that you'd gone over to speak with Will about it."

Karen nodded. "It was awful, Mom. You should have seen the look on Will's face when I asked if he was planning to leave the Amish faith."

Mom gave Karen's shoulder a gentle squeeze. "You had no way of knowing Will hadn't seen *The Budget*. You had no reason not to believe what Susanna Chupp said she'd heard."

Karen stared at a small hole in the tablecloth as she mulled things over. Would things have been better if she hadn't said anything to Will, or would he have found out on his own?

"Was there something more you wished to say?" Mom asked.

"Jah. I'm concerned because I wasn't able to really explain things to Will."

"Why not?"

"Because after he read the notice in *The Budget*, he rushed out the door."

"Why don't you go over and talk to Will this evening after dinner?"

"You think I should?"

Mom nodded. "If you're going to be his wife, you need to communicate with him about everything that's important, don't you think?"

"I do want to communicate with Will, but I don't want him to think I'm trying to be pushy or that I want him to do something he doesn't want to do."

"I'm sure he won't think either of those things."

"Who won't think what things?" Cindy asked as she stepped into the room.

"Karen and I were just discussing some issues," Mom said.

"What issues?"

"Never you mind. Now let's get breakfast on." Mom motioned to the refrigerator. "Cindy, why don't you get out some eggs and bacon while I get the stove warmed up?"

Karen rose from her chair. "Guess I'll set the table." As she opened the drawer to take out the silverware, she glanced out the window and realized it was snowing. She hoped it wouldn't be more than a light dusting and that the roads wouldn't get bad, because she really wanted to see Will.

CHAPTER 24

Megan paced the living room floor as she waited for Frank to get home. She had received a phone call from Regina Stoltzfus soon after Frank had left for work in reply to the notice she had put in *The Budget*. Since Frank wasn't at home when the call had come in and had left his cell phone at home, Megan had asked Regina to call again this evening.

I hope she doesn't call before Frank gets home, Megan fretted. *I know he'll want to talk to her. I wish I had insisted that she give me her number. I wish we had caller ID, because that would have given me her number.*

She went to the window and pulled the curtain aside. There was no sign of Frank's truck in the driveway or coming up the street.

"I'm hungry, Mommy," Kim said, tugging on Megan's hand. "When are we gonna eat supper?"

Megan looked down at her daughter and smiled. "As soon as your daddy gets home." She motioned to Carrie, lying on the sofa with a book. "Why don't you sit beside your sister and see if she'll read to you?"

"I don't want to read to her," Carrie mumbled. "She interrupts and asks goofy questions."

Kim thrust out her lower lip. "Do not!"

"Yeah, you do!"

Megan patted the top of Kim's head. "Why don't you go upstairs and play until Daddy gets home?"

Kim hesitated a moment but finally scampered out of the room.

Megan returned to the window to watch for Frank's truck.

"What are you doing?" Dad asked when Karen entered the barn.

"I'm getting my horse so I can go over to see Will."

"But it's dark outside."

"I've driven in the dark plenty of times, and I've always been fine with our battery-operated lights."

His forehead wrinkled. "But it's been snowing most of the day, and the roads might be bad."

"I saw a snowplow out on the main road when I left the store this afternoon, so I'm sure the roads will be clear enough. Besides, the Stoltzfuses' place isn't that far away."

"Even so, I don't see why you have to go there this evening. Can't it wait until tomorrow?"

She pursed her lips. "Didn't Mom tell you about that notice in *The Budget* and Will's reaction to it?"

"Jah, she mentioned it."

"Will was pretty upset, and we didn't get a chance to discuss things thoroughly enough, so I'd really like to talk to him before this day is over."

Dad massaged the bridge of his nose,

the way he always did whenever he was contemplating something. Finally he nodded. "Jah, okay. I'll help you get Ginger hitched to a buggy, and you can be on your way."

A short time later, Karen was headed down the road with her horse and buggy. Even though most of the snow had been plowed, Dad had been right—there were some slippery spots. She would have to be careful.

Karen held the reins tightly and clucked to the horse. "Easy, Ginger. Not too fast now, girl."

Things went along fine for the first mile or so. Then suddenly Ginger lost her footing, slipped on the ice, and nearly went down. The buggy rocked back and forth as it slid across the icy pavement.

Karen's heart hammered in her chest, and she clutched the reins so tightly that her fingers went numb. *I should have listened to Dad and waited until tomorrow to see Will. Maybe I'd better turn around and go home.*

As Karen tried to get Ginger to turn, the buggy wheels spun. She'd obviously hit another patch of ice! Ginger lurched to the right, pulling the buggy into a thick clump of snow and ice along the edge of the road.

Karen snapped the reins, hoping the horse could pull the buggy free, but the wheels only spun. Ginger whinnied as her hooves slipped on the ice. Karen was afraid if she kept pushing the mare, Ginger might collapse.

She grabbed her flashlight and climbed out of the buggy. "Guess we'd better walk home and get some help," she said as she unhitched Ginger. No way was she was going to leave the horse alone with the buggy. It wouldn't be safe.

"I'm heading out to see Karen now," Will called to Regina as he donned his jacket and zipple cap.

Regina glanced out the kitchen window. "Do you think that's a good idea? It's beginning to snow again, and the roads might be bad."

"I'll take it slow and easy."

"Can't it wait until tomorrow?"

"I'd really like to speak with Karen tonight, and the roads might be even worse by tomorrow."

"Are you going to discuss your response to that notice in *The Budget*?"

He nodded. "That, and a few other things."

"Have you changed your mind about contacting your daed?"

Will's eyebrows furrowed as he shook his head.

Regina nibbled on the inside of her cheek. Should she say anything more or drop the subject? *I'd probably better keep quiet about it for now,* she decided. *He'd be very upset if he knew about the phone call I made this morning.*

"I won't be gone long," Will said as he stepped out the door.

Regina stood at the window and watched until Will's horse and buggy left the yard; then she went to the living room where Mark sat reading one of his dairy farming magazines. "I'm going out to the phone shed to make a call."

"Jah, okay," he mumbled without looking up from the magazine. Regina figured he hadn't even heard what she'd said. Well, she wouldn't be gone long; he probably wouldn't miss her.

She hurried to the utility room, grabbed

her heavy woolen shawl and a flashlight, and went out the back door.

Frank had just stepped into the house when the telephone rang. He headed to the kitchen to answer it, but it stopped ringing. Then he heard Megan talking to someone. When he stepped into the room, she held the phone out to him as she covered the mouthpiece with her other hand. "It's Regina Stoltzfus," she whispered. "She wants to talk to you about that notice I put in *The Budget*."

Frank's mouth went dry as he took the phone from Megan. "Hello."

"Hello, Frank. This is Regina Stoltzfus. I wanted you to know that we saw the notice you placed in *The Budget*."

"You. . .you did?"

"Yes, and that's the reason I'm calling."

"The notice was actually my wife's idea."

"I know. I spoke with her when I called earlier today."

Frank looked over at Megan and covered the receiver with his hand. "Why didn't you call and let me know Regina had phoned here earlier today?"

Megan motioned to the counter across the room. "You left your cell phone at home, and when I tried calling your office number, your secretary said you would be out for the rest of the day."

"I had some errands to run, and I also made one quick delivery." Frank put the receiver back to his ear. "Where do you live now, Regina? When I went back to your place in Lancaster County, I discovered you had moved."

"Yes, we did, but not until you'd been gone nearly a year."

"So where'd you move to?"

"We live just outside of Middlebury, Indiana."

"What made you move there?"

"We bought a dairy farm, which Mark owns, and I run a health food store."

"Does Will still live with you?"

"Yes, he does."

A sense of relief flooded Frank's soul. "May I speak with him, please?"

"Uh. . .Will's not at home right now, and he doesn't know I've made this call."

"You didn't tell him about the notice in the paper?"

"He knows, but—"

"If he knows, then why didn't he call me himself?"

"After all this time without any word from you, I don't think Will quite knows what to say."

Frank swallowed hard. He didn't know what he would say to Will, either, but he knew lots of things needed to be said.

"When I spoke with your wife this morning, I learned that you not only remarried after you left Will with us, but you now have two little girls."

"That's true."

"I'm wondering something, Frank."

"What's that?"

"Could you help me understand the reason you never came back to get Will like you promised you would? Could you explain why you've waited until now to try to contact him?"

He swiped his tongue across his bottom lip. "It's a complicated story, and I'd prefer to wait and talk to Will about that, rather than him hearing it secondhand."

"I see." There was a long pause.

"Are you still there, Regina?"

"Yes, I'm here."

"Will you let Will know I called and ask him to phone me tomorrow?"

"I'll speak with him about it, but I can't promise that he'll call you."

"But I've got to talk to him. Please, can't you make him understand that?"

"I'll do my best."

"Okay, but before you hang up, could you give me your phone—"

"Good-bye, Frank." *Click.*

Frank hung up the phone and sank into a chair at the table.

"I take it you didn't get to speak with Will," Megan said, touching Frank's shoulder.

"No, and I didn't even get Regina's phone number. She hung up before I could ask."

"I didn't get it when I talked with her earlier today, either."

Frank grunted. "Want to know the worst part?"

"What's that?"

"Will didn't know Regina was planning to call me. She made it pretty clear that he doesn't want to talk to me. He probably hates me for leaving him the way I did."

Megan took a seat beside him and reached for his hands. "Let's pray about this and leave everything with God."

Frank nodded. Praying and leaving things in God's hands was a new concept for him, but he knew it was the right thing—the only thing—he could do.

As Will headed down the road in his buggy, he thought about the things he should say to Karen. He hoped she wasn't mad because he'd run out on her. He wanted to explain that he'd been upset and needed to be alone. He wanted her to understand the way he felt about his dad trying to contact him after all these years.

Will was halfway to the Yoders' when he spotted a buggy that appeared to be stuck in a pile of snow along the edge of the road.

He pulled over, grabbed his flashlight, and went to investigate. No horse was hitched to the buggy, and no driver was inside, either. But he recognized the quilt lying on the front seat and knew it was Karen's. He figured her rig had probably slid into the snow and gotten stuck. Karen must have unhitched her horse and headed for home.

Will climbed back into his buggy and continued toward the Yoders'. He'd only gone a short distance when he spotted Karen walking along the edge of the road, leading her horse.

He pulled up behind her and climbed down from his rig. "What happened? Are you okay?"

"I'm fine. I hit a patch of ice, and then my buggy slid into a mound of snow and got stuck. When I couldn't get it out, I decided to unhitch my horse and walk home to get help." She shivered. "Guess I should have listened to my daed when he warned me that the roads could be icy."

Will motioned to his buggy. "Hop in, and I'll tie your horse to the back of my rig. Then we'll go back and see if we can get your buggy pulled out of that mound of snow."

Karen nodded and handed Ginger's lead rope to Will. Then she climbed into his buggy while he hooked Ginger to the back of his rig.

"Where were you heading when you spotted us?" Karen asked after Will had joined her in the buggy.

"Over to your place. What brought you out on a cold night like this?"

"I was going to see you. I wanted to talk about what happened this morning and apologize for blurting out what Susanna had said."

"You had no way of knowing I hadn't read *The Budget*. You were only going on what you'd heard."

She reached across the seat and took hold of his hand. "Are you going to contact your real daed?"

"I don't think so."

"Why not?"

"You know, I used to dream about see-ing Pop again." Will sighed. "But he gave up the right to be my daed when he walked away and never returned, so why would I want to talk to him now? I mean, what would I say after all this time's gone by?"

"You could tell him the way you feel about having been abandoned, and you could let him explain why he left the way he did and never tried to contact you until now."

Will grunted. "Don't see what good that would do. If he didn't care then, I don't see why he cares now."

"The choice is yours, of course, but I really think you should pray about things and seek God's guidance before you make a final decision."

Karen's words jolted Will to the core as he gathered up the reins. He hadn't prayed about this matter or sought God's direction. Lately he'd been remiss in reading the Bible—not like when he'd gotten baptized and joined the church. Back then he'd been eager to spend time with God by reading the Bible and his little devotional book.

"I'll pray about the matter," he finally said.

She smiled. "I'll be praying, too."

As Will pulled his rig in front of Karen's buggy, she offered up a silent prayer. *Lord, please help Will get my buggy unstuck and help him see that he needs to speak with his daed.*

"Here you go," Will said, handing Karen the reins.

"What do you want me to do?"

"Just sit here in my buggy while I unhitch my horse and hook him to your buggy."

"My horse couldn't pull the buggy free from the snow, so do you really think your horse can do it?"

"Jah, I do. Blazer's a strong horse with a lot of spirit. Besides, my own buggy has been stuck in the snow a time or two, and I've always managed to get it out."

"Okay, but isn't there something I can do to help?"

He shook his head. "Just stay in here where it's warmer."

Will left the buggy, and Karen watched out the front window as his feet slipped on the ice while he attempted to unhitch Blazer from his buggy and then hitch him to hers. Once that was done, he waved at Karen and climbed into her buggy.

Karen started praying again, asking God to guide Will's hand and give his horse the strength to pull her buggy free.

The buggy wheels spun, and Will's horse appeared to be straining, but finally he pulled the buggy out of the mound of snow.

Karen breathed a sigh of relief. *Thank You, Lord.*

Will opened the door of the buggy and stuck his head inside. "I've got my horse hitched to my own rig again, and I'm going to hitch Ginger up to your rig. Then you can head for home, and I'll follow behind."

"Okay." Karen climbed out of Will's buggy and stepped into hers. As soon as he had Ginger hitched to the front, she took up the reins. She was thankful Will had come along when he did; she just wished she'd been able to make him see that he needed to contact his father.

CHAPTER 25

When Will and Papa Mark stepped into the kitchen the following morning, Will's nose twitched as a tantalizing aroma greeted him. Mama Regina had made his favorite breakfast food—buttermilk pancakes smothered in warm maple syrup.

"Guder mariye." Mama Regina motioned to the table. "If you two will take a seat, I'll bring the pancakes to the table."

"That maple syrup you've got heating on the stove sure smells good," Will said.

Mama Regina placed the platter of pancakes on the table in front of Will. "I know it's your favorite, and I haven't fixed it in a while, so I thought it would be a nice surprise."

Will nodded. "A very nice surprise on this cold November morning."

She smiled. "I've been planning our Thanksgiving menu, and I think maybe I'll make some White Christmas Pie, since I know that's one of your favorite desserts."

"That'd be real nice."

Everyone bowed their heads for silent prayer. As Will thanked God for the food he was about to eat, he remembered that he'd promised Karen he would pray about the situation concerning Pop. He'd been tired when he'd gotten home last night and had fallen into bed without praying.

Lord Jesus, he added to his prayer, *please give me a sense of peace about the decision I've made not to see Pop.*

Papa Mark cleared his throat, signaling that he'd finished his prayer, so Will opened his eyes.

"There's something I need to tell you," Mama Regina said, handing the platter of pancakes to Will. "And I hope you'll be receptive to it."

"What's that?"

"I spoke with your daed last night on the phone."

"Why would you call Papa Mark on the phone?"

"I was referring to Frank—your real daed."

Will's eyebrows shot up. "How'd he get our phone number?"

Mama Regina's cheeks turned bright pink. "I. . .uh. . .called him yesterday, but he wasn't home, so I called again last night."

Will gripped his fork so tightly that his fingers turned white. "Wh–why would you do something like that when you knew how I felt about things?"

She fiddled with the napkin beside her plate. "I thought he had the right to know where you are, and—"

"You told him where we live?"

"I just said we'd moved to Indiana and lived outside of Middlebury, but I didn't give him our address."

Will slowly shook his head. "I can't believe you would call him without discussing it with me first."

"I don't think your mamm felt she was doing anything wrong," Papa Mark cut in. "I'm sure she thought if she made contact with your daed and found out why he never returned or contacted us until now that you might be more willing to meet with him."

Will leaned forward in his chair as he looked at Mama Regina. "*Did* you find out why he never returned or why we haven't heard from him in all this time?"

She shook her head. "He said he wanted to talk to you, so I didn't press the issue."

Will's fork dropped to the table with a clatter. He couldn't talk to Pop. He wouldn't know what to say.

"Before we hung up, I told Frank that I would speak to you again and see if you'd be willing to meet with him." Mama Regina reached over and touched Will's arm. "I think it's important that you see your daed and let him explain things to you."

"I don't see how that's going to change anything. If he'd wanted to explain things, then he should have left me a note the day he left, like he told you he would." Will grunted. "He should have written some letters letting us know where he was, and he should have come back to get me." A lump formed in Will's throat, and he grabbed his coffee mug and took a drink, hoping to push it down.

"Maybe there's a good reason he hasn't contacted you until now," Papa Mark said.

Will shook his head. "There's no reason for a man to leave his son and wait nearly sixteen years to contact him." He looked over at Mama Regina. "Please don't call him again."

She slowly nodded. "All right, I won't call if you don't want me to."

"Danki." Will pushed away from the table and stood.

"Where are you going?" Papa Mark asked. "We haven't had our devotional time yet."

"I'll do mine later. I need to be alone right now, so I think I'll hitch up my buggy and take a ride."

Mama Regina pointed to Will's plate. "But you haven't eaten your breakfast."

"I've lost my appetite." Will slipped into his jacket, grabbed his zipple cap, and rushed out the door.

Frank paced in front of his office window. He'd been dealing with problems all morning, and his stomach felt like it was tied in knots. One of his trucks had broken down, so he'd had to send a tow truck out to get it. Then one of the loads they were supposed to deliver had gotten canceled, and another load had been delivered to the wrong place. On top of that, it had begun to snow, which meant the roads would probably be bad for all his drivers.

He glanced at his cell phone. He hadn't heard anything from Will or Regina yet and wished one of them would call.

If only I could talk to my son and explain things to him, we might be able to get back some of what we've lost. Maybe I should call home and see if Megan's heard anything yet.

He grabbed the phone and punched in the number. Megan picked up on the second ring.

"It's me, Megan. I was wondering if Regina or Will has called."

"No, Frank, not yet."

He sank into his chair and heaved a sigh. "Maybe I should go on the Internet and look for the Stoltzfuses' phone number. Regina said they live near Middlebury and that Mark runs a dairy farm and she has a health food store. I'm thinking either one of their businesses might be listed in the online phone directory."

"That may be, but I really think you should wait and see if one of them calls you."

"I've waited almost sixteen years to talk to my son—I'd say that's enough time, wouldn't you?"

"You're right; it is a long time, but I still think you should try to be patient. If Regina has talked to Will, then I'm sure one of them will call soon."

"I'll wait awhile longer, but the first chance I get, I'm going online to see if I can find their phone number. If you hear anything on that end, please give me a call."

"Of course I will."

Frank turned in his chair and glanced out the window. One of his trucks was just pulling in—the one that had picked up the wrong load. "I've gotta go, Megan. I'll talk to you later."

"Okay, Frank. See you tonight."

Frank clicked off his phone and hurried from the office.

The bell above the door of the dry goods store jingled, and Vonda entered.

"Wie geht's?" Karen asked.

"I'm doing fine." Vonda smiled. "I wanted to tell you that my folks are hosting a bonfire and wiener roast this Friday night. I'm hoping you and Will can come."

"A bonfire sounds like fun. I'll probably see Will sometime later this week. When I do, I'll ask if he'd like to go."

"My folks think I need to socialize more, so they're hoping we'll have a good turnout." Vonda started for the door but turned back around. "I. . .uh. . .was wondering if you think Leroy Eash might like to come."

"I'm sure he would. Why don't you stop by the blacksmith shop and ask him?"

Vonda's face turned crimson. "Oh no, I couldn't do that."

"Why not?"

"It would be too forward."

"I don't think Leroy would see it that way. He'd probably be glad for the invitation."

"You really think so?"

Karen nodded. She was tempted to tell Vonda that Leroy had an interest in her, but she remembered that he'd asked her not to say anything.

"I'll tell you what," Karen said, "if I see Leroy anytime this week, I'll be sure to let him know about the bonfire."

"Danki. I appreciate that." Vonda grinned and went out the door.

"Was that Vonda Nissley?" Cindy asked as she stuck her head around the corner of the shelf where she'd been filling boxes.

Karen nodded.

"She didn't stay very long. What'd she buy?"

"Nothing. She came to invite me and Will to a bonfire and wiener roast her folks are hosting this Friday night."

"What about me? Wasn't I invited?"

"She only mentioned me and Will."

Cindy's eyebrows scrunched together. "How come I'm always left out of everything?"

"You're not left out of everything."

"Sure seems like it." Cindy grunted. "It's always the same old story—I'm too young to be included in any of the fun things that go on around here."

"Why don't you plan something fun and invite some of the young people your age to join you?"

"Maybe I will—if I can think of anything fun to do."

"If the snow sticks around, you could get a group together and go sledding. That's always fun."

Cindy stared out the window with a wistful expression. "It would be a lot more fun than working in here."

The bell above the door jingled again. This time Will entered the store, wearing a grim expression. "If you've got a minute, I need to talk to you about something," he said, leaning over the counter where Karen sat.

She nodded then turned to Cindy. "Would you mind sitting behind the counter to take care of any customers who might come in?"

"Where are you going?"

"Will and I need to talk, so we'll be in the back room a few minutes. If you get too many customers and need some help, come and get me."

"Jah, okay." Cindy slipped behind the counter. "But I wish Mavis was working today," she mumbled.

Ignoring her sister's complaint, Karen followed Will. When they entered the back room, she turned to Will and said, "You look upset. Is something wrong?"

"Jah. Mama Regina called my real daed last night, without discussing it with me first. Now she wants me to call and talk to him." Will frowned and shook his head. "I never thought she would do something like that."

"She must have felt that it was the right thing to do."

"Jah, well, it wasn't right for me."

Karen touched Will's arm. "Are you sure about that?"

He drew back as if he'd been stung by a bee. "Of course I'm sure! I don't want anything to do with Pop. He had his chance to be my daed, but he walked away and never came back, so I'm not going to call."

"I thought you were going to pray about this, Will."

"I did pray." His face colored. "I prayed for peace about my decision."

"How can you know for sure what God wants you to do if you don't pray and ask Him to reveal His will for you?"

He shrugged. "I don't see how it could be God's will for me to see my daed when I'm feeling this way about things."

Karen wanted to argue further but could see how upset Will was, so she decided to change the subject.

"Vonda was here awhile ago. Her folks are hosting a bonfire and wiener roast on Friday night, and she wondered if we'd like to come."

He shrugged. "I guess we could. Maybe a night of fun will help take my mind off all the negative things going on right now."

Karen smiled. Maybe a night of fun was exactly what both she and Will needed.

As Regina stepped into the phone shed to check their answering machine, she heard a man's voice.

"This is Frank Henderson. I need to talk to Will, and I hope—"

Regina picked up the phone. "Hello."

"Regina?"

"Yes, it's me."

"I've waited for your call most of the day, but when I didn't hear anything, I looked for your phone number on the Internet and decided to give you a call."

Regina could hear the anxiety in Frank's voice and realized how desperate he was to talk to Will. "I'm sorry," she said, "but Will didn't want to return your call. He's upset that I contacted you without his knowledge."

Frank groaned. "Isn't there something you can say to get him to change his mind? I need the chance to make things right between us."

Regina didn't know what more she could say or do without causing a rift between her and Will. She offered up a silent prayer. *Lord, please give me the wisdom to know what to say to Frank.*

"Would it be all right if I come there?"

"Oh, I don't know if that's such a good idea."

"I'm begging you, Regina. Please don't keep me from seeing my son. I need to explain and make things right with him."

Regina drew in a deep breath and sighed. "Uh. . .I was wondering, how would you and your family like to join us for dinner on Thanksgiving Day?"

CHAPTER 26

As Megan sat with Frank in their living room late Friday evening, she reflected on the conversation they'd had after Frank had spoken to Regina for the second time. Frank seemed excited about joining the Stoltzfus family for Thanksgiving, but Megan had some misgivings she hadn't yet expressed.

She set the quilting book she'd been reading aside and looked over at Frank. "Can we turn the television down so we can talk?"

"What'd you want to talk about?"

"The trip to Indiana for Thanksgiving."

Frank grabbed the remote and muted the sound. "I guess you know I'm going to be a ball of nerves for the next few weeks while I'm waiting to see Will."

She left her chair and took a seat beside him on the couch. "Wouldn't you rather go there some other time? Mom and Dad are expecting us for Thanksgiving, and I hate to disappoint them."

"Are you saying you don't want me to meet my son?"

"I'm not saying that at all. I just think there might be a better time than Thanksgiving for us to go."

He shook his head. "We've spent every Thanksgiving with your folks since we got married. I don't see why we can't be away from them this once. Besides, Carrie will be out of school on Thanksgiving weekend, which will give us enough time to drive up to Indiana, have Thanksgiving with the Stoltzfus family, and get back here before she has to be back in school."

"You're right; it will give us enough time to make the trip." She sighed. "But not being with my folks on Thanksgiving isn't my only concern."

"What else is bothering you?"

"I'm worried about how things will go between you and Will. If he didn't want to talk to you on the phone, what makes you think he'll be pleased to see you in person?"

"I have no guarantees of that, but I'm sure Regina will tell Will we're coming and try to pave the way." Frank reached for her hand. "Please say you'll go with me to meet Will. I wouldn't want to go without you and the girls."

"I don't want you to go alone, either, and since I'm the one who put that notice in *The Budget*, I should be there to offer support when you meet your son." Megan squeezed his fingers. "I'll take care of making some hotel reservations for us right away, and then I'll explain to Mom and Dad why we can't be with them on Thanksgiving."

"I can't believe all this snow we've been having," Karen said as she and Will headed for Vonda's house. "We usually don't see this much snow in early November."

Will nodded. "That's true, but the weather seems to be unpredictable everywhere these days."

Karen peered out the front window of Will's buggy. "At least it's not snowing at the moment. Other than dealing with the cold, I think we should be able to have our wiener roast tonight."

"Don't see why not."

When they pulled into the Nissleys' place, Karen noticed several buggies parked near the barn, and then she spotted Leroy getting out of his buggy. Apparently Vonda had gotten up the nerve to invite him, because Karen hadn't seen Leroy to extend an invitation to him.

"I'll take the brownies I brought into the house and meet you by the bonfire," she told Will after he'd helped her down from the buggy.

"Sounds good. By the time I get my horse taken care of, I'll be more than ready to stand in front of a warm fire."

Karen picked up the pan of brownies and headed for the house. She entered through the back door and found Vonda and her mother bustling around the kitchen.

"I brought these to go with whatever you're planning to serve for dessert," Karen said, placing the brownies on the counter.

Vonda smiled. "Danki."

"Is there anything you need me to do in here?" Karen asked.

Vonda's mother, Dorothy, motioned to the packages of hot dogs and buns sitting on the counter. "You can take those out to the fire if you like."

"No problem."

"I'll be out with some condiments and a package of marshmallows," Vonda called as Karen went out the door.

Soon ten young people were gathered around the bonfire, roasting hot dogs and marshmallows.

"How's that new horse of yours working out?" Norman Yutzy asked Will.

"Fine. Blazer's a good, strong horse and very well-behaved."

"Not like my horse," David Graber put in. "That *glotzkeppich* critter has a mind of his own."

"Why don't you get rid of him and look for a new one if you think he's so stubborn?" Leroy asked.

"I probably will when I have enough money saved up."

"I got a good deal on my horse at the auction in Topeka, so maybe you—"

Will leaned closer to the fire as he tuned

out Leroy and David's discussion. It felt good to be here tonight with Karen and their friends. Visiting, eating, and sitting by the warm fire helped take his mind off his troubles.

Nathan jabbed Will's arm, and he jumped. "Hey! What'd you do that for?"

"Aren't you going to answer Harley's question?"

Will turned to face Harley. "What'd you ask me?"

"I was wondering if Luanne and I could come by to see the puppies soon. Since you used our cocker, Rusty, for stud service, you said we could have the pick of the litter."

"Come by anytime you like," Will said. "But the pups won't be ready to leave their mother until closer to Christmas."

Luanne smiled. "That's okay. A new puppy will make a nice Christmas present for my mamm. She's been really depressed since my daed passed away three months ago. Harley and I decided to give her the puppy we have coming, and we're hoping it will help make her feel better."

"That's a good idea," Karen put in.

"Having a pet can be a real comfort to someone who's grieving."

Will's mind slipped back in time as he thought about the comfort his first dog had given him. Mama Regina and Papa Mark must have known how hard he was grieving after Pop left, because it wasn't more than a few weeks later when they presented him with the copper-colored cocker he'd named Penny. Not only had the dog offered Will companionship, but she'd taught him how to be responsible. Penny had also taught Will about loyalty and trust—something Pop didn't know the first thing about.

"How'd you like to be our song leader tonight?" Nathan asked, nudging Will's arm again.

Will blinked and sat up straight. "Huh?"

"We're gonna sing some songs, and you've been elected to be the leader."

"Uh. . .no. Why don't you get someone else? I'm not really in the mood for singing."

"You *have* to be in the mood," Norman insisted. "A bonfire isn't nearly as much fun unless you sing some songs."

Will shrugged. "Okay, I'll sing along, but

you'd better choose someone else to be the song leader."

"I'll lead." Leroy looked over at Vonda, who sat to his left. "Do you have a favorite song you'd like us to start with?"

She smiled shyly and nodded. "How about 'Somebody Bigger Than You and I'?"

"Sounds good to me." Leroy led off, and everyone else joined in: *"Who made the mountains? Who made the trees? Who made the rivers flow to the sea? And who hung the moon in the starry sky? Somebody bigger than you and I."*

Will looked at the bright full moon and twinkling stars above. He had no doubt that Somebody bigger and smarter than he had hung the moon, stars, and sun in the sky. He also knew that Somebody was God.

When the song ended, several more requests came in, and when the singing finally died down, Leroy leaned over to Vonda and said, "How'd you like to help me build a snowman?"

She giggled shyly and nodded. "That sounds like fun."

Karen looked over at Will. "Why don't we make a snow-man, too?"

"Jah, sure," Will said with a nod. "It might be fun to act like a couple of kinner again."

"Let's have a contest to see which couple can make the most original snowman," Norman Yutzy suggested.

"That's a great idea." Nathan jumped up from the wooden bench where he'd been sitting and grabbed Mary Jane's hand.

"Why don't Luanne and I act as judges?" Harley suggested. "Since she's going to have a boppli in a few months, I don't think it would be good for her to be huffing and puffing while she tries to push a big snow-ball around the yard."

"Sounds good to me," Will said. "I'm sure you and Luanne will be very fair in picking out the best snowman."

Harley and Luanne remained in their seats by the fire, and everyone else raced into the yard.

Whoosh!—Leroy threw a snowball that hit Karen's arm. Her shoulders shook with laughter as she grabbed a wad of snow and threw it right back. Leroy ducked and scooped up another wad of snow. This one, he threw at Will.

"No snowball fights," Harley called.

"You're supposed to be building snow-men!"

Each couple hurried to get the body of their snowman made, and Karen shivered as the blowing snow tickled her face. "Whew, this is hard work, and it sure is cold," she said, slapping her hands together to remove the snow from her gloves.

"If you're cold, why don't you go back to the fire?" Will suggested. "I can finish our snowman on my own."

"No way! We started this together, and we'll finish it together."

"Aren't you the determined one to-night?"

Karen grinned. "I can be very determined when I want to be." She jerked the zipple cap from Will's head and plunked it on top of the snowman. "There now, that makes our snow-man complete!"

"No, it doesn't."

"Sure it does."

"Nope. Our snowman is married, so he needs a beard." Will slipped and slid across the yard and disappeared into the barn. A few minutes later, he returned with a hand-ful of straw. He handed half to Karen. "If we poke some of this in our snowman's chin, he'll have a nice long beard."

She smiled. "What a clever man I'm engaged to marry."

"I hope when we've been married fifty years that you'll still think I'm clever."

"I'm sure I will."

They finished up their snowman and moved back to where the others stood warming their hands by the fire. Harley and Luanne wandered back and forth across the yard, studying each snowman and trying to decide which one was the best. Finally they returned to the fire, and Harley announced, "The winners of our snowman contest are Will and Karen, whose bearded snowman is the most original."

Everyone clapped, and Will squeezed Karen's fingers. "I told you our snowman needed that beard."

Karen smiled. "You're the schmaert one, all right."

"Now that the judging is done, I'll go inside and get some hot chocolate, cookies, and the brownies you brought," Vonda said to Karen.

"Would you like some help?"

"I'd appreciate that."

"I'll be back soon," Karen said to Will.

He smiled. "I can't wait to taste some of those brownies you made. I'll bet they're almost as sweet as you."

The heat of embarrassment spread across Karen's cheeks. She was pleased to see Will in such a good mood. She'd been worried about him and the resentment he felt toward his father. Maybe on the ride home, she would try talking to him about it again.

CHAPTER 27

As Karen entered the house with Vonda,
she noticed how red Vonda's cheeks had
become. She had a hunch it wasn't from
the cold November wind. Vonda's flushed
cheeks probably had more to do with Leroy.

"It was nice of your folks to host this
get-together," Karen said as she lifted the
lid from her pan of brownies. "Everyone
seems to be having a good time."

Vonda nodded. "I'm glad Leroy could
make it."

"You like him a lot, don't you?"

"Jah."

"Don't tell him I said this, but he likes you, too."

"Are you sure about that?"

Karen nodded. "I wasn't supposed to say anything, but I think you need to know that Leroy has wanted to ask you out for some time."

"Then why hasn't he?"

"He's been afraid you would say no."

"Why would I say no? I just told you, I like Leroy." Vonda picked up the container of popcorn her mother had made while they'd been outside and turned to face Karen. "There's just one problem."

"What's that?"

"I feel so shy whenever I'm around Leroy that I can get all tongue-tied and don't know what to say."

"You could start by asking him some questions."

"What kind of questions?"

"You might ask about the things he likes to do, places he likes to visit, or ask for details about his blacksmith shop. Just get him talking. I'm sure he'll take it from there." Karen gave Vonda's shoulder a gentle squeeze. "You may even discover that you and Leroy have several things in common."

"You really think so?"

"Jah."

Vonda picked up the pot of hot chocolate from the stove and poured it into two large thermoses. "When we were building our snowman out there, Leroy asked if I'd like to go out to supper with him sometime."

"What'd you say?"

"I said I'd have to check with my folks and let him know."

Karen clicked her tongue. "Vonda Nissley, how old are you?"

"Twenty-two—you know that."

"So do you really think you need your parents' permission to have supper with Leroy?"

Vonda dropped her gaze to the floor. "I—I guess not."

Karen lifted Vonda's chin with her thumb. "I think the two of us should take these refreshments out to our friends, and then I want you to tell Leroy that you'll be glad to have supper with him one night next week."

Vonda blinked a couple of times before a slow smile spread across her face.

"You're sure schmaert, you know that? No wonder Will's so anxious to marry you."

Karen chuckled. "I don't know how smart I am, but one thing I do know is that I'm just as eager to marry Will as he is to marry me."

"Are you about ready to go home?" Will asked Karen as things began to wind down.

"I'm ready whenever you are."

"Okay. If you'd like to wait here by the fire, I'll get Blazer hitched to my buggy."

"That's fine with me. It's turned into such a cold night, I'll be happy to stand here and enjoy the warmth of the fire awhile longer."

"I'll pull the buggy over this way when I'm ready to go." Will said good-bye to Vonda and the others who were still huddled around the fire; then he sprinted across the yard.

When he guided his horse and buggy up the driveway close to where the bonfire was, he discovered Karen standing off to one side, talking to Leroy. Usually seeing the two of them together would have upset him, but not tonight. After observing the way Leroy had hovered around Vonda all evening, Will figured he could put his fears to rest. He had a hunch it wouldn't be long until Leroy and Vonda started officially courting, and that thought made him quite happy.

As soon as Will's rig came to a stop, Karen left Leroy and hurried toward the buggy.

"It's been a fun evening," she said as Will helped her into the passenger's side. "But I'm glad we're going home, because I'm tired and cold."

"Me, too, but it might not be much warmer in my buggy." He leaned over and lifted the buggy robe from the floor. "We can drape this over our laps, and it should help some."

"At least we'll be out of the wind. I think that's what's making it seem so cold." Karen snuggled under the robe and leaned her head on Will's shoulder. "I hope it's not this cold on our wedding day."

"Won't matter if it is," he said, guiding his horse onto the main road. "We'll be indoors most of the day where it'll be nice and warm."

"That's true, but if the weather is bad, it may keep some of our guests away."

"I don't think we'll have to worry about that. Unless we have a blizzard, I'm sure everyone will make it."

"You're probably right. I think I must be turning into an old worrywart."

He chuckled. "At least I know for sure that you're *my* worrywart."

"What's that supposed to mean?"

"After seeing the way Leroy hovered around Vonda all evening, I've got a hunch that he's got his eye on her."

"You're right; he does. I've known for some time about Leroy's interest in Vonda. Since she's so shy, he didn't know how to approach her, so he's asked me several times for some suggestions."

"Are you saying that's the reason Leroy's been hanging around you so much—because he wanted your advice on how to make Vonda take an interest in him?"

"That's mostly it, but as I've told you before, Leroy and I have been friends since we were bopplin, so sometimes he just likes to gab with me about things."

"When I saw you with Leroy at Das Dutchman, were you talking about Vonda?"

She nodded. "The reason I didn't tell you before this is because Leroy asked me not to say anything."

"Guess I've been worried all this time for no reason at all."

She needled him in the ribs. "I've been trying to tell you that nothing's been going on between me and Leroy."

He needled her right back and chuckled.

"What's so funny?"

"Here I was trying to get Leroy and Vonda together, and the whole time, he already had an interest in her."

"That's right, and even though Vonda's been too shy to let on until tonight, she's had an interest in Leroy, too."

Will groaned as he shook his head. "What a dummkopp I've been. When things didn't go as I'd planned with Leroy and Vonda, I tried to get Mary Jane to take an interest in him, but she had her eye on Nathan." He reached across the seat and took Karen's hand. "I'm glad everything's settled between us."

"It always feels good to get things settled," she agreed.

They rode in silence as Will kept his focus on the road and made sure he had good control of his horse. He didn't want to slip on the ice or end up stuck in the snow.

"You're really cold," Will said when he noticed Karen shivering. "We're almost to my folks' place, so I think I'll stop in and get another blanket."

"I'll be okay. We're not too far from my house now."

"Even so, I think I'll stop for a blanket." He squeezed her fingers gently. "I won't have my bride-to-be freezing to death."

Karen snickered. "I'm glad to see you're in such good spirits. That must mean you had a good time tonight."

"Jah, it was good to set my worries aside and have a fun evening with you and our friends."

"I wonder how the young people are faring in this cold weather," Mark said as he and

Regina sat on the sofa, enjoying the warmth that spilled from the fireplace and filled the room with a woodsy aroma.

Regina smiled. "We never let a little cold weather keep us from having a good time when we were courting."

He chuckled. "That's true enough."

"Do you think I did the right thing by inviting Frank and his family here for Thanksgiving dinner?" she asked.

"I hope so. Guess we'll have to wait and see how it goes."

"My main concern is how Will's going to deal with seeing his daed again." Regina sighed. "I still haven't decided if I should keep quiet and let Will find out about it on Thanksgiving Day, or if it would be better to tell him now in order to pave the way."

"Pave the way for what?" Will asked as he and Karen stepped into the room.

Regina's heart gave a lurch. How much of their conversation had Will heard?

"Wh—what are you doing here?" she sputtered. "I figured you'd still be at the Nissleys' place."

"We left awhile ago because things were winding down," Will said. "It was cold in my buggy, so I decided to stop here on my way to Karen's and pick up another blanket."

Regina rose from the sofa. "I'll get one for you."

Will held up his hand. "Before you do, I'd like to know what you were talking about when we came into the room. You said something about me and paving the way."

Regina looked over at Mark, hoping he might come to her rescue, but he sat with an unresponsive look on his face.

She cleared her throat and groped for the right words. "I. . .uh. . .spoke with your daed again the other day."

"What'd you speak to Papa Mark about?"

She shook her head. "I was talking about Frank, your real daed."

Will frowned. "I thought you agreed not to call him again."

"I didn't; he called me. He sounded desperate to see you, Will."

"He can't be too desperate, or he would have contacted me long before now."

Regina drew in a deep breath. "I. . .uh. . .hope you won't be too upset about this, but I invited Frank, his wife, and their daughters to join us for dinner on Thanksgiving Day."

The color drained from Will's face, and he grabbed the back of the closest chair as if needing it for support.

Karen stepped up beside him and touched his arm. "Are you okay? Maybe you should sit down."

Will groaned. "If that man is coming for Thanksgiving, I won't be here!"

"But where would you go?" Regina asked.

"I'll go to one of the shelters in South Bend with some of my friends who plan to help feed the hungry that day."

"It's a charitable thing they're planning to do," Mark commented, "and if you were going to help for the right reasons, I would encourage you to go with my blessings." His eyebrows furrowed. "But to go to South Bend just so you don't have to see your daed is not a good enough reason."

"I think your daed's right," Karen put in. "Helping out at the shelter should be done with the right intentions."

Will's face softened a bit as he slowly nodded. "All right, I won't go to South Bend on Thanksgiving, but I won't stay here and be forced to speak with someone who doesn't love me, either."

Regina shook her head. "You don't know that he doesn't love you, Will. You haven't heard Frank's reasons for not coming back to get you."

"I don't care. I don't want to hear his reasons."

Karen put both hands on Will's shoulders, causing him to look directly at her. "Would you do it for me?"

Regina held her breath as she waited for Will's answer. When he finally nodded, she breathed a sigh of relief. She hoped and prayed that whatever Frank had to say to Will on Thanksgiving Day, healing would come for Will's troubled soul.

CHAPTER 28

Frank gripped the steering wheel and grimaced as he headed down the road with Megan and the girls in their minivan. Ever since they'd left Pennsylvania, he'd been having second thoughts about going to Indiana to see Will. *What if Will isn't happy to see me? What if he refuses to listen to what I have to say? How will Megan and the girls fit in with Will's Amish family? Will they understand why there's no TV or electricity in the house? Will they wonder why Regina and Mark are dressed differently than we are? Will Carrie and Kim ask a bunch of silly, embarrassing questions?*

Frank had tried to explain things to the girls before they'd left home, but the hardest part was telling them about their half brother whom they'd never met and explaining how Will had come to live with an Amish couple. He didn't know how much they understood, but he hoped things would go okay on Thanksgiving Day.

"You look tired. Would you like me to drive awhile?" Megan asked, gently nudging Frank's arm.

"I'm okay. I just need to stay focused on my driving and quit thinking about how things will go when I see Will tomorrow."

"I've been praying that your son will listen to what you have to say."

"I've been praying the same prayer—and a lot more, too."

"Are there other things you're concerned about?"

Frank glanced over his shoulder and saw that Carrie and Kim were asleep in the backseat. "I'm worried about how the girls will react to being in an Amish home and meeting their half brother who's more than twice their age."

"You've explained things to the girls, so hopefully it won't be a problem. Most kids usually adapt to their surroundings fairly well."

"I wonder how easy it was for Will to adapt to the Amish way of life after I left him with Mark and Regina."

"That's one of the things you can ask him tomorrow."

"Yeah. There are a lot of things I'd like to know, and he'll probably have plenty of questions for me, too."

"I'm sure he will."

They rode in silence for the next several miles, until the girls woke up and started fussing at each other.

"Kim's pinching me," Carrie complained.

Megan turned around. "Please keep your hands to your-self, Kim."

Kim started to cry, and Carrie followed suit.

Frank grimaced as he gripped the steering wheel tighter. He'd be glad when they stopped for the night, and he hoped the girls would be in happy moods when they arrived at the Stoltzfuses' place tomorrow afternoon.

As Will scrubbed the milking apparatus and then the floor in the milking barn, a multitude of thoughts swirled around in his head. *Just one more day until Thanksgiving. Just one more day until I see Pop again. Has he changed much in sixteen years? I sure have. He probably won't recognize me.*

Will doubted that he and Pop would have anything in common to talk about, although he had to admit he was curious to know whether Pop still drove a truck for a living. He was also curious about the woman Pop had married. What was she like? How long had they been married? And what about the two little girls Mama Regina had told him that Pop and his new wife had?

That means I've got two half sisters I've never met. If Pop hadn't left me with Mama Regina and Papa Mark, I wonder if he would have remarried. Maybe the two of us would have kept

traveling around the countryside while Pop made deliveries in his semi.

Will grabbed the hose and turned on the spigot to rinse what he'd just scrubbed. *But if I'd stayed with Pop, I never would have gotten to know Mama Regina and Papa Mark. I wouldn't be engaged to marry Karen, either. Maybe it's a good thing Pop never came back for me. Maybe I should thank him for that when I see him tomorrow.*

Will clenched his fingers around the hose. He didn't know if he could even speak to Pop, much less thank him for anything. He didn't know if he could stand to look at the man who had abandoned him.

"I'm a Christian, I shouldn't be thinking these thoughts or feeling the way I do," he mumbled.

"What was that?"

Will whirled around. He hadn't realized Papa Mark was nearby. The last time he'd looked, Papa Mark had been outside talking to the milk inspector.

"I. . .uh. . .was talking to myself."

"I gathered that much." Papa Mark

touched Will's shoulder. "Do you want to talk about what's troubling you?"

Will shrugged. "Don't see what good it'll do to talk about it."

"You never know; it might do more good than you think."

Will turned off the water and took a seat on a nearby stool. Papa Mark pulled up another stool and sat down.

"I'm having some qualms about seeing Pop tomorrow," Will said. "I'm not sure I can face him, and I know I'll have trouble believing anything he says."

"It's understandable that you would have some doubts and concerns. It's hard for any of us to understand why Frank left the way he did and never returned or tried to get in touch with us." Papa Mark shrugged. "But until we've heard his reasons, I think we need to give him the benefit of the doubt, don't you?"

"I guess so, but it sure won't be easy."

"Never said it would be." Papa Mark punched Will playfully on the arm. "How about the two of us go inside now? Maybe we can see if we can talk your mamm into letting us have a taste of one of those delicious desserts she's been baking all morning."

Will smiled, despite his misgivings about tomorrow. "She said she was going to make some White Christmas Pie. That's my favorite dessert this time of the year."

"Jah, it's mine, too." Papa Mark rose from the stool. "So let's go find out for sure if your mamm's put White Christmas Pie on our Thanksgiving Day menu."

CHAPTER 29

Will's palms grew sweaty as he stood in front of his bedroom window, staring down at the snow-covered yard. In less than two hours, Pop and his new family were supposed to arrive.

He gripped the edge of the windowsill until his fingers began to ache. *I don't know if I can do this. I only agreed to meet with Pop because Karen asked me to, and I have no idea what I should say when I see him. Maybe I should have gone to the homeless shelter to help feed the hungry, after all.*

But it was too late for that. Will's friends who'd been planning to go to South Bend had probably left already.

He glanced at the clock on the table beside his bed. It was almost a quarter to one. He needed to head over to the Yoders' and pick up Karen. If he didn't go now, they might not be back before their company arrived.

Will turned from the window and started for the door. *At least having Karen here today will give me some extra support. I have a feeling I'm going to need all the support I can get.*

As Regina scurried about the kitchen getting things ready for their Thanksgiving meal, she glanced at the clock. It was one thirty, and Will wasn't back with Karen yet. He'd left forty-five minutes ago, and since Karen's house wasn't that far from their place, she was sure he and Karen would be here any minute.

"Do you need any help in here?" Mark asked, poking his head through the kitchen doorway.

Regina smiled. She appreciated the fact

that her husband had always been willing to help in the kitchen. "I probably won't need your help until it's time to carve the turkey, but if you'd like to sit and visit while we're waiting for our company to arrive, that would be real nice."

"Sure, I can do that." Mark poured himself a cup of coffee and took a seat at the table. "I wonder what's keeping Will," he said, glancing at the clock. "He ought to be back by now."

"I've been thinking the same thing. Maybe Karen wasn't ready when he got there, or maybe the roads are icy, so he's taking it slow."

"That could be."

Regina heard a car pull into the driveway and rushed to the window. "Ach, Mark, there's a minivan in our driveway. I think Frank and his family are here."

Mark rose from his seat. "Do you want me to answer the door?"

"Let's do it together."

"Don't be nervous now," he said in a reassuring tone. "God will see us through this day."

"I've been praying for that."

Regina followed Mark through the living

room and opened the front door. A red-haired man stood on the porch, and a petite, pretty woman with shoulder-length brown hair stood beside him. In front of the woman stood two little girls—one with curly red hair, the other with dark hair worn in a ponytail. Except for a few gray streaks in the man's red hair and the tiny wrinkles around his vivid blue eyes, he looked a lot like Will.

"Hello, Frank," Regina said. "It's good to see you again."

"It's good to see you, too." Frank extended his hand, first to Mark and then to Regina. He motioned to the woman at his side. "This is my wife, Megan."

Megan smiled and shook their hands. "These are our daughters, Carrie and Kim," she said, resting her hands on the girls' shoulders.

Regina opened the door wider. "Please, come in out of the cold."

Once Regina had hung up their coats, she suggested that everyone take a seat.

Frank glanced around nervously. "Uh. . .where's Will? He's here, I hope."

"He went to pick up his girlfriend," Mark

said. "Since they're getting married in a few weeks, we figured you would like to meet her."

Frank nodded. "Yes, yes, I sure would."

Regina looked at the clock on the fireplace mantel. It was almost two. She hoped Will hadn't become so nervous about seeing his dad that he'd decided to stay at the Yoders' for Thanksgiving dinner. *Should I send Mark over to see?*

As if Mark could read her thoughts, he touched her arm and said, "I'm sure Will and Karen will be here soon." He looked over at Frank and smiled. "How was your trip from Pennsylvania? Did you have any problems with icy roads?"

"Not until we got to northern Indiana," Frank replied. "We were surprised to see how much snow you have."

"It's not the norm for the end of November," Mark said. "But it does give us some much-needed moisture after the dry summer and fall we had."

"We had a light dusting of snow in Harrisburg a few weeks ago, but it only stuck around a few days."

"If you folks need a place to spend the

night, you're more than welcome to stay here," Regina said to Megan.

Megan smiled. "That's kind of you, but we have reservations at the Country Inn & Suites in Shipshewana."

Regina glanced at Frank's daughters, who stood with their noses pressed against the front window. She left her seat and joined them there. "Would you girls like something to color?"

They both nodded with eager expressions.

Regina took a coloring book and a box of crayons from the bookshelf in the corner of the room. "I like to keep a few toys available for children who come to visit," she said, placing the items on the coffee table.

"Girls, what do you say to Regina?" Megan prompted.

"Thank you," they said as they took a seat on the floor.

"If you'll excuse me, I need to check on things in the kitchen," Regina said.

Megan rose from her seat. "Do you need any help?"

"That'd be nice." Regina glanced at the men and was pleased to see that they were engrossed in conversation. "The kitchen's this way," she said to Megan.

Megan followed Regina into the other room. "Mmm, something sure smells good in here."

"It's probably the turkey." Regina opened the oven door and checked the meat thermometer. "It's definitely done. As soon as Will and Karen get here, I'll ask Mark to start carving." She poked a fork into one of the potatoes simmering on a back burner. "These are almost done, too, so I hope they get here soon."

Megan glanced around the large, cozy kitchen. A few feet from the gas-operated stove sat a refrigerator, probably run on gas, too. A scenic calendar hung on the wall near the door, and the large table in the middle of the room was set with fine china, glasses, and silverware for eight people. Above the table hung a gas lamp, and another lamp sat on the floor across the room.

"What can I do to help?" Megan asked.

"You can make the gravy after I take the turkey out." Regina motioned to a plastic pitcher on the counter near the sink. "In the meantime, you can fill the glasses on the table with water."

Megan went to the sink and turned on the faucet. She had never been inside an Amish home before and hadn't known if they would have indoor plumbing or not. Apparently they did.

She knew from what Frank had told her that Regina and Mark were kind and gentle people. That had been evident when Regina made them feel welcome and gave the girls the coloring book and crayons.

"It was nice of you to invite us to join your family for Thanksgiving dinner," Megan said as she filled the water glasses. "Frank's been excited about coming here ever since you extended the invitation."

Regina removed a tossed green salad from the refrigerator and placed it on the table. "We wanted to give Will the chance to spend time with his father and get to know him again, and we thought he'd be more relaxed sitting around the table with all his favorite foods."

Megan smiled. It was obvious that Regina was a mother who knew her son well. "Despite Frank's excitement about coming, he's been a ball of nerves ever since you responded to the notice I put in *The Budget* on his behalf."

"Nervous about seeing Will?"

"Yes. At first, he was afraid no one would respond to the notice, and then after you did, he was upset because Will didn't want to talk to him."

Regina glanced at the clock above the refrigerator and grimaced. *I'm afraid the reason Will's late is because he doesn't want to see his daed.*

CHAPTER 30

As Will and Karen headed toward Will's house, his heart began to race like a runaway horse. His palms grew so sweaty he could barely hang on to the reins. He didn't know how he was going to face his dad or what he would say. What could he say, really—that he still felt resentment because Pop had left him with an Amish couple he'd barely known? Should he say that he was angry because Pop never came back or contacted him until a few weeks ago? Should he tell Pop how he'd cried himself to sleep for weeks after he'd left, or should he pretend that he didn't care about any of these things?

"How come we're going so slow? Aren't you worried that we'll be late for dinner?"

Karen's questions drove Will's thoughts aside, and he turned to look at her. "I'm. . .uh. . .being careful so my horse doesn't slip on the ice."

Karen's forehead wrinkled. "The road doesn't seem icy to me. Blazer hasn't slipped even once."

"That's because he's been going slow."

She reached across the seat and touched his arm. "Are you okay? You seem really tense."

Will loosened his grip on the reins a bit. "I am feeling tense, and it isn't just my concern that the road might be icy. I'm worried about seeing my daed again."

"I figured as much."

"I'm glad you're with me, though. I don't think I could do this on my own."

She smiled. "I'm confident that you'll have the words to say when you see your daed."

"Sure hope so, because we're here." Will guided his horse and buggy up the driveway, and his heart gave a lurch when he spotted a light green minivan parked near the house.

"Looks like your company beat us here," Karen said, pointing out the front buggy window.

"I'll bet Mama Regina is fit to be tied because we're late." He halted the horse in front of the hitching rail. "If you'd like to go inside, I'll get my horse put away."

"I'd rather wait with you, and we can walk in together."

"Jah, okay." Will had a hunch that Karen figured if she went in alone he might decide to hang out in the barn until their company left. Truth be told, he wished he could do just that, but he knew it not only would be rude but would upset Mama Regina. Besides, once Karen went inside, if Will didn't come in soon after, Papa Mark would probably come out to the barn looking for him.

As if Karen could read Will's thoughts, she smiled and said, "Everything will be okay; you'll see."

When a young, red-haired man wearing Amish clothes stepped into the living room,

Frank's breath caught in his throat. It had to be Will! Except for the clothes he wore, he looked just like Frank had at that age. A pretty, blond Amish woman stood beside Will, and Frank figured she must be Will's fiancée.

"Sorry we're late, Papa Mark," Will said, looking only at Mark. "I was worried that the roads might be icy, so I took it slow."

Frank winced when he heard Will call Mark "Papa," although he realized that for the last sixteen years, Mark had been Will's only real father.

"I'm glad you're okay; I was starting to worry." Mark moved over to Will and motioned to Frank. "In case you don't recognize him, this is your daed."

"I figured as much," Will mumbled, making no eye contact with Frank.

An empty feeling settled in the pit of Frank's stomach. Wasn't Will happy to see him? Didn't he care at all?

Resisting the temptation to grab Will in a hug, Frank stood and held out his hand. "It's really good to see you, Will."

An awkward silence filled the room as Will shifted from one foot to the other.

Finally he gave a curt nod and shook Frank's hand.

"This is Karen Yoder, Will's fiancée," Mark said, looking at the young woman beside Will.

She smiled and shook Frank's hand. "It's nice to meet you."

"It's nice to meet you, too." Frank motioned to Carrie and Kim, kneeling on the floor with the coloring book Regina had given them. "These are my daughters, Carrie and Kim."

Will only grunted when the girls looked up at him, but Karen squatted beside them. "You're doing a nice job with those pictures you're coloring," she said.

Carrie smiled. "Thank you."

"My wife, Megan, is in the kitchen with Regina," Frank said.

Will nodded. "I see."

Feeling the need to break the ice and hopefully put Will at ease, Frank motioned to the sofa. "Why don't we have a seat so we can visit?"

Will seemed reluctant at first, but he finally took a seat on one end of the sofa. Frank sat on the other end, and Mark seated himself in the rocking chair across from them.

An awkward silence filled the room as they sat staring at each other. The only sound that could be heard was the steady *ticktock, ticktock* of the clock on the fireplace mantel.

Frank cleared his throat a couple of times as he searched for the right words to say to Will. "Mark and I were talking before you got here, and I understand that you've become quite the dairy farmer."

Will shrugged.

"I'll bet working with cows is interesting."

"Uh-huh."

"Maybe after we eat, you can show me the cows."

"That's a good idea," Mark said. "We'll be doing the afternoon milking at four thirty, so we can show Frank how it's done then."

Regina poked her head into the room. "I thought I heard voices in here." She smiled at Will. "I'm glad to see you made it. I was beginning to worry."

"Will thought we should go slow in case

we hit ice on the road," Karen explained from her seat on the floor beside the girls.

Regina smiled at Karen. "I see you've made a couple of new friends."

Karen nodded. "I'm watching Kim color a picture of a cow."

"And I'm coloring a horse," Carrie put in.

"That's real nice." Regina looked over at Mark. "The turkey's ready to be carved."

"All right, then." Mark left his seat and headed for the kitchen.

"I'll go with you," Karen said, rising to her feet. "I'm sure there's something I can do to help get dinner on."

Regina glanced down at Frank's girls. "Why don't you two come with us? Maybe there's something you can do, as well."

Frank was quite sure Regina had suggested that everyone but him and Will leave the room so the two of them could talk in private. He felt grateful for the opportunity to be alone with his son and knew he'd better take advantage of this opportunity. It might be the only time he and Will were alone all day.

"Regina and Mark seem as pleasant as

I remember," Frank said to Will after everyone had vacated the room.

"Uh-huh."

"It seems that they've done well by you."

"They've been real good parents." Will leveled Frank with a piercing look that went straight to his heart. It was a look that let Frank know that in Will's eyes he'd messed up as a parent.

"You seem to have adjusted to the Amish way of life."

"Yeah."

"Are you happy being Amish?"

Will nodded. "The Plain life suits me just fine."

"I can see that. You look healthy and strong."

Will fiddled with the piping on the small pillow lying beside him. "I understand you're living in Harrisburg now."

"That's right. I have my own trucking business there." Frank shifted restlessly, wishing he didn't feel so nervous. Seeing Will again was bittersweet. Will had changed so much—they both had, really. They were like two strangers trying to get to know each other for the first time, even though neither of them knew quite what to say. Not that Frank didn't have a lot he wanted to say, he just didn't think he should say it too quickly. They needed the chance to get to know each other again—feel at ease in one another's presence.

"Are you still driving a semi?"

Frank shook his head. "Only when one of my men is sick or we have a lot of deliveries to make and need the extra manpower."

"So you never found another job besides trucking?"

"No, I—"

"How was your trip to Indiana?"

"The girls got restless, and we had to stop more often than I would have liked, but all in all, the trip went well." Frank grimaced. If they kept up this idle chitchat, he'd never get the chance to say what was on his mind. He needed to find a way to bring up the past—explain to Will why he'd left and hadn't returned.

"So how long have you been married to Megan?"

"Almost ten years."

"How'd you meet her?"

"She was working as a waitress at a truck stop."

"And now you have two daughters."

"Yeah, Carrie and Kim are good girls." Frank cleared his throat a couple of times. "There's. . .uh. . .something I'd like to say, and I hope you'll hear me out."

Will shrugged. "That's what you came here for, right?"

"Yes, it is. That and to get to know you again." He moistened his lips. "I've really missed you, son."

A muscle on the side of Will's neck twitched. "If you missed me so much, then why'd you leave? You could have at least said good-bye."

"I wanted to; believe me, I did. But I was afraid if I told you what I planned to do, you'd want to—"

"Regina wanted me to tell you that dinner's on the table," Megan said, stepping into the room. She looked over at Will and smiled. "You must be Frank's son. You look so much like your dad—same red hair and blue eyes."

Will gave a quick nod.

"This is my wife, Megan," Frank said.

"Nice to meet you," Will mumbled.

"It's nice to meet you, too. I've heard a lot about you, Will."

"We'd better get in there before the food gets cold." Will stood and rushed out of the room.

"Sorry for interrupting," Megan said to Frank. "But I figured we should eat since Regina has everything ready."

"It's okay. Things are a bit awkward between Will and me right now, and we didn't get very far in our conversation." Frank slipped his arm around Megan's waist. "I'll try talking to him again after we eat. Maybe he'll be more willing to listen when his stomach is full."

CHAPTER 31

As Will sat at the table across from Frank, he was thankful Karen sat beside him. He needed her for moral support. It wasn't easy trying to make conversation with someone he hadn't seen in almost sixteen years. He and Pop were like two strangers, each not knowing what the other wanted him to say.

Will wished he could blurt out everything that was on his mind, and if he and Pop hadn't been interrupted when Megan had come into the living room, he probably would have asked some of those questions.

"Do either of you girls like dogs?" Papa Mark asked, smiling across the table at Carrie and Kim.

They both grinned and bobbed their heads.

"We're hoping we'll get a puppy for Christmas," Kim said around a mouthful of mashed potatoes.

"Will has a nice cocker spaniel, and she had a batch of pups several weeks ago," Papa Mark said. "Maybe he'd be willing to take you out to the barn for a look-see after we're done eating."

The girls turned expectant gazes on Will, and their eyes brightened like shiny new pennies when he nodded. "I think you'll enjoy seeing Sandy's five squirming hundlin."

"Who's Sandy, and what's a hundlin?" Carrie wanted to know.

"Sandy's my cocker spaniel. Hundlin is the German-Dutch word for puppies."

"What's German-Dutch?" Carrie's eyebrows furrowed as she tipped her head and stared at Will.

"German Dutch, or Pennsylvania Dutch, as some call it, is the language Amish people speak when they're not talking English," Pop said.

"Hmm. . ." Carrie reached for the plate of pickles then plunked one on her plate and one in her mouth. "Yum! This is good. I love dill pickles!"

"Everything tastes delicious," Megan said to Mama Regina. "You really outdid yourself on this meal."

"Thank you. Be sure to save room for dessert."

Papa Mark nodded enthusiastically. "We're having White Christmas Pie, and it's one of the tastiest pies you'll ever eat."

"How come we're havin' a Christmas pie on Thanksgiving?" Carrie questioned.

"It's a special pie my grandma used to make," Mama Regina explained. "She used to fix it on Thanksgiving so we'd be reminded that Christmas was just around the corner."

Kim's freckled nose turned up as she looked at the kitchen door and squinted. "Christmas has corners?"

Everyone laughed, including Will. He was actually beginning to relax a bit.

"'Around the corner' means it's coming

soon," Pop explained. He looked at Kim with such affection that it pricked Will's heart. These two girls had been given the privilege of growing up with their real father. Will had been cheated of that opportunity.

"Do you fix White Christmas Pie again at Christmas?" Megan asked Mama Regina.

"Yes, it's a family tradition." Mama Regina looked over at Karen and smiled. "I'm hoping my future daughter-in-law will continue with the tradition after she and Will are married next month."

"I'd be happy to keep up the tradition," Karen said, "but I'll need the recipe for the pie."

Papa Mark chuckled. "My wife has made that pie so many times I think she knows the recipe by heart."

Pop scratched the side of his head. "White Christmas Pie. Didn't you serve that when Will and I spent Christmas with you sixteen years ago?"

Mama Regina nodded.

Pop looked over at Will. "Do you remember that, son?"

Will gave a quick nod. He may have

been only six years old at the time, but he remembered eating the pie. He remembered a whole lot more about that particular Christmas, too.

"That was a tough year for Will and me," Pop said. "Having just lost Will's mom less than a year before and then struggling to find a job that wouldn't keep me on the road all the time. . ." His voice trailed off, and he blinked a couple of times.

The room got deathly quiet. Will hoped Pop wasn't going to break down and cry. *It's me who should be crying,* he thought ruefully. *It was me who got left behind. It was me who cried himself to sleep every night for days and days after Pop left. I'm the one who's spent the last sixteen years wondering why my daed stopped loving me and didn't want to be with me.*

Pop reached for his glass of water and took a drink; then he looked over at Will again. "Sixteen years is a long time. I've really missed you, son."

Will's face heated up like an oven turned on high. "If you missed me so much, then why'd you leave?"

"I had a delivery to make in Texas, and then I was going to look for another job—one that would keep me closer to home so we wouldn't have to traipse all over creation in our home on wheels."

"Too bad you forgot to tell me you were going."

"I didn't forget. I left you a note."

"What note? I never saw any note."

"I left it on the kitchen counter."

Will's eyes narrowed. "No note was found in the kitchen or anywhere else in the house."

"I'm sure there was a note. I put it there before I left that morning. The night before, I even asked Regina to tell you that I'd be leaving a note for her to read to you." Pop looked over at Mama Regina. "You must have found the note when you went to the kitchen to fix breakfast."

Mama Regina shook her head. "I do remember you saying that you planned to leave Will a note, but I found no note after you left, Frank."

Will's lips compressed as he folded his arms. "If there had been a note, Mama Regina would have read it to me."

"Oh, but I'm sure—"

"Forget about the note!" Will stared hard at Pop as his face became hotter. "Why didn't you come back for me or at least send some letters? Just tell me why!"

"I—I couldn't, Will. I—"

"Sure you could. It's not like you weren't able to read or write."

Karen reached for Will's hand under the table and gave his fingers a gentle squeeze. He knew she was trying to calm him down—probably wanted him to drop the subject before it got out of hand. But he didn't know if he could calm down. Not until he'd said what was on his mind. Not until he got some answers.

Pop's face turned crimson. "The reason I couldn't write to you is because—"

"Because you didn't care! You just dropped me off in Pennsylvania and left me with two people I barely knew." The anger bubbling in Will's soul spurred him on to say exactly what was on his mind. "I guess you figured you'd be happier on your own and could make a new life for yourself if I wasn't around. I guess you cared more about your own happiness than you did mine!"

Will stopped talking long enough to draw in a quick breath. It was then that he noticed the stunned look on Megan's face.

Even Frank's girls were wide-eyed. Karen looked mortified, and the expressions he saw on Mama Regina's and Papa Mark's faces let Will know they were shocked by his outburst and had been deeply hurt by what he'd said.

Will hadn't meant to hurt his folks. Papa Mark and Mama Regina had been good to him all these years, treating him as if he were their own son. He loved them both and appreciated all they'd done for him. He couldn't imagine how his life might have been if they hadn't taken him in. But he was so upset right now that he couldn't find the words to say he was sorry. And he didn't want to say anything more to the man who used to be his father. All Will wanted was to be alone. He needed time to think. Needed time to sort out all the thoughts swirling around in his brain like windmill blades spinning in a very strong wind. Will knew if he didn't leave the room he might say more hurtful things, so he pushed away from the table.

"Where are you going?" asked Papa Mark.

"Outside. I need some fresh air."

"Please stay, Will. We need to talk things out." Mama Regina's voice was pleading.

Will shook his head. "I've gotta go." He grabbed his jacket and cap from the wall peg and rushed outside.

Karen's hand shook as she reached for her glass of water. She'd been afraid something like this would happen today. Will was just too hurt by what Frank had done to listen to anything the man had to say.

Frank groaned. "Maybe we should go. It's obvious that Will doesn't want to hear anything I have to say." He looked over at Megan. "We shouldn't have come here today. It was a big mistake."

"No, no, we're glad you came. Please stay," Regina said. "Will just needs a little time to calm down and work things out in his mind. I'm sure he'll be back soon, and then we can have our dessert and talk things through."

Karen knew Regina was right; Will needed some time alone. Even so, she wanted to be with him—to comfort him and tell him what she thought about the way things had gone with his father.

"Let me help with the dishes," Megan said as Regina and Karen began clearing the table.

"I appreciate the offer, but the dishes can be done after we've had our dessert." Regina smiled, although it appeared to be forced. Karen was sure Will's mother felt as much concern for Will as she did. She also knew from Mark's and Regina's expressions when Will had begun spouting off that they'd been hurt by some of the things he'd said. He'd made it seem as if his life had been miserable without his dad. Did Will actually think he would have been happier driving around the countryside with Frank than he had been living with a sweet, caring couple who had loved and nurtured him as if he were their own?

Tears welled in Karen's eyes. *If Will hadn't come to live with Mark and Regina, he and I never would have met. I need to talk to Will. I need to know if he's sorry he joined the Amish church and asked me to marry him.*

Karen motioned to the fluffy white pies sitting on the counter across the room. "Maybe I can coax Will inside if I remind him that you made his favorite dessert."

Regina shrugged. "It's worth a try."

Karen picked up one of the pies and opened the back door. She was relieved when she spotted Will sitting in a wicker chair on the other end of the porch. "Your mamm's about to serve some of this," she said, holding the pie out to him.

He grunted.

"Aren't you coming inside for dessert?"

"I've lost my appetite."

"But it's cold out here. Please come in and have a piece of pie with us."

Will shook his head.

"Don't you think you should apologize for the things you said in there? Don't you think—"

"I didn't mean to hurt Mama Regina or Papa Mark. I'll talk to them about it after our company leaves."

Karen grimaced. She knew she couldn't force Will to go inside or speak to his dad. Maybe if he sat in the cold long enough, he would come to his senses. "Okay, suit yourself."

When Karen returned to the kitchen, she placed the pie on the counter and turned to Regina. "Will says he's not hungry and wants to be left alone. So why don't you go ahead and serve your guests while I go back outside and try again to talk some sense into him."

Regina nodded. "I pray he will listen."

"I know the things Will said must have hurt you," Karen whispered, "but I'm sure he didn't mean them."

"I'm sure you're right. Will is hurting and spoke out of anger and frustration."

Karen hugged Regina then draped her shawl over her shoulders and went out the door.

"Why'd you come back outside? I thought I told you I don't want any pie," Will mumbled when Karen took a seat in the chair beside him.

"I'm here to keep you company."

He stared straight ahead. "I'm not good company right now."

"That's okay; I understand."

He jerked his head. "I don't see how you could. You've never been abandoned by anyone."

"I'm not saying I understand how you feel about your daed having left you, but I think I do understand why it's so hard for you to talk about your feelings."

"Would you like to know what I'm feeling right now?"

"Jah, I would."

Will grunted. "I'm feeling that you might be better off without me in your life."

Karen's mouth fell open. "How can you say something like that?"

He scrubbed his hand down the side of his face. "I don't know what kind of husband or father I would make. What if I take after Pop and do things to hurt my family?"

"Oh, Will, I don't think—"

"Maybe I shouldn't have joined the Amish church. It might have been better if I'd gone English and moved away."

Karen shook her head. "You can't mean that, Will. You love the Amish way of life; you've told me so many times."

"Jah, well, that was before my daed showed up and made me feel so *verhuddelt*."

"The only reason you're feeling confused is because you haven't talked things through with him. You need to tell your daed what's on your heart. You need to let him explain why he never returned or contacted you."

"He had the chance to explain it while we were at the table. And what did he do?" A muscle on the side of Will's neck quivered. "He lied and said he'd left me a note!"

"Maybe he had planned to leave you a note but forgot to do it in his haste to leave."

"I don't think he ever planned to leave me a note. I think he decided to sneak off during the night so he wouldn't have to explain anything to me. I bet he was just looking for the opportunity to find another wife and begin a new life without me in the way."

Karen wasn't sure how to respond to Will's last comment. She didn't know Frank Henderson well enough to know if he was capable of walking out on his son so he could start a new life. But the desperate look she'd seen on Frank's face while they were sitting at the table made her think he was hurting as much as Will right now.

Will rose from his seat and walked to the other end of the porch. "I need to get away from here for a while. I need time alone to think things through."

"Where are you going?" Karen called as he tromped down the stairs.

"For a buggy ride."

As Karen watched Will walk away, tension knotted her stomach, and she felt herself on the brink of tears. She had a horrible feeling he wasn't just going for a buggy ride—he was walking out of her life forever.

CHAPTER 32

Karen returned to the kitchen with her shoulders slumped and her head down. Regina felt immediate concern. "Where's Will? Couldn't you talk him into joining us for dessert?"

Karen shook her head and sank into her chair at the table. "He went for a buggy ride, and I—I don't know when he'll be back."

Frank grimaced. "It's because of me that he's gone. He wouldn't listen to anything I had to say. I didn't even get to tell him the reason I never wrote or came back for him."

Regina handed Megan a piece of pie. "How would it be if we let the girls stay here at the table to eat their pie while we adults take ours in the living room?" She glanced over at Frank. "It will give us a chance to talk about some important things."

Megan nodded. "That's a good idea."

"I think so, too," Karen agreed.

Regina was relieved when the girls didn't argue. In fact, they dug into their pie as soon as Regina set the plates in front of them. Then she gave each of them a writing tablet and some pencils. "When you girls are finished eating, you can draw some pictures if you like."

"What about the puppies?" Carrie asked. "I thought we were gonna see Will's puppies."

"If Will's not back soon, I'll take you out to see the puppies," Mark said.

"Okay!" Kim bobbed her curly red head as she grinned up at him. "I'm gonna draw a picture of the puppy I'm hopin' we'll get for Christmas!"

The adults followed Mark out of the kitchen, and once they were seated in the living room, Regina placed a dessert tray and a pot of coffee on the small table in front of the sofa. Then she handed everyone a piece of pie.

"I do remember eating this now," Frank said after he'd taken his first bite. "It tastes, how do you say it. . .*wunderbaar*?"

Mark chuckled. "That's how we say it, all right."

"What's wunderbaar mean?" Megan asked.

"It means 'wonderful.' That and the word *jah* were the only German-Dutch words I learned during my brief stay with Mark and Regina."

"If you'd stayed longer, you'd have probably learned a lot more of our words," Mark said.

Frank looked over at Regina. "Are you sure you didn't find that note I left in your kitchen the morning I left Will with you?"

"I found no note."

Frank's forehead wrinkled as he rubbed the back of his head. "Well, I thought I left it in the kitchen. After my accident, some things were kind of sketchy, and it took me awhile to piece things together."

"What accident?" Regina asked.

"A few days after I left Will with you, I

was involved in a bad accident and ended up in the hospital in serious condition." Frank paused and drew in a quick breath. "Once I regained my memory and was well enough to return to Lancaster County, I was shocked to discover that you had moved and had apparently taken my boy with you."

"Of course we took Will." Mark's cheeks reddened. "We could hardly leave him in a house that was being sold to someone else."

Frank grunted. "I wasn't saying you should have left him there. I just think you should have left word with a neighbor, so that when I returned, I would know where you had moved."

"We did leave word," Regina was quick to say.

"But I asked the neighbors living closest to you, and they said they'd heard something about an Amish couple living there at one time, but they didn't know who they were or where they'd gone."

"That makes no sense." Mark pulled his fingers through the ends of his beard. "What were the neighbors' names, do you know?"

Frank shook his head. "I never asked."

"What'd they look like?" Regina questioned.

"As I recall, the woman had dark curly hair, and the man had light brown hair."

"That wasn't the Johnsons, then." Regina pursed her lips. "John and Ellen Johnson must have moved from their place by the time you came back to get Will."

"Did you check with any of the other neighbors?" Karen questioned.

Frank nodded. "I did, but no one knew anything."

"All of our closest Amish neighbors moved about the same time we did," Regina explained. "Some came here to Indiana, and some went to Ohio."

"Why did you leave Lancaster County?" Megan asked.

"Because we wanted to go someplace where we could buy more land and wouldn't have to deal with so much traffic." Mark smiled. "I grew up on a dairy farm and liked working with cows, so when I was offered the opportunity to buy this farm in northern Indiana, I jumped at the chance."

Frank reached for his cup of coffee and

took a drink. "I hate to admit this, but when I came back and found you had moved, I decided that you must have left the area deliberately."

Mark's eyebrows furrowed. "Why would we do that?"

"Well, uh. . .I figured maybe you'd done it so you could raise Will as your son."

Regina gasped. "We would never do such a thing! Why, you'd been gone almost a year without making any contact with us before we moved to Indiana. By that time, we were convinced you weren't coming back for Will."

"Even so," Mark put in, "we did leave word with our neighbor so you would know where to find us."

Frank stared into his cup as he slowly shook his head. "Guess I jumped to conclusions."

"I can only imagine how horrible you must have felt," Karen said.

Megan reached over and clasped her husband's hand. "Until I got the idea to put that notice in *The Budget*, Frank had lost all hope of ever seeing his son again."

Regina rose from her seat and peered out the window. "I wish Will would come back. He needs to hear what you've told us, Frank."

Mark glanced at the clock on the mantel. "Speaking of Will, it's almost time to milk the cows, and since he's not back yet, it looks like I'll have to do it alone."

"I'd be glad to help," Frank said, "but unfortunately I don't know the first thing about milking a cow."

"No, but I do." Regina smiled at Mark. "Since Will's not here, I'll help with the milking tonight."

"Maybe I should take the girls out to see the puppies first," Mark said. "I wouldn't want to disappoint them."

"Why don't we all go out and take a look?" Regina suggested.

"That's a good idea," Megan said. "I'd like to see the puppies myself."

Mark rose to his feet. "Then let's get the girls and head out to the barn."

Megan smiled as she watched her daughters, down on their knees in one corner of the barn, playing with Will's honey-colored cocker spaniel and her five lively pups.

"They're sure cute little things." Megan

nudged Frank's arm. "Don't you think we should consider getting the girls a puppy for Christmas?"

"I'll think about it. Right now I have more important things on my mind." He glanced at the barn door. "Sure wish Will would come back. There are so many things I didn't get to say. I'd hate to leave without talking to him again."

"Can you come back tomorrow?" Regina asked. "By then, Will might be more willing to listen to what you have to say."

Frank nodded. "I guess we could come by here before we head for home."

"What time did you plan to leave?" Mark asked.

"Right after breakfast. I'd like to be on the road by nine or ten at the latest."

"We're always up early for milking, so come by anytime in the morning."

"Thanks." Frank looked over at Megan. "I think it's time for us to head for the hotel now, don't you?"

Megan nodded. "I'm kind of tired, and I'm sure the girls are, too."

As Frank rounded up their daughters and herded them out the door, Megan stepped up to Regina. "It's been nice meeting you. Thanks again for inviting us to share Thanksgiving with you today."

"You're welcome. It was nice meeting you, too." Regina sighed. "I just wish things had turned out better between Will and his dad."

"I wish they had, too. Frank's waited a long time to see his son again, and if we have to return home without him being able to explain things to Will, I'm afraid he'll sink into depression."

Regina nodded. "And if Will doesn't hear the truth about why Frank left and never returned, I don't think he'll ever come to grips with his past."

As Will guided his horse and buggy down the road, his mind replayed the events of the day. He felt bewildered and exhausted from all the things that had been said. Even the things that hadn't been said filled his thoughts and caused his heart to ache. Should he have stayed and listened to what Pop had to say, or had he done the right thing by leaving?

Nothing would have been gained by us rehashing the past, he finally decided. *Pop wouldn't admit that he hadn't left me a note. He's just a big liar. I wish Mama Regina had never invited Pop and his family for Thanksgiving dinner. I wish he'd stayed out of my life forever!*

A car sped past, going much faster than it should in snowy conditions, causing slushy snow to splash against the buggy's front window. Blazer shook his head and whinnied loudly as some of the slush hit his face.

Will grimaced as he gripped the reins and strained to see out. The roads were worse tonight than they had been all week.

The buggy vibrated as it swayed precariously, and Will continued to fight for control. "Hold steady there, Blazer. Easy, boy."

Blazer reared up, lifting the front of the buggy clear off the pavement.

"Whoa! Whoa!" Sweat rolled down Will's forehead.

Blazer reared again, and when his hooves thudded against the pavement, he stumbled and fell. He thrashed around for a bit but, with Will's encouragement, finally managed to get up.

Before Will could gain full control of the

situation, the horse took off at a run. The buggy whipped across the slippery road like a leaf being tossed in a strong wind, and nothing Will did brought it under control.

Blazer's hooves slipped again, and he jerked to the right. The buggy careened off the road and—*crash!*—slammed into a telephone pole, smashing Will's door and tossing him to the passenger's side of the buggy. He screamed as the buggy toppled over and searing pain shot through his leg. When he reached down and touched it, something warm and sticky oozed between his fingers. *Blood!*

As Will lay there, light-headed and unable to move, an image of Karen popped into his head. He didn't know how badly he was hurt or how his horse had fared, but he prayed someone would find them—and soon.

CHAPTER 33

While Regina and Mark did the milking, Karen finished cleaning up the kitchen. It gave her time to reflect on everything that had happened and evaluate her relationship with Will. As much as she hated to admit it, things hadn't been right between them since he'd read that newspaper article about the little girl who'd been abandoned by her parents and left in a park. He had even become more jealous of Leroy during that time, too, and Karen figured it was probably due to the insecurities he felt from having been abandoned by his father. Then after Will learned that his father was trying to contact him, she'd realized that not only was Will dealing with jealousy and insecurity, but he was full of bitterness. It was obvious that he had never come to grips with his past or forgiven his dad. Until he did that, Karen didn't see how they could be married.

As Karen wiped the table with a sponge, tears rolled down her cheeks and splashed onto the front of her dress. *Maybe Will and I aren't meant to be together. Maybe I shouldn't have agreed to become his wife.*

When the back door creaked open and clicked shut, she wiped her eyes with the palm of her hand.

"Mark and I got the cows milked, and now he's cleaning things up in the barn. How's it going in here?" Regina asked, stepping into the kitchen.

"Fine. I've gotten most everything cleaned up."

Regina glanced around. "Looks good to me. Danki for taking care of this so I could help Mark with the milking."

"You're welcome."

Regina stared at Karen. "Have you been

crying? Are you still upset because Will took off the way he did?"

Karen nodded.

"You know Will—he needs to be alone when he's upset about something. I'm sure after he's had some time to sort things out that he'll come home and we'll work everything out together."

"I hope that's the way it goes."

Regina opened a cupboard door and removed a recipe box. "You mentioned that you'd like the recipe for White Christmas Pie, so I'd like to give it to you now." She handed the box to Karen. "It should be filed in the pie section."

"I. . .I still want the recipe, but I'm not sure Will and I will be getting married, so—"

"What do you mean?" Regina looked stunned.

Karen sighed deeply. "After what happened today, I'm having second thoughts about marrying Will."

"You can't mean that. Will loves you, Karen."

"I love him, too, and Will has many fine qualities, but it's obvious that he's still deeply troubled over his past and is full of bitterness toward his daed. I'm afraid things will never be right between Will and me unless he and Frank are able to make their peace."

"You're right, and I'm hoping when Frank comes back tomorrow that he can tell Will what he told us this evening and Will is willing to listen." Regina hugged Karen. "Please don't give up on Will. He needs you in his life."

Karen sniffed. "I'm not giving up on Will, but I won't marry him until he sets things right with his daed."

"Then we'll have to pray that he does. And now," Regina said as she headed for the stove, "I think I'll pour myself a cup of coffee while we wait for Will. Would you like one, too?"

"No thanks. I'll just look for that recipe." Karen opened the box and flipped through the recipe cards until she came to the pie section. When she found the recipe for White Christmas Pie, she removed it and read the ingredients. "This looks fairly simple. Is there more on the back?" She turned the card over and gasped. "Regina, you'd better take a look at this!"

"What is it, Karen?"

"Frank was telling the truth about the note he wrote for Will. It's right here—on the back of this card."

Regina rushed across the room and peered over Karen's shoulder. "I remember seeing the recipe card on the counter the morning Frank left our home in Lancaster County, only the card was faceup with the recipe showing. I had no reason to turn it over." She clicked her tongue as she slowly shook her head. "So that's why I didn't see Frank's note. I put the recipe back in the box and, until today, never took it out."

Tears flowed down Karen's cheeks as she pressed her weight against the counter and stared at Frank's note. "Will needs to see this. He needs to know that his daed wasn't lying when he said he left a note."

"You're right. Once Will sees the note on the back of the card, he'll finally believe." Regina glanced at the clock. "I'm really beginning to worry. Will's been gone almost two hours. I think he should have been back by now."

"I'm worried, too. I'm afraid he might

have decided to leave for good and never come back."

Regina shook her head. "Will wouldn't do that. I'm sure he wouldn't."

"Sometimes when people are under pressure and unable to deal with a problem, they do things they wouldn't otherwise do."

Mark stepped into the kitchen just then. "I got the milking apparatus and barn all cleaned, but there's still no sign of Will." He looked at Regina. "I don't know about you, but I'm getting concerned."

"We're worried about Will, too, but you need to look at this!" Regina handed Mark the recipe card. "Frank did leave a note for Will. He wrote it on the back of my recipe card for White Christmas Pie. It must have gotten turned over, because I never saw the note when I put the card back in the recipe box."

Mark studied the card. "You're right; this was written by Frank. Will needs to see it so he'll know his daed was telling the truth."

Regina glanced at the clock again. "I wonder where he went and what could be keeping him."

"Maybe he went over to the Chupps' to see Nathan. Want me to drive over there and find out?"

Regina nodded. "That's a good idea."

"The Chupps' place is on the way to my house, so since you'll be heading that way, would you mind giving me a ride home?" Karen asked.

Regina's eyebrows furrowed. "Aren't you going to wait here for Will?"

Karen shook her head. "If Will wanted to be with me, he wouldn't have run off like he did. I think it's better if I'm not here when he gets home."

Regina touched Karen's arm. "I'm sure he didn't leave on your account."

"That's right," Mark put in. "The reason Will left was because he couldn't deal with seeing his daed."

"Even so, I'm tired and I'd appreciate a ride home."

"I'll get Bob and hitch him to my buggy right away."

"I wish you could have worked things out with Will today," Megan said as they neared Shipshewana.

Frank sighed. "I wanted that, too, but as you saw, Will did not."

Megan glanced in the backseat and was relieved to see that the girls were asleep. She didn't think they needed to hear this conversation. They'd heard enough during dinner.

"It's only natural that things would have been strained," she said, turning back to look at Frank. "After all, you and Will haven't seen each other in a very long time."

"I keep asking myself if there was anything I could have said or done today to make things right between me and Will."

"You did the best you could, but there was no way you could get through to Will when he wouldn't listen. Maybe when we stop at the Stoltzfuses' tomorrow morning, things will go better. A good night's sleep can do wonders for a person's frame of mind."

"Are you saying I was in a bad mood today and that's why things went wrong?"

"Of course not. I'm just saying that Will might be more willing to listen to your side of things after he's had a good night's sleep."

Frank grunted. "If Will's even there tomorrow. When he took off after dinner, I got a horrible feeling that I might never see him again."

As Karen and Mark headed for her house, she decided to bring up the situation with Will and Frank again.

"If Will sees the note Frank wrote on the back of Regina's recipe card, do you think things will work out between him and his daed?" Karen asked.

"I hope that's the case. Even though Regina and I think of Will as our son, we'd like to see him have a relationship with Frank."

Karen sighed. "What if Will isn't there when Frank returns to your place in the morning?"

"Where else would he be?"

"What if he doesn't come home tonight? What if—"

"Look over there!" Mark shouted as he pointed to the other side of the road. "I think that's Will's buggy tipped on its side. Ach, what a mess!"

Karen's breath caught in her throat. *Dear Lord, please don't let it be Will's.*

Mark guided his horse to the side of the road and pulled the buggy in behind the other rig. Then he grabbed a flashlight and jumped out of his buggy.

Karen was right behind him, her heart hammering in her chest.

Mark shined a beam of light onto the buggy. The door on the driver's side was pushed in, and the shafts that had been connected to the horse were broken. As Mark shined the light around more, Karen recognized Will's horse lying several feet away from the buggy. He wasn't moving.

"Will! Can you hear me?" Mark shouted, cupping his hand around his mouth.

No response.

"I need to get in there!"

Karen clutched Mark's arm. "Please, let me go."

"All right, but I'll need to get some tools from my buggy so I can clear the front window out of Will's buggy. It's the only way you'll be able to get in."

Karen nodded, feeling numb. Everything seemed to be happening in slow motion.

Tears flowed down her cheeks, and her body trembled as she stood helplessly waiting for Mark to return with the tools. What if Will was dead? What if she never got to tell him how much she loved him?

Mark stepped up to her, holding a crowbar and a hammer, with his flashlight tucked under one arm. "You'd better stand back while I get the window pulled free."

Karen moved aside, watching, waiting, and praying. Finally the window released, and Mark tossed it to the side of the road. "You'd better take this," he said, handing her the flashlight. "You'll need it to see how things are once you're inside."

Karen took the flashlight, and with her heart thudding and legs shaking, she crawled inside. She spotted Will right away, scrunched against the passenger door. He wasn't moving. With a shaky hand, she slipped her fingers around his wrist to check for a pulse. She felt a pulsation beneath her fingertips, but it was very weak. She leaned close to Will and put her face in front of his mouth. A faint breath blew against her cheek, and she felt a sense of relief knowing he was still alive.

"How's Will?" Mark called.

"He's unconscious, and his pulse is awfully weak." Karen's voice quavered, and she drew in a shaky breath. *Dear God, please let him live.*

"Can you tell how badly he's been injured?"

She lifted the flashlight and spotted a bump on Will's forehead, and then she saw a huge tear in his pants and gasped. Blood squirted from Will's leg like a gusher of water spurting from a well.

Knowing she needed to get the bleeding stopped, Karen shined the light around the buggy and was relieved when she found a lightweight blanket on the floor. She scooped it up and, using one corner of the blanket, applied pressure to Will's leg.

"I checked on Will's horse, and he's dead," Mark said when he stuck his head inside the buggy a few minutes later. "How's Will doing?"

"He's unconscious. It looks like his leg's been cut, and it's bleeding really bad. I've applied pressure, but he needs to get to the hospital right away."

"We're close to the Chupps' place, so I'll go there and call for help while you stay with Will and keep pressure on his leg."

Karen swallowed against the bile rising in her throat. "Okay."

"I'll be back as quick as I can." Mark disappeared into the night.

It seemed like an eternity until Mark returned to the buggy.

"I called 911 from the Chupps' phone shed, and help is on the way," he panted. "How's Will doing?"

Tears welled in Karen's eyes as she spotted blood seeping through the blanket. "Not so good. I haven't been able to get the bleeding stopped."

"The ambulance should be here soon. Nathan's gone to my place to get Regina, and he's lining us up a ride to the hospital."

"I'd like to ride in the ambulance with Will, if you don't mind," Karen said, swallowing hard.

"That's fine. We'll meet you at the hospital."

Karen looked down and gulped on a sob. "I love you, Will. Please don't die."

CHAPTER 34

Danki," Regina said when Mark handed her the cup of coffee he'd gotten from the vending machine outside the hospital waiting room.

Mark looked over at Karen. "Are you sure you don't want some?"

She shook her head. "I'm afraid coffee would make me feel shakier than I already am."

Regina glanced at the door. "I wish we'd hear something. I can't stand this waiting."

"Will's only been in surgery a short time," Mark said. "I'm sure someone will come and give us some news soon."

She shuddered. "When you came back to the house and said Will had been in an accident, I was afraid we might never see him again. All I've been able to do since then is pray."

Karen nodded. "I've been praying, too."

"That's all we can do right now," Mark said. "Will's in God's hands, and we have to trust that he'll be okay."

"Frank should be notified about Will's accident," Regina said.

Mark nodded. "What hotel did he say they'd be staying at tonight?"

"I believe Megan said it was the Country Inn & Suites," Regina said.

Karen stood. "Would you like me to look up the number and see if I can reach Frank there?"

Regina nodded. "Jah, please do."

Karen hurried from the room.

A few minutes later, a doctor entered and stepped up to Regina and Mark. "Mr. and Mrs. Stoltzfus?"

They nodded.

"Your son is out of surgery now."

Regina jumped to her feet. "Is he all right?"

"He's got some bumps, bruises, and a

couple of broken ribs, but his worst injury was the main artery in his leg that was severed."

Regina gasped, and Mark groaned.

"He lost a lot of blood, and he'll need a transfusion." The doctor looked at Mark. "I'm sure you know that your son has a rare blood type."

Mark looked at Regina then back at the doctor and shook his head. "We didn't know."

"The thing is, no blood of his type is available locally right now and it might take awhile for us to get some." The doctor paused. "Will's very weak, and he needs that blood as soon as possible."

Tears stung the back of Regina's eyes. "Is. . .is he going to die?"

"We got the bleeding stopped, so if we can get the blood Will needs, he'll recover." The doctor looked at Mark again. "Since blood types are inherited from the parents, you're the most likely ones to donate the blood Will needs."

Mark shook his head. "I'm sorry, but we can't do that."

"Why not?"

"Will isn't our son. I mean, we raised

him from the time he was six, after his real father, who isn't Amish, left him in our care."

"Oh, I see. Do you know where Will's biological parents are?"

Regina nodded. "His mother's dead, but his father's staying at a hotel in Shipshewana. Will's fiancée is trying to reach him on the phone right now."

❦

Frank was about to turn on the TV in their hotel room when the phone rang. Since Megan had just put Carrie and Kim to bed, he grabbed the receiver.

"Hello."

"Is this Frank Henderson?"

"Yeah. Who's this?"

"Karen Yoder, Will's fiancée."

"Did Will make it home okay?"

"No, he's—" Karen's voice faltered.

"What is it, Karen? What's wrong?"

"Will was in an accident with his buggy. I'm at the hospital with Mark and Regina, and Will's still in surgery."

Frank's heart thudded against his chest. "How bad is he hurt?"

"I'm not sure. He was unconscious when

we found him, and his leg was bleeding really bad." There was a pause. "I applied pressure, but it just kept bleeding."

"What hospital is he in?"

"We're here in Goshen. The hospital's not hard to find. If you'd like to come, I can give you directions."

"Of course I want to come. I'll be there as soon as I can." Frank grabbed a notepad and pen. "I'm ready. Go ahead and give me the directions."

Moments later, Frank said good-bye to Karen, hung up the phone, and turned to Megan. "I've got to go."

"Go where, Frank?"

"Will's been in an accident. He's at the hospital in Goshen."

"Oh, Frank, I'm so sorry. How serious is it, do you know?"

"Karen said Will's in surgery, and it doesn't sound good."

"Should I wake the girls so we can go with you?"

Frank shook his head. "I might be gone awhile. I think it would be best if you and the girls stayed here and got some sleep."

Megan slipped her arm around his waist. "I won't be able to sleep until I know how

Will's doing. Please call when you know something, okay?"

He nodded. "I'll let you know as soon as I can."

"I'll be praying."

"I spoke with Frank, and he should be on his way to the hospital right now," Karen told Regina and Mark when she returned to the waiting room.

Regina clasped Karen's hand. "I'm so glad. The doctor was just here, and he says Will has a rare blood type that they don't have in stock and that Frank's blood may be a match. They need to give Will a transfusion because he lost so much blood."

Karen sank into a chair. "Frank seems to care about Will. I'm sure he'll be willing to give his son the blood he needs."

Regina nodded and moved over to the window. "I just pray Frank gets here in time."

CHAPTER 35

Will moaned as he slowly opened his eyes. Three figures stood at the foot of his bed, but he couldn't make out who they were. "Wh–where am I?"

"You're in the hospital."

"Karen?"

"Jah, Will, it's me." Karen moved to the side of Will's bed, and her face came into view.

"What happened to me? How come I'm in the hospital?"

"You were in an accident," Papa Mark explained. "I was taking Karen home, and we found your mangled buggy on its side along the edge of the road."

"What about Blazer? Is he okay?"

Papa Mark slowly shook his head. "I'm sorry, son, but your horse is dead."

Will grimaced. First Ben and now Blazer? He was beginning to think he wasn't supposed to own a horse.

"We're sorry you lost your horse, but we're thankful you're going to be okay," Mama Regina said as her face came into view.

"I don't feel okay." Will groaned. "My leg feels like I've been kicked by a cow."

"You've got several bumps, bruises, and a few broken ribs, but the worst part of your injuries was the artery in your leg that was severed. The doctors did surgery, and your daed gave you some of his blood, so you're going to be okay," Mama Regina said, patting his hand.

A lump formed in Will's throat as a sense of gratitude welled in soul. "Danki, Papa Mark, for giving me some of your blood."

Papa Mark shook his head. "It wasn't me. Frank saved your life."

"Pop gave me blood?"

"That's right," Karen said. "When I phoned his hotel to let him know you'd been in an accident, he came to the hospital right away. And when he learned that you have the same rare blood type as he does, he didn't hesitate to give you some of his blood." She leaned closer to Will's bed. "There's something else you need to know."

"What's that?"

"It's about the note your daed left you sixteen years ago."

"There was no note."

"Jah, there was." Karen opened her pocketbook and removed the recipe card she'd put there before leaving Will's house. "After you left the house and the company had gone home, your mamm gave me the recipe for White Christmas Pie, and I discovered Frank's note had been written on the back side of it." She held the card in front of Will's face.

He squinted. "I can't make out what it says. Could you please read it to me?"

Karen nodded and cleared her throat. "'Dear Will, I'm going to make my delivery, and then I plan to look for another job. I'll be back for you soon. Mark and Regina will take good care of you until then. Love, Pop.'"

"So there really was a note."

"I found the card on the counter the morning your daed left," Mama Regina said. "But it was lying faceup, and I didn't turn it over before I put it back in the recipe box."

Will swallowed hard as tears clouded his vision. "I need to see Pop. Do you know where he is?"

"He's in the waiting room," Mama Regina said. "I'll go get him."

For the last fifteen minutes, Frank had been pacing the floor of the waiting room, berating himself for the things he had done in the past. He had so many regrets. . .so many things he wished he could change.

He sank into a chair, closed his eyes, and let his mind carry him back in time. . .back to the day of his accident. . . .

Frank flipped on the radio and searched for a country-western station. He needed something to lift his spirits and take his mind off the guilt he felt over leaving Will behind.

He felt sure Will would be well cared for while he was gone, but that wouldn't make him miss the boy any less.

He finally found a station playing his favorite kind of music, but he couldn't seem to relax. Besides the fact that the roads were icy, making him feel tense, he couldn't stop thinking about Will.

Does Will understand the reason I left? How did he react to my note? Will my boy be happy living with people he hardly knows? Does he realize how much I love him?

Frank strained to see out the window. It had been snowing hard ever since he'd crossed into North Dakota. His windshield wipers could barely keep up with the moisture hitting the front window.

I'll pull over at the next truck stop. Maybe a cup of coffee and a sandwich will revive me a little.

The car in front of Frank swerved unexpectedly to the left. He figured the vehicle must have hit a patch of ice, so he lowered his speed. The car swerved again, this time to the right.

Then it spun around and headed straight for Frank's truck!

Frank turned the wheel sharply to avoid a head-on collision, but as his tires slipped on the ice, he lost control. As the car collided with Frank's truck, he held on to the steering wheel and screamed, "Somebody help me! I've got to get back to Will!"

"Frank. Frank, are you sleeping?"

Someone touched Frank's shoulder, and his eyes snapped open. Regina stared down at him with a peculiar look on her face.

"I. . .I wasn't sleeping," he mumbled. "Just remembering some things from the past."

"I came to tell you that Will's awake, and he wants to see you."

"He. . .he does?"

"Yes, but before we go in, there's something I think you need to know."

"What's that?"

"After you left our house last night, I gave Karen the recipe for White Christmas Pie."

"What's that got to do with anything?"

"Karen found your note—the one you wrote for Will and asked me to read to him after you left."

Frank's mouth dropped open. "Where'd she find it?"

"On the back of the recipe card."

A tremor shot up Frank's spine as a rush of memories washed over him. "Now that I think about it, I did write the note on the back of a recipe card and I left it lying on the kitchen counter."

"I'm sure you did, but the card must have gotten turned over somehow; I ended up filing it away without seeing the note. The card's been in my recipe box all these years, and that's why we never knew you had written a note."

Frank pulled his fingers across his stubbly chin and shook his head. "No wonder Will didn't believe me."

"Would you like to see Will now?"

He swallowed around the lump in his throat. "Yes, I would."

"I still can't believe you found Pop's note," Will said as he looked up at Karen. "I really thought he was lying."

"Sometimes when we've convinced our-selves of something, it's hard to believe the truth even when we hear it."

Will grimaced. "What I still don't under-stand is why Pop never came back to get me or wrote any letters letting me know he hadn't forgotten me."

"Why don't you ask him about that now?" Mama Regina said as she slipped in be-side Karen.

Will turned his head in time to see Pop enter the room. At that moment, he re-membered Papa Mark saying to him, *"God has a reason for bringing people into our lives at certain times." Could God have brought Pop here to save my life? No mat-ter what's happened in the past, at least Pop and I are together again.*

"Hello, Will," Pop said. "I'm relieved to know you're going to be okay."

"I understand I have you to thank for that. I hear you gave me the blood I needed."

Pop nodded and moved to the side of Will's bed. "I'm glad I could do it, but it doesn't make up for the years we've spent apart."

Will drew in a quick breath. "Karen told

me about the note she found on the back of the recipe card. I'm sorry I didn't believe you."

"Since you didn't see the note after I wrote it, it's understandable that you wouldn't believe me."

Will swallowed hard. "I. . .uh. . .need to know one thing."

"What's that?"

"Why didn't you come back for me, or at least write and let me know why you weren't coming back?"

Pop leaned closer to Will. "I'd planned to write, but a few days after I left you with Regina and Mark, I was in an accident that landed me in the hospital, where I stayed for many months, thanks to my injuries. Once I was well enough, I headed to Pennsylvania to get you. Unfortunately you weren't there. Someone else was living in Mark and Regina's house."

"We left word with a neighbor so that if your daed came to get you, he would know we had moved," Papa Mark said. "I guess by the time your daed showed up, our neighbor had also moved."

Frank grimaced. "I was so shook up when I found out you were gone I could barely function. If I hadn't met Megan when I did, I might never have gotten my life straightened around."

Will stared at the ceiling as he mulled things over. He'd been so sure Pop had abandoned him on purpose. He hadn't figured Pop might have had a good reason for not contacting him.

"'And ye shall know the truth, and the truth shall make you free,'" Will said, quoting John 8:32.

Pop tipped his head. "What?"

"It's a verse from the Bible. Jesus was telling those who believed on Him that they would know the truth and be set free from their sins. The verse reminds me of my situation," Will said. "I've been holding a grudge against you all these years because I didn't know the truth. But now the truth has set me free."

Pop nodded. "Megan quoted that verse to me not long ago. Afterwards, I prayed and asked God to forgive my sins."

"I'm happy to know you're a believer." Will reached out and touched Pop's arm. "Will you forgive me for not believing you wrote a note and for holding a grudge against you all these years?"

Pop nodded as tears trickled down his cheeks. "If you'll forgive me for not being there during most of your childhood."

"I forgive you, Pop." Will looked over at his folks. "I've always been thankful that you took me in and treated me like your own son, and I'm sorry if the things I said during our Thanksgiving dinner hurt your feelings. I love you both so much."

"We love you, too, Will." Tears shimmered in Mama Regina's eyes.

"And we've been glad we could raise you," Papa Mark added.

Will smiled at Karen. "I'm also thankful to God for giving me a special woman to share my life with—if she still wants to marry me, that is."

Karen nodded as tears sprang to her eyes. "Jah, Will, I do."

"Before we pass the box of tissues around, I'd like to know one thing," Frank said.

"What's that?" Will asked.

"Am I invited to your wedding?"

"Yes!" Will and Karen said in unison.

Frank clasped Will's hand. "I'll have to head home with Megan and the girls tomorrow, but I promise to stay in touch, and we'll be back for your wedding in December."

Karen smiled at Frank. "We'd like to have your family join us for Christmas, too, wouldn't we, Will?"

Will nodded. "Maybe by then I'll be well enough so we can go outside and build that snowman we never got to make sixteen years ago."

"I think my girls would enjoy that, too." Frank grinned like a boy given a new toy on Christmas morning.

As Mama Regina, Papa Mark, and Pop moved away from Will's bed, Will reached for Karen's hand. "Even though I had some doubts about being your husband, I know I could never be truly happy without you in my life."

She gave his fingers a gentle squeeze. "I wouldn't be happy without you, either."

EPILOGUE

Ready or not, here we come!" Pop shouted as he and Kim raced across the yard with arms full of snowballs and a honey-colored cocker spaniel puppy nipping at their heels.

Will smiled as he thought about the Christmas present he'd given his half sisters earlier today. The girls had named the puppy Shadow because it liked to follow them.

"No snowball fight yet," Carrie squealed. "Mommy and I aren't ready."

"How about you, Will?" Pop called. "Are

you and Karen ready to make a few snow-balls?"

Will looked at Karen, who stood by his side, red faced and full of smiles. "Would you rather watch from the sidelines, or would you like to take part in the fight that's about to begin?"

She pulled the collar of her coat around her neck and shivered. "I got cold enough building our snowman, so I think I'll watch the snowball fight from the porch where it's warmer."

"Guess I'll sit this one out, too," Will said.

Whoosh!—a snowball flew across the yard and hit Will's arm. "We'd better get out of the line of fire before I change my mind and start making a few *schneeballe.*"

"If you'd like to join the fun, I'll stay on the porch and cheer you on," Karen said.

Will shook his head. "No way, I'd rather be with my *schee* fraa."

The color in Karen's cheeks deepened when he called her his pretty wife. He loved the way she blushed so easily. Will took her hand and led her over to the porch.

"I can't believe we've been married a whole week already," he said as a surge of joy swept over him. He envisioned how sweet and beautiful Karen had looked on their wedding day as they'd stood before the bishop and repeated their vows. It had been a wonderful day, and having Pop and the rest of his family there to share it with them had made it especially memorable.

"I'm glad we were able to postpone our wedding by one week so you could have more time to heal. I'm pleased your daed and his family could be here for the wedding and stay through Christmas, too."

"Jah, it made the day even more special." Will nuzzled the back of Karen's neck with his cold nose. "Is being married to me all you'd hoped it would be?"

She shivered. "It's all that and more, but if you keep doing things to make me feel colder, I'm going to drag you into the yard and douse your face with snow."

He chuckled. "Is that a challenge?"

She shrugged. "Take it however you like."

Will was about to respond when Mama Regina and Papa Mark joined them on the porch.

"I've got some hot chocolate heating on the stove," Mama Regina said. "Whenever everyone's ready for a break from all this merriment, we can have some of Karen's White Christmas Pie to go with it."

Will smacked his lips. "That sounds good to me. Should I see if I can get our snowball throwers to stop so we can go inside?"

Papa Mark shook his head. "We're not ready to go in just yet."

"How come?"

"Your daed and I have a surprise for you." He pointed to the horse and buggy coming down the lane. "And here it is now."

As the rig drew closer, Will realized it was Nathan's. A shiny black horse trotted behind the buggy.

"That's enough with the snowballs," Pop shouted to Megan and the girls. "Will's Christmas present has arrived!"

Will looked over at Papa Mark then back at Pop, who was heading for the porch. "My Christmas present?"

Pop nodded, and a wide smile spread across his face. "I figured you'd be need-ing a new horse to replace the one you lost in your buggy accident, so Mark went with me to pick it out a few days ago." His smile widened as Nathan untied the horse. "Aaron Chupp agreed to keep the horse in his barn until Nathan brought him over here today."

"It's another trotter," Nathan said as he led the horse closer to the house.

"So what do you think?" Pop asked. "Do you like the horse we chose?"

Will nodded. "He's real nice. Thank you, both, so much."

"You're welcome."

Will reached out and touched the horse, letting his fingers glide through its silky mane. "I hope I have better luck with this one than I had with my other two."

"You know what they say about the third time around," Nathan said with a chuckle.

Will rubbed the horse's muzzle. "Any idea what I should name this one?"

"How about Pie?" Pop suggested. "After all, it was the recipe for Regina's White Christmas Pie that brought us together."

"What kind of name is Pie for a horse, Daddy?" Carrie asked.

"You're right. It is a silly name." Pop grinned at Will. "It's your horse, so you choose a name."

"How about I call him Pop? That way, whenever I'm with the horse, I'll think of my daed and be reminded of how much I love him."

Tears welled in Pop's eyes, and he gave Will a hug.

"I don't know about the rest of you, but I'm cold and hungry," Mama Regina said. "How about we go inside for a piece of Karen's White Christmas Pie?"

"Sounds good to me," Megan agreed. "My nose and toes are about to fall off from being out here in all this cold snow."

Nathan grinned at Will. "I'll put Pop in the barn, and then I'll join you."

"And I'll put the girls' puppy away until it's time for us to go," Pop said, turning toward the barn.

As the others headed for the house, Will touched Karen's arm and turned her to face him. When he saw the peaceful look on her face, he felt a sense of joy and hope for the future. He couldn't imagine what more he could want than having his family together on Christmas Day. He couldn't conceive of being married to anyone but Karen. And it was all because of a note that had been written on the back of a recipe card.

RECIPE FOR WHITE CHRISTMAS PIE

1 tablespoon Knox gelatin
¼ cup cold water
1 cup sugar, divided
4 tablespoons flour
½ teaspoon salt
1½ cups milk
¾ teaspoon vanilla
¼ teaspoon almond extract
½ cup whipping cream, whipped until
  stiff
3 egg whites
¼ teaspoon cream of tartar
1 cup flaked coconut
2 (9 inch) baked pie shells

In small bowl, soak gelatin in cold water; set aside. In sauce-pan, mix ½ cup sugar, flour, salt, and milk. Cook over low heat, stirring until mixture comes to a boil. Boil for 1 minute; remove from heat. Stir in softened gelatin. Cool. When partially set, beat until smooth. Blend in vanilla, almond extract, and whipped cream. In separate bowl, beat egg whites and cream of tartar until stiff. Add ½ cup sugar and beat until soft peaks form. Fold into gelatin mixture;

then fold in flaked coconut. Divide equally into baked pie shells. If desired, sprinkle with additional flaked coconut. Store in refrigerator until ready to serve.

ABOUT THE AUTHOR

Wanda E. Brunstetter enjoys writing about the Amish because they live a peaceful, simple life. Wanda's interest in the Amish and other Plain communities began when she married her husband, Richard, who grew up in a Mennonite church in Pennsylvania. Wanda has made numerous trips to Lancaster County and has several friends and family members living near that area. She and her husband have also traveled to other parts of the country, meeting various Amish families and getting to know them personally. She hopes her readers will learn to love the wonderful Amish people as much as she does.

Wanda and her husband have been married over forty years. They have two grown children and six grandchildren. In her spare time, Wanda enjoys photography, ventriloquism, gardening, reading, stamping, and having fun with her family.

In addition to her novels, Wanda has written several novellas, stories, articles, poems, and puppet scripts.

Visit Wanda's Web site at www.wandabrunstetter.com and feel free to e-mail her at wanda@wandabrunstetter.com.